DIZZY

A STEEL BONES MOTORCYCLE CLUB PREQUEL

CATE C. WELLS

Cover art and design by Clarise Tan of CT Cover Creations.
Edited by Tiffany Mills.
Proofreading by Jean McConnell of The Word Forager and Nevada Martinez.
Special thanks to Erin D.

Thanks for reading! Like what you read? Please do me a solid and leave a review.

❀ Created with Vellum

1

FAY-LEE

Chaos, that flaky bastard, is gone, and I'm royally screwed.

I sink to the curb in front of the Steel Bones clubhouse. I stare at my knees and pick at the frayed edge of my jean shorts.

I've looked everywhere, and I've waited for almost two days now. No one's seen him. His bike's gone. This rager is finally fizzling out. People are gonna start noticing that I'm not going home.

My backpack was in Chaos' saddlebag, so I've got no change of clothes. No makeup. Somewhere along the line, I lost my phone.

This is not the worst situation I've ever been in—that'd be the shed incident, hands down, and I'm not gonna think about that now. This predicament is small potatoes. No need to panic.

There's a nip in the air, but the sun's shining. Everyone's mindin' their own business. Prospects are cleaning up inside. Over by the garage, a monstrously large and shaggy brother is showing his two boys how to change the oil on a white SUV.

In broad daylight, this ain't a scary scene. Shit gets wild after dark, but I can handle myself. I've been sticking with the sweetbutts until they all pair up, and then I sit with the old-timers at the bar.

I just stayed up all night listening to a dude with no legs named Boots tell stories about a wild woman he knew who left for California and never came back. At heart, it was a tragic story, but my belly muscles still ache from laughing.

I'm three hundred miles from home, and three hundred more miles away from New York City. It took me two weeks to get this far, hitchin' and walkin' when I couldn't find a ride. It's early fall now, but the weather's gonna turn soon.

What am I gonna do?

I got lucky with Chaos. Or so I thought. When he picked me up at that rest stop, he said he was heading up to Newfoundland, and I could ride with him all the way to New York State. He took my last twenty for gas, but he didn't try that hard to fuck me, or at least, he hadn't yet.

He'd said we'd only be stopping in Petty's Mill for a few nights. Petty's Mill is every small town, everywhere. Historic downtown along the river. A gas station, a fast food joint, and a tractor supply on the road in. Probably on the way out, too, but we didn't get that far.

Chaos said he had business with some old friends. It wouldn't take long. Now he's disappeared, and no one seems to know or care where he went.

No use crying about it. I need a plan. I keep plucking at the loose threads on my shorts and try to think.

Over by the garage, the shaggy dude has taken off his T-shirt, and he's got it hanging from his back pocket. He's got a nice body. He's thick, solid, but he's got what my oldest sister calls "painter's back." All those muscles a man gets from manual labor, day in, day out. She should know the name for it. Her first husband hung drywall, and he was ripped. We all thought he was a catch until he brought home the clap.

I tear my eyes from the man's muscles. I need to focus. Men are trouble, and I'm in enough as it is.

If I had my phone, I could ask one of my older sisters to send money. Dee would probably tell me she's got her own problems, but Carol's a soft touch. Only problem is her case number ends in eight, so she doesn't get her benefits until the seventeenth of the month.

Heh. The shaggy dude's oldest boy, a skinny kid maybe eight or nine, is taking his shirt off, too, but he doesn't have a back pocket to shove it in. He tucks it in the elastic waist-band of his shorts instead. I don't particularly like kids, but that's cute.

The boy has to stand on the bumper to see under the hood. They're both so serious—him and his daddy—deeply considering the engine in manly silence. The younger boy's gettin' bored. He's sittin' in the gravel, drawing in the dirt with a stick.

Mama's boyfriends never do shit like change their own oil. She likes flashy men who spend a lot of time in the bathroom. A man who can bullshit you into abandoning your better sense. Charmers. They don't stick around long after she turns up pregnant, but damned if they don't always come around again when their luck runs out. Like bad pennies.

I'm nearly nineteen, and since I can remember, I've been raisin' Mama's kids. And my sisters'. I've been cleanin' up other people's messes and fixin' their problems and bailin' them out of trouble, and I'm done with it. If I have to, I'll walk to New York.

I sure as hell ain't never goin' back home.

That ain't even an option.

But still. I'd rather not walk. The blisters on my heels from the day I walked out of Dalton to the interstate to hitch my first ride are still pink and a touch raw.

Over by the SUV, the younger boy's gotten bored, and he's wandered off toward the dumpster and the line of recycling bins on the side of the garage. This is how you know you're not in Kentucky. People here separate their paper and biodegradables. Back home, we burn it out back in the same trashcan.

This is a strange motorcycle club all around. They've got more money than most. The clubhouse is huge, and they're building an addition. It ain't a riding club or a gang so much as a business. Half the parking lot is taken up by yellow construction equipment: excavators, loaders, dozers. My nephews would be in heaven.

They've got other hustles, too, like a garage. Most of the sweetbutts work at their strip club, The White Van. A few girls have half-heartedly tried to convince me to talk to Cue, the brother who runs the place, but reading between the lines, they don't believe I have the shape for it. I'm too skinny, and I'm an A cup. Another difference between here and back home. The club in Dalton would hire you on the day you turned eighteen, no matter how you looked.

Still, I could give it a go. Search out Cue. He should be easy to find. Bald as his name, apparently. I'd make an awful stripper, but all I need is one paycheck to buy a bus ticket. I could do it if I were drunk.

Uh, oh. The little guy has spotted something on the roof

of the garage. The sun's glinting off a hunk of glass in the gutter. I scrub my dry, bleary eyes. Is that a beer bottle?

Now, he's pulling himself up on the dumpster. He barely makes it. His feet scrabble against the sides as he drags himself up by his lil' chicken arms. Kid's no more than six or seven. Adventuresome, though.

Reminds me of when one of my nephews found a way into the crawl space and set himself up a hidey-hole down there with a beach chair, sleeping bag, and snacks. He was pretty much living down there until the rats ran him out.

Now, there's an idea. This place is sprawling. The main clubhouse, the garage, the huge yard with its makeshift stage and firepit, the woods beyond. And then there's the frame and scaffolding for the addition. There's got to be a nook where I can hunker down. I'll think better after getting some sleep.

Thunk. Thunk. The little dude is jumping, trying to grab the gutter. The plastic lid bows under his weight. Like his daddy, he's sturdy. Hope it holds.

The other two haven't even noticed he's wandered off. The shaggy dude's bent over—long, wild black hair falling in his face—straining with a wrench. Sweat's glistening on his back, muscles tensing under his ink. His tattoos are faded and old school. A skull with a sword through the eye socket. A cross. Dog tags clutched in an eagle's talons. A heart wrapped in banners reading Sharon, Parker, and Carson.

There's a sword through the center name, blood dripping from the tip. Guess things didn't work out with Sharon.

I rub the stars on my inner wrist. My brother did them with a needle and thread before he left for Florida, and we never heard from him again.

Thud. The intrepid explorer has landed flat on his ass in

the dirt. My body tenses, anticipating the wail, but this guy's a tough customer. Hops up, doesn't bother dusting himself off, and clambers right back up. Kid just might make it.

I should get a move on. The place is clearing out, and soon, someone's gonna notice the raggedy chick poppin' a squat out front.

I stand, hand instinctively reaching for my phone. Damn. I can't believe someone stole it. I was sitting at the bar, and I swiveled on the stool for a second, and it was gone. Well, maybe it was longer than that. And maybe I left it while I went to pee, but still. It's gone.

I head back for the clubhouse, but a clatter, a grunting, and a flailing catch my eye. *Holy crap.* The little guy's dangling from the roof. He found some milk crates and stacked them on top of the dumpster. He must have kicked them over when he grabbed for the gutter. Now he's twisting and turning, trying desperately to walk the wall and hoist himself up, but he hasn't got the strength. His knuckles are white, and his eyes are glued on the prize.

Oh, my lord. He's letting go with one hand to try and grab the bottle.

I have only known raccoons with this level of determination.

I bolt over, vault up on the dumpster—gross—and grab him by the calves.

"Stop! I almost got it!"

Fair enough. I brace him with my chest and lift him higher. The plastic lid sways, creaking under our combined weight. If we crash into this dumpster, and I'm somehow stabbed to death with that damn broken bottle, I'm gonna haunt this kid for the rest of his life.

"Got it!"

I lower him down, my arms shaking. He's a husky one.

"Thanks, lady."

Before I can say boo, he jumps off the dumpster, waving a shard of glass, shouting, "Parker! Look what I got!"

I leap down and lope off before his hot daddy looks over this way. Last thing I need is to draw the attention of one of the brothers of the Steel Bones Motorcycle Club. Not when I plan to squat in their digs and riffle through their shit until I have enough cash to blow town.

I'VE BEEN an uninvited guest of the Steel Bones MC for a week. I'm freezing. I'm starving. I'm sick to death of classic rock, and I stink.

I hope that when the club kills me, they make it quick. I'm so freakin' cold, all they'll need to do is give me a good wallop, and I'll shatter into pieces.

And they are gonna catch me soon and kill me, 'cause my luck has always been shit, and I ain't cut out for bein' stealthy. Besides, my feet are so numb, I'm trompin' around like a slutty, grubby Frankenstein.

Geese honk high overhead, and the dark is easing to gray as I slowly turn the knob to the clubhouse's back door. It's dawn. Frost covers the yard. You can see my boot prints clear as day, coming from the woods.

The sun better melt that soon, or I'm gonna be busted in a comically Scooby Doo fashion. Tell the truth, I can't believe I've evaded detection this long.

I gently nudge the door. Sweet. It's unlocked. In the week since Chaos bailed, the door's been fifty-fifty. Drunk bikers ain't the most conscientious. The club's also hectic with all the construction mess. A whole chunk of wall is nothing but plastic sheeting. Guess they figure if a person can bust in like the Kool Aid Man, why lock a door?

I pad down the hall past the offices, heading straight for the kitchen. My stomach is pretty much gnawing on itself at this point. The clubhouse was a ghost town last night, so I couldn't crash the party like I have been—defrost, chow down, lift cash from whoever passes out.

It's so blessedly, beautifully warm in here. My frozen skin prickles, burning as it thaws. I ain't gonna last much longer sleeping rough.

I'm still wearing the clothes I was wearing when Chaos left—a short-sleeved belly shirt that says *Cute But Psycho*, jean shorts cut up to my ass, and combat boots. Thank goodness I was able to snag a wool horse blanket that was covering a bike out in the garage, or I'd have frozen to death days ago.

Luckily, I've only had to "head on home now" for a few hours each night. Steel Bones party hard; they start early, and they go late. Last night was a fluke. If it happens again, I'm gonna have to fuck a dude to get a bed. It's getting too cold. That's a last resort, but I'm a practical girl.

That's tomorrow's trouble, though. Right now, I'm in heaven: an industrial kitchen, clean as a whistle, pantry stocked full. I swing open a cabinet. Oh, yeah. Bread. Peanut butter. I pile my arms up and move to the fridge. There's jelly. Grape and strawberry. Every condiment you can image. A whole row of mustards. Glory day.

I grab what I need and head for a counter, slapping down ten slices like I do making lunches for the kids at home. I spread the peanut butter thick and glop the jelly on with a spoon.

I rummage through a few drawers, but there's no wax paper I can find, so I stack the sandwiches and put 'em in a plastic grocery bag. Whoever runs this kitchen, she's got those cutesy sacks where it's sewn to look like a cat with a big ol' skirt, and you pull the bag out of the cat's ass. Adorable.

I use the heel of bread to wipe the last of the peanut butter out of the jar and eat it as I root through the cabinets. Tuna, pasta, mayonnaise. No good. Chips, pretzels. I pop a bag open and munch as I scan the shelves. There's a bag of mixed nuts. Jackpot. That goes in the bag. I grab some beef jerky and a box of snack cakes, 'cause I'm only human, and I head out, snagging a few bottled waters as I go.

I should go walk the woods for a spell and come back in the afternoon. Wait in the tree line for a car load of sweet-butts to roll up and slide on in with them. But the feeling is just coming back in my thighs, tingling and sharp. And the woods are spooky as hell when you're alone.

Besides, the clubhouse is dead. From the hallway, I can see the commons—the bar running the length of the converted five-bay garage, the pool tables and jukebox, the vintage doors that slide open on tracks. There's no one in sight. Not even a dude passed out on the ripped leather sofas.

This is a first.

I do a lap around the commons, checking once again for the phone I lost that first night. You never know. Maybe it fell down a crack. As I root around the bar—no phone—I grab a bottle of vodka. That'll help me pass the day. I should count myself lucky and scurry back to my makeshift camp until tonight.

Or I could go upstairs. Find an empty bunk. Get a shower. Sleep in a bed.

Do I dare?

There's a dozen or so rooms in the annex. As I've learned

this past week, only five brothers actually live here full time. Heavy, the club president. He's a giant beast of a man with a voice like the crack of doom. He stomps around, sending folks fleeing in his wake.

There's Wall. Bodybuilder type. Says ma'am. I think his wife put him out. He's a nice guy.

Then there's Nickel and Creech. They are not nice. Nickel's a brawler. He's gotten into a fight every night I've been here, and he hasn't lost once. He's not interested in the ladies that I can tell. Not so Creech. He's a tattoo artist. Inked head, full sleeves, gauges. Grabby, pervy, and a huge asshole.

An older guy lives here, too. He looks like Superman if Superman had gray hair, a stoop, and a two-pack-a-day habit.

Five guys. A dozen rooms. Those are good odds. If it were the Lotto, I'd be emptying my pockets.

I listen hard, holding my breath. No signs of life. Maybe the guys are out on a run? It's a work day, but you can already tell that the weather's gonna be gorgeous and clear.

I tiptoe to the stairs, holding my bag of sandwiches and vodka behind my back. If I get busted on the second floor without a brother, I'm gonna look guilty as hell, but I've gotten away with bolder shit by battin' my eyelashes and keeping it movin'.

As far as I can tell, the guys who live here have the bigger rooms at the end of the hall. I take a gamble on the first door I come to. It opens no problem, and I slip inside, quickly shutting the door behind me.

Empty. Score.

This must be a crash pad. There's a twin bed. Faded navy fitted sheet, nothing else. A low dresser with an old, filmy mirror. No bottles or knickknacks. An overflowing ashtray on a wooden stand like my Meemaw had. And an empty bottle of Southern Comfort on its side on the floor. I can see a toilet through an open door past the dresser.

Dare I dream? I hustle over. There's a shower stall! And a worn towel hanging from the rod. No soap or anything, but it's clean enough. Oh, it's on.

I rip my shirt over my head as I kick off my shorts. My fingers are still a bit numb from the cold, so it takes me the longest time to untie my shitkickers.

My panties come off last. Whew. Shameful. I rinse them in the sink, wring them out, and hang them to dry. Wet panties are gonna suck if I have to go back outside. Maybe I'll leave 'em here, and come back for them later tonight.

I run the shower as hot as it'll go, and the small room fills with steam. I hop in, and oh, the Lord loves me. Water pressure! The water drums on my back, sore from sleeping on the hard ground, and streams down my body, warming me through and turning my skin a rosy red.

There's even a bottle of shampoo. It's practically empty, but I add some water and shake, and there's more than enough to wash my skinny self and lather up my hair.

This is amazing. My hair is long and straight—I had aspirations of growing it as long as Crystal Gale when I was a kid, but it won't grow past the small of the back—so it doesn't show the dirt when it's unwashed. My scalp, though, itches like hell. I use my fingertips, scrub real hard. I love the feel of suds slipping down my bare back.

I'm done in less than five minutes. I shower quick. I hate running out of hot water with my hair lathered up.

I grab the towel and sniff. Could be worse. I squeeze my hair dry, wipe the steam from the mirror, and smile. Still crooked. And there's the scar from when I tripped and busted my mouth open on a curb. It needed stitches, but

Mama left it too long. The scar's not so bad, though. Only a thin white hash mark across the corner of my lips.

I wish I had a comb. Shit, I wish I had a toothbrush. I check the medicine cabinet. There's an open box of condoms and floss. I grab the floss, wind it around my fingers. What the hell? It's something.

I should take the condoms, too.

I've rifled through a half dozen purses, and I have exactly seventeen dollars hidden in the sole of my left boot. The chicks who hang with Steel Bones seem to operate purely on credit, and the brothers don't ever leave their wallets unattended.

A bus ticket to New York City is thirty-nine dollars. I'm not desperate enough yet, but I could make that twenty-two bucks in fifteen minutes in a dark corner. My sister Dee goes down to the truck stop sometimes, and she'll get thirty for a blow job. I grab the box of condoms, tucking the floss inside.

Maybe there're warmer clothes in the dresser. Life's got to throw me a break at some point, right?

I step into the room, naked as a jaybird except for the towel wrapped around me, clutching a box of condoms, and my heart stops.

Sitting on the bed, bare-chested, is a huge, red-eyed man with wild black hair halfway down his back, and a wiry black beard, almost as long. It's the dad with the white SUV.

He looks like the bastard child of a bassist from an 80s metal band and that god with the lightning bolts. Up close, I can tell he's younger than I thought. He's in his thirties. His tattoos curl around his hunched shoulders, and he's wearin' the most hangdog expression I've ever seen on a man outside of a funeral or a court date.

He's swigging from the bottle of Southern Comfort.

Guess it wasn't empty after all. In his other hand, he's holding a thick flannel shirt.

Well, let's make lemonade. I ignore my thumping heart, smile wide, and cock a hip.

"Hey, mister," I say. "I'll show you my titties for that shirt."

2

DIZZY

I wake up on the floor, in the crack between the bed and the wall.

It's not my bed.

And it's not so much *waking up* as *coming to*.

I clamber upright and stumble around to sink onto the bed. My head is pounding, my mouth tastes like tire, and last night is a blank. But there *is* a bottle of SoCo on the floor.

I fold at the waist and reach to scoop it up, every muscle and joint protesting.

I'm too old for this shit.

I swirl the bottle. Sweet. There's a quarter left. Hair of the dog has never done me wrong. I take a swig.

What fuckin' day is it? It ain't Friday. I get the boys on Friday. Goddamn, it's bright in here. And there's someone in the bathroom.

Did I get laid?

I got morning wood despite my condition. That don't tell me shit. I always wake up hard.

My head pounds. I chug, trying to work up the energy to stand again. Get moving.

And then the prettiest little thing, naked and wrapped in a towel, sashays into the room, stops dead in her tracks, and does a double take.

What's that she's holdin'? A box of condoms?

She smiles. It's wonky, lop-sided, and sweet as hell. My cock jerks and chafes against my jeans. Well, hallelujah, I got pants on.

"Hey, mister," she purrs and winks. "I'll show you my titties for that shirt."

I ain't wearin' a shirt.

She nods at my hand. I'm holdin' a flannel. Oh. There's my shirt.

She raises an eyebrow. Big brown eyes full of mischief. Jet black hair drippin' on the carpet. She ain't got much meat on her. Firm little titties under that towel, though.

Fuck.

"How old are you, girl?"

"Twenty-one."

"Bullshit."

"Okay. Twenty."

"Where's your ID?"

"What? Are you the bouncer? Wanna see my titties or not?"

I do. She's the prettiest thing I've seen in years. Her smile kind of quirks at the corners. Like the Joker, but not insane.

"Why do you want my shirt?"

"I'm into grunge. Why the fuck you care?"

"Watch your mouth."

I don't like this sweet girl talkin' like she's hard. She's curlin' her bare toes, squirmin', goosebumps all up and down her arms. I set the bottle on the floor.

I've never seen her around before. Could be a new sweetbutt. I don't pay much attention. Even after the divorce, I'm more into bikes than chasing pussy.

Shit. This girl might be with one of the younger brothers.

"You property?"

She shakes her head. "Are you?"

"Nope." Not since Sharon bailed. "Why do you want my shirt?"

"I'm cold." She bites her bottom lip, blinks at me from under thick black lashes, and my abs tighten. My cock wants out. In. Whatever it can get.

"It's my favorite shirt."

"I have amazing tits."

I shrug a shoulder. Ain't no arguing with that. "Okay."

"No touching."

"I'm familiar with the rules of the champagne room." Steel Bones owns a club. The White Van. I do security there on occasion when they need a shift covered. So, yeah. I guess I am the bouncer.

She narrows her eyes, shoots me a look. I keep real still. I'm totally invested in this now. My head don't hurt anymore, and the fog's clearing. I'm harder than I've been in a long time. I don't know what I did to deserve this, but I ain't ever looked a gift horse in the mouth.

"Okay." She exhales, drops the box of condoms, and tugs the towel loose, letting it fall. She squeezes her eyes shut. Her nose wrinkles like a rabbit.

Her tits are gorgeous, small, no bigger than those apples you buy in bulk. She's got puffy nipples that peak like sugar cones. Perfect. I bet I could fit a whole tit in my mouth.

She pops her eyes open. Her shoulders relax when she sees I'm still sitting on the bed.

"You're gonna stay right there?"

"I'm gonna do whatever you want."

She narrows her eyes, weighin' me up, and then she seems to make a decision and her lips curve. She's gettin' a little confident, arching her back, and resting a hand on her hip. She's slim, but her waist nips in, and she's got that womanly figure.

"Like what you see?" she asks.

"Hell yes."

There's a bush between her thighs, as dark as the hair on her head, beaded with droplets from her shower. Haven't seen that in a long time. Sharon and the dancers at the club keep it waxed. Reminds me of the chicks in the porno mags the old-timers keep in a crate by the jukebox. I like it.

"So, what do you want me to do?" She tries a new pose, sticking her ass out.

My cock begs to be touched. What I'd give for her to come over here and go to her knees, suck me with that sassy mouth. But she's skittish. I don't want to scare her off.

"Show me more, baby."

Her forehead furrows. Her arms fall to her sides. She's at a loss.

Yeah, she's bold, but I don't think she does this on the regular.

"Turn around."

She raises an eyebrow. I raise one back. She stiffens her spine and turns.

She's got a juicy, heart-shaped ass. My mouth waters. I want to take a bite. I've always been an ass man, and hers is exquisite. Enough heft so it'll jiggle when you slap it, but firm. Taut. Perfect handfuls.

"Go to that bureau. Bend over it." My breath is coming quick. My forehead's broken out in sweat.

"You got a jacket?" Her chin lifts.

"A jacket?"

"You want me to bend over, that'll cost a jacket."

"Yeah. I got one around here somewhere." She wants a coat? I'll buy her a coat. Fur. Leather. Whatever. I want to see that ass spread wide. Damn, it's been so long since I wanted anything but a fuckin' nap.

Her gaze darts around the room. "You sure?"

"Yes, baby. Go bend over that bureau."

She gnaws the inside of her cheek, staring past me at the wall. She's thinkin'. Please Lord don't let her think better of this.

Finally, she seems to come to a decision and flashes me another adorably askew grin.

"Like this?" She pads over to the bureau, folds at the waist, and looks at me over her shoulder, tossin' her wet hair so droplets splatter on the wood.

I can see her sweet titties dangle in the dull mirror. Oh, yeah. Blood's pulsing to my cock. My body primes. It takes every inch of my self-control to stay where I am, hands at my side.

"Widen your stance."

She carefully lowers to her forearms and inches her legs apart.

"Arch your back."

There it is. I groan. "You're so beautiful, baby."

Her pussy lips spread, and I can see her slick, pink folds. She's creamed herself, and her clit has popped from its hood. Her shoulders are rising and falling, but not so quickly as mine.

"You've got such a pretty pussy."

Our eyes meet in the mirror. Her lips turn up in a small, wary smile. "I do?"

She cranes her neck to try and see. I can't help chuckling.

"What makes it pretty?" she demands.

Ain't that a hell of a question.

"Look how wet and slippery it is for me. Touch it, baby."

She shifts her hips and pushes up on her arms, nervous. I love watching her face. She's sneaking peeks at me in the mirror. My face. My chest. The tent in my jeans. I like her eyes on me.

She's waiting for something.

Maybe for me to go first.

I unzip my pants. My cock springs free. She smothers a gasp. Yeah. I'm one that's big all over.

"We really doing this?" she pants, breathless.

"We're really doing this." I stroke my cock. It can't get no harder, though.

She works her hand between her legs. Her delicate fingers slip-slide through her juices. She keeps darting shy glances at me in the mirror.

"Show me how you like it." I don't know where this bossy shit is coming from. It ain't my usual style. She's seems down with it, though. "Show me what you do when you're alone."

Her face is flushing, her expression dazed. She finds her clit, circling the nub with her middle finger. She neglects her slit, shiny with cream. I want to fill her. I want to slam my aching cock into that tight hole. She's so hot, her eyes now glued on my cock as I work myself hard, smearing precum root to tip.

"Does that feel good?" I ask.

She mumbles.

"Squeeze that titty. Pinch the nipple. Hard."

She has to push up to do what I say, and she readjusts

her stance, tilting her hips higher until I can see deep in her sweet, dewy pussy.

She's fuckin' beautiful.

"Now show me. Show me those puffy nipples." She half rises, cupping herself, offering herself to me in the mirror. She's into it, biting her lower lip in concentration, bright red from her chest to her cheeks.

My lower spine's tingling, and my balls are getting tight. Would she let me cum on those sweet tits, rub my cum on those rosy, raw nipples?

This is a dream—the best dream. I don't even want to cum, not before she does.

"Flick that clit. Come on, now. You're close, aren't you?"

She nods, gasping, holding onto me with those big brown eyes. Her knees are wobbling now.

"Cum for me, baby. Let me see you cum."

She moans out loud, and my pants vibrate.

A country twang singing "Forever and Ever, Amen" comes muffled from my pocket.

Fuck.

Sharon.

Not now.

I groan.

"One minute, okay? Stay right there." I hold up a finger as I stand, jerkin' my pants to my waist. "I gotta take this. It could be an emergency. But you stay right there. I'll be right back. You're gonna stay right there for me, aren't you, baby?"

I'm aware I'm begging, but I'm past pride. The hazy look is gone from my girl's eyes, and she's straightening up. She won't meet my eye.

Goddamn. "Just one minute. I'll be right back."

The phone keeps singin', so I tap to answer as I cram my dick back in my jeans and step into the hall. I need to change that ringtone. Sharon put it on my phone for our anniversary. Seven or eight years ago.

"Sharon? What's up?"

My heart was already pounding, and now it's stuck in my throat. Ever since we split, whenever she calls, my first thought is, *Are the boys okay?*

Ain't gonna lie. They're wild. Carson in particular is accident-prone. We got three broken bones between the two of them at this point, and four concussions.

"Dwayne!"

There's an unholy ruckus at the end of the line. TV blaring. Dogs barking. Carson's hollering. He don't sound hurt.

"Yeah. What's up?"

"You need to take the boys tonight."

"All right." I force myself to swallow what I really want to say, and I head further down the hall. "When?"

The judge gave me every other weekend and a few hours on Wednesday nights. When we went to court, Sharon pulled some shit about how I'm never around and painted me as a degenerate 'cause I'm in an MC. She tried to get full custody, which is a joke 'cause she's always asking me to take the boys early or keep 'em late. I don't mind. I'll take 'em whenever. They're my kids. I miss 'em.

Still. I was the one who had to assure the judge I was gonna put the boys first before he gave me four fuckin' days a month.

"Carson, handle it yourself! I'm on the phone with your father!" she shouts. "Can you pick them up from Steve's after school?"

Steve's the dude she was fuckin' when we split. He was her boss at the real estate agency then, but he's her bitch now.

"I can get 'em from school. No problem."

"No. I'm picking them up. Just come get them from Steve's. Four or five. I need you to get them by six, though. I have reservations. It's a business thing."

Sharon's got a lot of "business" things after hours these days. Steve better keep an eye out.

"Okay. I'll pick 'em up from school."

"No. That's already on my schedule. Just get them from the house."

Sharon don't like me showing up at the school, lookin' like I do. A few years back, when she got her real estate license, she started takin' issue with my tattoos and my clothes. When we were in high school, my long hair revved her engines. Made her cry when I had to cut it for basic.

People change. Sharon's become a person I don't even recognize. I deal with her like I deal with a shitty customer. They want to act the boss, but that don't mean they know shit about engines. I make it quick, and I move on with my day.

What is it they say? If you argue with a dumbass, you're the dumbass.

It's getting louder in the background. Parker's shoutin' at his brother now about some video game controller. Jesus. Pain spears my temples. I need an ibuprofen.

"And can you just keep them through the weekend? I'll get them Sunday. Or you could drop them here. Yeah, that's easier. Let's do that."

"Fine."

"Don't forget Carson's inhaler."

"I told you I got one at the house."

"Okay. Six o'clock?"

"Six o'clock."

She hangs up first.

I scrub my neck. I ain't gone grocery shopping. I've been crashing at the clubhouse, eating here. The house is a wreck. I never got around to cleaning up after the last weekend with the kids. Ah, hell.

But all that can wait.

The throb in my head eases, and my limp cock twitches, rising to attention. There's a sweet piece of ass waitin' for me, legs spread, right down the hall.

I grin. It feels so damn rusty.

I shove my phone in my pocket as I jog back to the room.

The door's open.

My shoulders slump.

There's a wet towel and a box of condoms on the floor. My shirt and the bottle of SoCo are missing.

The girl is gone.

~

"CHURCH!" Mikey hollers, way too loud. I try to punch him in the side of the head as he trots by, but he's too fast. "Church in five!"

Damn prospect. It's only nine o'clock in the morning. Shouldn't he be passed out under a pool table somewhere? Not prancin' around, chipper, like some coked-up town crier.

What's Heavy doin' callin' church this early with no notice, anyway? And on a weekday.

I groan. I searched for my ghost girl high and low before I gave up. I showered, I'm on my second cup of coffee, and my headache is back with a vengeance.

I should've never left the room. Kept my eyes on her. I don't even know her name.

She didn't get her jacket. It's warming up. It's fifty-eight now, but tonight, it'll get down into the thirties. Why don't she have a jacket? For that matter, why did she need my shirt? Where's her clothes? Goddamn.

"Coming?" Grinder slaps me on my back. My head pounds.

"Yeah, man. After you."

Grinder's my dad's age, but we're both doing the old man shuffle toward the boardroom.

"Rough night?" I ask.

"Ernestine put me out."

"She gonna stop cookin' again?" Ernestine runs the kitchen. She makes a mean brisket.

"Probably not. She likes y'all."

"She'd like you too if you didn't fuck the club pussy." Might as well tell a man like Grinder to stop breathin', but it's true.

"Hey. The club pussy fucks me."

"Fell into it, did you?"

Grinder grins. "It was the damnedest thing."

Oh, shit. What if he knows my ghost girl? My stomach sours. He's too old for a girl like her. Hasn't stopped him the past. And my girl seemed desperate.

"You ever seen a girl around here, twenty or so, long black hair. Smile tilts funny?"

Grinder gives me the side-eye. It ain't like me to inquire after a woman. Engine parts and vehicles, yes. Females, no. I'm a mechanic. What can I say? A man don't ever get over his first love. God don't make nothin' as perfect as a shovelhead.

"Can't say that I have. She do you right?"

I shrug as we file into the boardroom. The table's only half full, not surprising considering the day and time.

Boots and Eighty are down at the old-timer's end of the table. Boots has nodded off in his wheelchair. Par for the course. Most of the time, he only bothers to wake up when Grinder needs him to pass a vote.

The club's in a weird place right now. We voted in Heavy as president when his old man passed, right after I got out of the service. Heavy's a few years younger than me, and he's got his crew: Charge, Scrap, Forty, Nickel.

Nickel's the only one present, pacing by the window. Charge is probably on a job site. Scrap's upstate, has been for the past six years. He's doing a dime bid for manslaughter. Forty's on deployment.

So, Heavy's the man, but he don't always have the numbers. He's gotten us out of running cigarettes and doing bitch work for the Renelli organization up in Pyle. Now we're in construction and vehicle mods. That's how I spend most of my time, rigging out cars and bikes like Q from James Bond.

See, our clientele is interested in a little something extra. And one hundred percent discretion. Rooms that don't show up on blueprints filed with the county. Compartments and defensive equipment that isn't apparent to the casual observer.

We do your basic construction projects, too, and that's bringing in more and more cash, but at the beginning, it was the vehicles we modified for the Renellis and shadowy dudes from overseas that paid the bills.

The old-timers are pissy about the change. Eighty don't want to wear any kind of helmet, hard hat included. They don't trust anything new. Heavy's crew backs him unconditionally.

That leaves us guys in the middle—me, Jed, Wall, Pig Iron—to break the ties. Thankless fuckin' position.

I take a chair, and Heavy ducks through the door. He's got his laptop. I still can't get over the fact he went to college. I wonder how many times he got security called on him. Once, at night, he was in the yard, and I mistook him for a bear.

Heavy lowers himself and turns the laptop to face us. There's a screensaver of a cherry-red Road King. Sweet.

Grinder takes the seat to Heavy's right, and Gus shuffles in, beer in hand.

"All right, brothers," Heavy begins.

"We don't have a quorum," Eighty pipes up from the foot of the table. Three years ago, dude didn't know a quorum from his asshole, but Heavy's big on proper procedure, and so Eighty picked it up right quick so he can be a dick about it.

"Don't need a quorum," Heavy says. "We ain't voting on a motion. We got a problem."

Shit. I was hoping to get home, get some work done on the sportster. Big George has us working out of our home garages while he renovates the Autowerks, another part of Heavy's master plan. We're getting a new hangar out back to do custom jobs. It's gonna be epic.

"What problem?" Grinder folds his hairy arms. Grinder's the kind of guy that if he don't know about it, it can't be a thing.

"We got an uninvited house guest." Heavy clicks the mouse pad, and there in grainy black-and-white is my ghost girl, sitting on a parking stop out in front of the clubhouse.

She looks even younger than she did this morning. Her hair's in pigtails, and her knees are tucked to her chin. Her face is tight. Worried.

My heart rate kicks up.

"Since when we sticklers about random pussy hangin' out?" Eighty snorts.

"Since she rode in on the back of Chaos' bike," Jed answers.

Oh, fuck.

The mood gets stone cold sober in an instant. Chaos is— was—a hang around. A dude we rode with for years. About a week ago, the night of the rager, Pig Iron busted him in Heavy's office in the dark, hunched over the blueprints for the facility we're building for the Wade Group up by Pyle, phone out, taking pictures.

Of course, those were the papers filed with the county. The real schematics, the one with the subterranean storage rooms, those are in the vault. Still, if he knew enough to look at blueprints, he knew something.

Maybe the Feds got to him.

Maybe the Rebel Raiders did. The Raiders have been feuding with Steel Bones since the clubs split back in the 90s.

Maybe he came up with his own scheme to blackmail the Wade Group. The family owns half of the state.

Heavy's working it out. The *why* wouldn't have changed anything, though. At church, the vote was unanimous. He betrayed us, risked our livelihoods, our freedom.

Chaos is gone. His bike is at the bottom of the Lucka-hannock. No loose ends.

Except my ghost girl. I slump, my heart sinking. Goddamn. If it ain't one thing, it's another. Nothing can ever be easy.

"Who is she?" Jed asks, glaring at the screen. Jed's an enforcer. Takes his job very seriously. Kind of a bitch, in my opinion. Weak chin. Wears a lot of camo, but he never served, and he don't hunt.

My muscles tense. She's a tiny slip of thing. He don't need to be staring at her like he's gonna shank her.

"Deb says her name's Fay-Lee," Pig Iron says. Deb's his wife. She does the books, fusses over the sweetbutts. Her and Sharon never got along. "From Kentucky."

Heavy taps the computer, zooms in on her face. You can see the scar on the corner of her lip. "We've got video of her in the yard. By the garage. All hours."

Heavy's sister Harper, the club lawyer, don't allow CCTV in the clubhouse. She says if we want to document our crimes, we should get social media like normal Americans. There's surveillance all over outside, though.

"Fuck." I close my eyes, bend my head.

"You see her?" Heavy asks.

"Shit. This the bitch you were lookin' for this morning?" Grinder snorts.

Now everyone's lookin' at me.

"I woke up. She was comin' out of the bathroom."

"Where?" Heavy swings the door open, snapping for a prospect.

"My old bunk. This was hours ago. She's long gone."

Heavy barks at Mikey to get some boys and go clear the rooms upstairs.

"Who is she to Chaos?" My blood courses faster through my veins. Chaos was not a good dude. Even before the spying. He had a dog, Spiro. German Shepard. When he tried to start over in Florida, he left the dog, didn't tell no one. Hobs ended up takin' him in.

Pig Iron shrugs. "Not clear. But she's got to be wondering where he got to."

Chaos is buried under a sapling at the top of Half Stack Mountain. Heavy, Nickel, Bullet, and I planted him three days ago. Saw a twelve-point buck on our way down, and we brought our bows for a cover story, but none of us got our license yet this year, so we had to let him go.

"Was she in on it?" A bitter taste fills my mouth.

"That's not clear, either. It'd be strange for her to hang around if she was. Unless the price placed on those blue-prints make the risk worth it." Heavy readjusts the laptop, sizing her up. My shoulders tense. "We'll find out when we catch her."

That really sets my hackles off. "Where's she hidin' out?"

"Don't know. She's been slippin' in with other folks. On occasion, she walks right in." Heavy taps the space bar and flips to a picture of her waltzing in the back door. "Deb thought she was friends with Angel. Angel thought she was with Creech. I spent an hour of my life havin' *Who's on first?* conversations with sweetbutts this morning."

"How do you know she's squatting here? She could be couch surfing with a hang around. Did you talk to all the sweetbutts?" Eighty asks. He's not gonna miss an opportunity to play devil's advocate. He can't stand that a brother his kid's age wears the *President* patch.

"Matter of fact, Ernestine brought it to my attention," Heavy says.

Grinder's ears perk up.

"She's complained to me three times this week that someone's been in her kitchen."

"We're in her kitchen all the time," Eighty observes. Grinder casts him a dirty look.

"We eat her food. We don't steal her can openers," Pig Iron points out. "And none of us is short enough to need an overturned milk crate to reach the shit on the top shelf of the pantry. I asked Crista to eyeball the bar just now. She's missing a bottle of vodka and a bottle of SoCo."

I don't feel the need to say shit about the Southern

Comfort. Dues come out of my paycheck, same as everyone else.

"Holy crap," Boots cackles. He must've woken up at some point. "We got a Goldilocks infestation! Who's been drinkin' my hooch? Who's been openin' my cans?"

That earns a chuckle. My chest eases. That sweet little thing who spread her pussy lips for me ain't a threat. For all her bravado, no one could mistake her for hard. If she's involved, she was put up to it.

"She's probably down on her luck. I mean, she was ridin' with Chaos." I still don't fuckin' like that.

"We'll find out when we catch her." Jed cracks his knuckles.

The fuck you say. I push back from the table, and my chair screeches. "No one touches her."

Heads swivel, eyes blink at me. Yeah. I ain't one to speak up at church. Or anywhere else, really. I'm a fairly mild-mannered man, and I don't generally have opinions about shit other than engines and craft beer. It tastes like piss.

Everyone's gawking at me like I got two heads.

"She's mine. Anyone finds her, they bring her to me." I push back from the table and stand. I couldn't say why I'm so sure about this. But ain't no other man here gonna lay hands on her. That's just crystal clear in my mind.

"You know her?" Jed asks.

"No."

"You got some kind of claim on her?" he pushes.

"What just came out my mouth? You wanna go?"

There's a ripple of *whoa*s and *holy shits*.

"You ever see the boy fight?" Boots whispers to Eighty, loud enough the whole room hears.

"Can't say I have. Fifty bucks says he knocks Jed out in one."

Boots shakes his head. "Sucker bet. Ain't takin' that."

"You want to weigh in on this bullshit, President?" Jed sucks his teeth.

Everyone looks to Heavy. He's studying me, brow furrowed.

Folks say we look like brothers. We got the same wavy black hair and wiry beards. I'm big—six foot two, two hundred forty pounds—but he's got four inches and thirty pounds on me. It might not be coincidence. Parties got wild back in the day. Still do.

Regardless, I don't doubt for a minute that he'll back my call.

That's what guys like Eighty and Jed don't quite *get* yet. Heavy Ruth ain't his dad. He don't live for the club. He lives for his brothers. And there's a difference. He don't always know what's right, but I have never once had cause to doubt his motivations.

We might or might not be blood, but we're family, without doubt.

"All right, brother," he agrees. "You gonna lead the hunt?"

Blood rushes to my cock, an image of that sweet ass jigglin' as she lifts her knees high and sprints away, her laughin' brown eyes sparklin'. A jolt of adrenaline puts my hangover on mute.

Then, I remember. The kids. "I got to get the boys by six."

"Okay. Until then, you work with Nickel and organize sweeps. I've called in the prospects. We'll set them up on the perimeter, cordon off the search grid." Heavy's in his element. He fuckin' loves logistics.

He carries on, arguing with Grinder about who should pay a visit to the sweetbutts to see if they have a houseguest.

My eyes are drawn back to the laptop. My stomach tight-ens, and my cock pulses. I ain't felt like this in a long, long time. If ever.

Excited.

Alive.

And ready, willing, and eager to beat the ass of any man who dares lay a hand on the pretty girl in pigtails.

I'm not that guy. I go along, get along. Mind my own business. If the pussy's easy, I don't say no. Don't go lookin' for it either.

But I don't let no man touch my bike. Or mess with my kids. And, apparently, I got a similar view about my ghost girl.

"Hey," Boots interrupts. "Dizzy? Ain't that your boy?" He's pointing at the laptop screen.

Well, I'll be damned.

Heavy's zoomed out on the picture of my girl sittin' in front of the clubhouse, and there's Carson in the back-ground, dangling from the edge of the garage roof, about to fall on his ass.

I'd like to say I'm surprised.

But I ain't in the slightest.

∾

EVEN THOUGH I ALREADY DID, we check out every nook and cranny on the property. When we don't find her, we start sweeping the woods. Truth be told, Heavy's directions get taken more as suggestions as the day wears on and everyone gets bored and then smashed.

There's no sign of Fay-Lee before I got to go get the boys. I leave with the understanding that if she's found, no one touches her 'til I get back.

I'm unsettled. She's real thin, and the sun's goin' down. There's a bitter wind kickin' up. My plan is to bring the boys back, let 'em loose, and resume the search. They'll be stoked. My boys are drawn to trouble like bugs to a porch light, and there's no end of shit they can get into unsupervised at the clubhouse. Ain't a problem. No one would let 'em come to any real harm.

I roll up to Steve's place at the same time as Sharon. The boys spill out of her white Suburban, iced coffees in hand.

I wait by the truck as the boys come runnin'.

"Dad!" Carson bumps my fist. "We gonna watch *Rocky* tonight?"

"That's the plan." I tousle his hair. It's stiff. There's gel in it. What the hell? He goes to hop in the cab. "Hold up. Not 'til you finish that." I nod at his drink.

I'm not cool with a seven-year-old chugging fancy coffee, but I'm even less cool with cleaning it out of my upholstery.

Parker runs into the house for something as Sharon makes her way over, bags dangling from her elbows. She goes up on her toes to peck my cheeks. She never did that when we were married. I think she picked it up from bein' in real estate.

"Thanks for watching them, Dwayne. You're a life saver."

I ain't "watching" them. They're my kids. But as a rule, I do not start shit with the mother of my children if it can be helped. She can put things however she wants.

Parker hurries back outside, letting the screen door slam. He's got his gaming console, wires dangling. It's gettin' harder and harder to tear him away from that machine. He's always been interested in how shit works, so I can keep him off it if we're workin' on dirt bikes or swappin' out the HVAC filter. He don't ever want to throw a ball around, though. As soon as there's no project to work on, he's back click-clackin' those buttons.

Carson's the opposite. He's a real physical kid. Uncoordinated but thick-skinned, like I was.

Parker piles into the back. I shut the door and head for the driver's side. Sharon lays a hand on my arm.

Fuck.

"I need just a minute, Dwayne." She guides me away from the truck.

This ain't good.

"What's up?"

"Listen. You remember how I was telling you about that new development that the Wade group's putting up outside of Hazleton?"

I do not remember, but that don't mean she didn't tell me.

She rolls her eyes. "Fifty single family homes on three acre lots? Starting in the low five hundreds?"

We bought our house for two hundred when I got back from my final deployment. Paid cash.

"I told you how Baker and Coyne are going to be the exclusive agents? We're doing a blitz? All units sold before the New Year?"

This is not ringin' a bell.

She drops her head back and closes her eyes. "I'm expecting that Bill will tell Steve and I tonight that we're lead agents. We'll have to get a room at an extended stay. Petty's Mill to Hazleton is a two-hour commute, both ways. This is gonna be a one-month full court press. All hands on deck. It's a once in a lifetime opportunity."

Six years ago, right after Carson was born, she took a class to get her real estate license, and overnight, she started talkin' like she's selling time-shares.

"You're gonna be out of town for a while?"

"Yes. At the end of next month." She starts to sigh in aggravation, but she catches herself. "Which means Parker and Carson are going to have to stay with you. Are you going to be up for that?"

I'm clenching my jaw so tight, my molars ache. I force myself to take a deep breath. "Yup."

She waits like she's expecting me to say something else. "We can work out the details later."

"All right."

"I haven't mentioned it to the boys yet. Carson's going to be upset. You know he's a mama's boy. He's going to need support with the transition."

"Okay." I have no fuckin' clue what that means.

Her face is turning pink. She's gettin' frustrated, but I don't know what she wants me to say.

"This is a great opportunity for Steve and me. We have a chance to take it to the next level. A six-figure month."

She looks at me, expectant.

I shove my hands in my pockets and nod.

She needs something from me, but I don't know what. That was the story of our marriage. I did all the things my pops did. Mowed the lawn, kept her gas tank topped off, worked my ass off so she could buy whatever she wanted. Enlisted in the National Guard so she could move out of the townhouse my folks helped us buy and get a house with a yard.

My mom was a happy woman. Pops and her both passed when the kids were babies, less than a month apart, and I don't remember either sayin' a harsh word about the other.

Get Sharon started, she can go on all night about me. At least she could when we were married. I'd piss her off, and she'd spend hours on the phone, whisperin' to her friends, bitchin' me out to one lady after the next.

She taps a pristine white sneaker on the driveway.

Shit. What do I say?

"Congrats."

She throws her hands up and blows out her cheeks. Guess that wasn't what she was lookin' for.

"We can talk it through later," she says. "You're dropping the kids off at school Monday, right?"

"You said I should bring 'em here Sunday night."

"Fine," she huffs. Without a word to the boys, she turns on her heel and flounces into the house.

Parker and Carson are both starin' out the truck windows at her. Carson's bottom lip is wobbling. Damn. He's so big; sometimes I forget he's only seven. And he is a mama's boy.

I hop into the truck and give 'em a smile. "How about we stop for pizza?"

The mood instantly lifts. I crank the tunes, and Carson starts tellin' me about how he shimmied all the way up the flagpole at school before the principal caught him.

I wonder if the guys have found Goldilocks.

My heart still kicks up a notch at the thought, but there's a taint to the excitement now.

In case I forgot, life ain't a fairy tale. Goldilocks don't sneak in your room to rock your world.

More likely than not, the princess is sick of you, and you ain't the prince. You're the fuckin' dancing candlestick.

"Hey, Dad. Can we ride dirt bikes tomorrow?" Parker pipes up from the back seat.

That's my boy. "Hell, yeah."

Life ain't so bad, either. I got my boys in the back, *Rocky* on Blu-ray, and a fresh memory to keep me warm when I pass out alone in my bed later tonight. In the meantime, we'll drop by the clubhouse, and the boys can play their video games while I go for round two on my little mouse hunt.

I spend the rest of the drive tryin' not to think about what I'll do when I catch her.

3

FAY-LEE

I didn't go back to the clubhouse last night. I could hear the bass beat all the way at my makeshift camp, and smell the smoke from the bonfire, but something told me not to press my luck.

So I got shitfaced under a pine tree to keep warm. Even drunk, I was bored as shit. No phone. No TV. I curled up to conserve heat and renamed the constellations after characters from *In the Arms of Love*, my favorite soap.

A lot of people think there aren't any soaps on anymore, but that's not true. There's five of them still running, but *In the Arms of Love* is my favorite. It's set in Manhattan. That's what gave me the idea of heading that way.

I'm not naïve. I'm not trying to make it on Broadway or anything. I can't sing worth shit. I just figured I want the opposite of Dalton, Kentucky. It doesn't get more different than New York City, or so I imagine.

Honestly, I didn't have much of a plan when I left. After the shed incident, I left as soon as I could.

Pure spite fueled me for the first few days, even though I was so physically weak after the hospital that I couldn't manage to walk more than a few miles a day at first. I finally cooled down halfway through West Virginia.

Wish I could summon up that rage again now. It's mid-morning, but I'm still numb with cold. The flannel helps, but when the wind gusts up, it has a wicked bite. I wrap the shirt tighter, hold the collar to my nose, and inhale. Whiskey and motor oil.

My cheeks burn. I can't believe I did that—what he asked me to do. I'm no virgin. Rylan Dorset sweet-talked me out of my V-card the summer after ninth grade. But I have four sisters with nine kids and no husbands between them. Men lost their shine for me about the same time as my youngest sister brought home her third baby.

I know better than to fall for male bullshit. Most men leave you worse than they found you, that's the long and short of it. It's like the opposite of taking only pictures, leaving only footprints. They take only whatever they want, leave when you need them most.

I'm sure there're good men out there. In real life, Luke Lamore from *In the Arms of Love* helps rehome pets when their elderly owners pass. Still. It's beyond foolish to sit around waitin' for a man to rescue you.

I should go for a walk, get the blood flowing. It's a damn miracle I didn't freeze to death when I passed out last night. The blanket didn't do much. Too thin. I stand, flick off the pine needles stickin' to my thighs, and head in a direction away from the clubhouse, deeper into the woods.

The quiet is strange. I've never been alone before in my life. I can appreciate the beauty, but it creeps me the fuck out.

Truth is, I might be getting a little homesick. Not for the people. Screw them. But for a place to be where all I've got are my old, familiar problems.

In retrospect, I might have gone off half-cocked. What happened with the shed was an accident after all.

A suffocating feeling seizes my chest. I wiggle my fingers, reassure myself. My nails have grown back. I'm alive. No permanent harm done.

I stomp my feet, jog a few feet, shake out my arms. Fight through the residual panic.

Anyway, home wasn't perfect—not by far—but at least I had a room, even if I had to share, and we had electric most months. I had a bed, and when the heat got turned off, nieces and nephews would always end up crawling in for body heat, and it'd be cozy, if crowded and stinky.

I can't believe Chaos just took off, no word. I should have kept an eye on him. A name like that—I can't say I wasn't warned. He seemed pretty steady, though. Didn't drink much. Spent a lot of time texting on his phone.

I head off uphill, toward the low mountain rising in the distance. There are tons of trails back here, mostly narrow ruts for dirt bikes. I kick up the pace, and my heart starts pumping. My joints loosen as I limber up.

It's a beautiful day. Perfect blue sky. Wispy white clouds. Red and yellow and orange leaves rustling overhead.

Will I even like living in a big city? Is it true you can't see the stars 'cause of all the streetlights? That would suck.

A stiff breeze carries a faint whining buzz, coming from up ahead. Someone's out riding the trails. They're far away, though, heading toward the mountain.

I stick to a trail that curves and winds. I hop stones to cross a creek, and pick it up again on the other side.

If I hate New York, there's no saying I have to stay there. *Love Another Day* films in Burbank, California. I could try my luck there. It'd be warmer, that's for damn sure. *The*

world is your oyster as Gram used to say. I'll get more enthusi-
astic for the adventure once I get somewhere.

My spirits are rising with my body temperature as I
round a bend in the trail.

I gasp.

Holy shit.

There in a forest green flannel and dark jeans is the
shaggy dude from the bedroom, kneeling beside a dirt bike
lying on its side.

He surges to his feet, and his eyes go wide.

I freeze in the middle of the trail.

"Don't run," he says, raising his palms. "We just want to
talk to you."

We? Oh, hell no.

I bolt into the underbrush.

"Hey!" he barks.

His footsteps thud in the dirt behind me, and I pump my
arms, lift my knees high. Thorns tear at my skin; vines wrap
around my ankles. I trip, biting my cheek. The terrain's
uneven, all ditches and slopes. Felled branches and bram-
bles block my way.

They're on to me. They know I've been sneaking in. I'm
dead.

I clamber up a bank, skirting a massive, mossy trunk,
forcing a path through. Prickles catch my shirt, tangle in my
hair.

Leaves crunch as he tears through the woods behind me.

I push harder. He's so big. There's got to be a narrow gap
I can slip through, a thicket I can wriggle into and hide,
where he can't follow. A hollow log. Something.

My lungs burn.

We just want to talk to you.

That's never the truth. Not from the cops. Not from

outlaw bikers who catch you trespassing on their property. I lengthen my stride, landing funny on my ankle. There's a sharp twinge, but I'm not stopping. I limp on, favoring the other leg, and then there's a clearing ahead.

A creek with wide, pebbled banks runs through it.

"Baby. Stop!"

I pump my arms. Sticks crack and boots pound behind me. I'm not goin' down easy. I'm—

Flying through the air, twisting, limbs flying, wrapped in impossibly strong arms. I land with a jolt on top of a huge, hard man. The impact knocks the breath from my lungs.

Before I can blink, he's flipped us so I'm underneath him, smooth stones pressing into my back. The creek babbles a few feet from my head.

He's panting, smiling ear-to-ear, his bright black eyes crinkling at the corners. His beard scratches my upper chest. During the chase, the flannel I stole from him flew open.

"Caught you," he says.

I don't know what to do. This can't be good. Why's he smiling?

Well, when in Rome? I offer him a tentative grin in return. "Want to go again?" I pant between gasps.

He laughs, low and gravelly. It vibrates against my belly. He's lying on top of me, but he's keeping most of his weight off me. My legs are pressed together, his knees bracketing my thighs, my hands braced against his chest. He could do whatever he wants. He's double my size.

My heart skips, and heat flows to my pussy. Dumb body. I should be fighting. Struggling. Instead, I gently press my fingers into his pecs, test the muscle. He's as solid as a rock.

The woods are silent except for the wind in the treetops and a goose honking high overhead. I spread my fingers. His heart thumps against my palm. He doesn't stop me. He lets me explore. I run my hands up and over his shoulders.

"Come on. It'll be fun." I try a flirty smile. His lip curls. He has really nice teeth.

"You don't stand a chance. You're slow as shit." He smooths my hair from my face, plucking stickers and leaves free.

I stay real still. His fingers skim down my jaw.

"Then why are you out of breath?" I ask.

"Out of practice."

"Bet you couldn't catch me if we went again."

He chuckles. "I know better than to take that bet." He runs a calloused thumb across my lower lip, rubbing at my scar. "How'd you get this?"

"I'll tell you if you let me up."

He shifts so that he's between my legs. I can feel his hard cock against my lower belly. I suck in a breath and tuck my arms back tight to my chest. His mouth turns down.

"Ain't gonna hurt you, baby."

"You tackled me to the ground."

"You're all right." His brow creases. He pushes up on his arms, biceps flexing, and scans my body. "Shit. You tore your legs to hell."

"*I* didn't do it. It was the sticker bushes."

He's got my boot by the laces, and he's tugging my leg up so he can get a closer look, rising to his knees. He's really big. I'm still pinned underneath him, his massive thighs bracing mine apart.

My heart races, as fast as when I was running.

I'm scared. But also, I'm not. He's not moving fast, pushing and pushing, like men do when they're trying to get somethin'.

"It hurt much?" He plucks a splinter from my ankle. It stings.

I shake my head.

His lips are pressed in a tight line, his eyes hooded. He's got so much hair and beard, if you don't look close, you miss the expressions flitting across his face. Like now. Fun is over. He's gone serious.

"We got to get back to the clubhouse, clean these up."

Okay, now I'm scared again. This guy seems to have a soft spot for me, but Heavy and the others? Women are nothing but pussy to that kind of men. I know that.

I paste on my sweetest, most innocent smile. "Or you could let me go. Pretend you never saw me. I'll disappear. I won't cause any more trouble."

He gently lowers my leg and rests his huge hands on my hips. My breath catches. His thumbs touch and fingers wrap almost all the way around my waist.

I feel very small.

"I ain't lettin' you go."

Shivers dart down my spine.

"If you take me back there, they'll hurt me." I wish I was playin' him, but the pit in my stomach says it's the truth.

"No, they won't. They just want to ask you some questions. They been lookin' for you."

I've watched every detective show there is, walking the floor with colicky babies. That is a line of bullshit.

"I won't tell anyone that you let me go." I don't think this man would care if I tattled, but I'll try anything. Is there a rock around here? I could bash him in the head like on TV.

"You lookin' for something to hit me with?" He grins. Damn but he does have really white, even teeth. They come as a shock on a man as hairy and rough around the edges as him.

"Nope. I wouldn't."

He tightens his grip on my middle. Not so much that it hurts, but my hands fly to his forearms. They're hard as steel. I couldn't budge this man an inch if I tried.

"Don't lie to me." There's a warning in his tone. Little zings skitter across my bare skin.

"Maybe." Why is my voice breathless?

I recognize that this situation is deadly serious. Steel Bones knows I've been squatting, and I guess they've been hunting me down.

So why does this feel like he and I are playing a game?

I should claw at his eyes. Fight for my life.

But my pussy's getting wet. That's stupid, stupid, stupid.

I squirm. His grasp doesn't give, not even a little.

"What are you gonna do to me?" My voice is a whisper. I curl my fingers around his forearms, test the skin with my nails.

It's like yesterday in the room. Longing swirls in my belly, halfway between an itch and a craving. I don't get this way with guys. I can see to my own needs, and I appreciate a well-made man as much as the next girl, but nothing they *do* moves me much.

Except this man.

Everything he does makes my body do tricks. My tummy flips, my tits ache, my pussy throbs, tender against the seam of my shorts.

"Baby, you gotta stop lookin' at me like that," he growls.

"Why?" What is he going to do to me if I keep it up? My heartbeat kicks up a notch. I shouldn't ask. I don't want to know, right?

But I also really, really do.

There's a shout in the distance. His gaze hardens, and suddenly, he's all business.

"Up you go." He pops to his feet, hauling me up after him, enveloping my hand in his huge paw. I tug. He squeezes tighter. "Come on."

He pulls me back the way we came. When I drag my feet, he doesn't give an inch, but he stays in the lead, blocking the sticker bushes, swinging me over fallen logs.

"When we get to the boys, you don't say nothin'. Don't try to run."

The boys?

The whine of engines grows louder as we near the trail.

He stops, and I nearly slam into his back.

"You hear me?" he asks over his shoulder.

He doesn't wait for an answer. He jerks me forward, and as we step out of the underbrush, two little boys on dirt bikes come flying toward us. They skid to a stop, sending up clods of dirt.

Show-offs.

"Hey, where'd you go? We saw your bike—" The older one stops mid-sentence when I step out from behind his dad.

"Hey, lady." The younger one waves in recognition. "Where's your bike?"

"What happened to your leg?" The older one's nose is wrinkled up.

I look down. There's a smear of blood down my calf. Gross.

A bullfrog honks.

Leaves rustle.

I look up.

All three of them are staring at my leg, waiting for me to answer the question.

This is utterly surreal.

"Sticker bush," I say.

The older boy nods, satisfied. "You gonna ride two-up?" he asks his father.

"Gonna have to. You take Carson back. We'll be behind you."

"What's her name?" The husky one from the garage—Carson—flips up the visor on his helmet to get a better look.

I go to answer, but the big man beats me to it. "Fay-Lee."

He knows my name.

That's not good.

But still, my chest warms.

"So what's your name?" I crane my neck and yank my arm, but he's still got an iron grip on my hand.

"Dad's road name is Dizzy. But his real name's Dwayne. You can call him whichever you want." Carson lifts his chin at his brother. "He's Parker. I'm Carson."

Why do they both have last names as first names?

"Dizzy," the dad corrects. "Call me Dizzy."

"Okay, Dwayne." It flies out of my mouth. I don't even think about it.

A split second later, Dizzy drops my hand and lands a walloping slap to my ass. I sway forward.

"Hey!" I grab the cheek and rub. It didn't hurt. Not really. But it did surprise the shit out of me.

Parker snorts.

Carson shakes his head. "You can't do that to a woman, Dad. She's gonna be mad."

"You mad?" Dizzy's eyes are twinkling, his mouth quirked up at the corner amid that thick beard.

I should be. I narrow my eyes.

"Yeah, she's mad." Carson nods. "Look at her face."

"I better get her back to the clubhouse, then. Feed her. Patch her up."

"Yeah." Carson snaps his visor back down. "I'm hungry, too."

Parker revs his engine. In some kind of silent accord, both boys tear off, mud spraying behind them in all directions.

Dizzy tugs me toward his bike.

"You can't just kidnap me with your kids right there."

"I'm not kidnapping you."

We come up along his two-wheeler. "We're not both gonna fit on that."

He's sizing it up, eyeing me. I'm skinny, but the laws of physics still apply, and he's gargantuan.

He grunts. "We'll walk back. I'm not confident about that patch anyway."

"I don't know. If you leave it here, someone might take it. You go ahead and ride it back. Fix it up. I'll follow."

He snorts, grabs my hand again, and drags me off in the direction of the clubhouse. His stride is long. I scamper to keep up.

My brain's spinning a mile a minute. If he loosens his hold for just a second, I can run. Didn't work last time, but if I stick to the trail, I'll have a better shot. I'm younger than him by a lot. I've got stamina.

And an empty belly and an aching ankle.

Maybe the club really just wants to ask me a few questions. Maybe they want to know how I dodged their security. This could be like the hacker who gets hired by the FBI 'cause her skills are so crazy good.

Yeah, right. That's not what's happening here.

They know my name. They've been looking for me. I'm no fool. No one knows that I'm here except Chaos, and the Lord only knows where he is. They're gonna kill me. Make an example. I struggle for breath, not from the pace, but the growing panic.

I should have left when I had the chance. What are blisters to being murdered and buried in an unmarked grave in the back of a biker compound?

We're closing in on the tree line. I can see the makeshift stage in the yard and the picnic table pavilion.

I dig in my heels. Dizzy's still moving, so he nearly yanks my arm from the socket.

"Let me go." I'm not joking anymore. My brave front's gone. My eyes are prickling, and my nose is burning. I'm gonna start bawling. "I promise I'll disappear. I'm not gonna be any more trouble for you guys."

He stops, gazes down at me, forehead furrowed. He drops my hand and raises my chin with the knuckle of his index finger.

"I said no one's gonna hurt you."

"I don't believe you." It's a whisper.

"Baby," he says. "You don't have a choice."

A cry echoes in the yard, and in seconds, huge, tattooed men in leather and chains are trotting toward us, surrounding us, and there's no way out. I'm trapped.

Everything goes red.

They're not taking me without a fight.

My elbow connects with a slab of muscle, and I keep going, eyes screwed shut, desperate and wild.

All I can hear through the roar in my ears is Dizzy shouting, "Back the fuck off."

4

DIZZY

She loses her mind.

Mikey and another prospect lope over with Jed and Bullet, and she freaks out. I got my arm around her waist before she can run, but she fights, flailing, nails me in the ribs with a bony elbow.

Thank goodness the boys ain't around. They're probably in the kitchen by now.

I hold her firm against my chest, arms pinned to her sides, and I try to hush her. She don't like that. She windmills her legs. Jed lunges for her, and before I can warn him off, she nails him in the solar plexus. He snarls, raising a fist.

On instinct, I spin with her, give him my back. A weird growl comes from my chest. I cough to clear my throat.

"Back up, dude, and she won't kick you." I jiggle her a little. "Calm down now."

"Let me go," she screams.

I can feel her chest expand as she gets ready to howl. I slap a hand across her mouth, careful to leave her nose free.

"No one's gonna hurt you. They just wanna ask you some questions."

Even to my ears, I sound full of shit.

No one's gonna touch her, though. No one but me.

She keeps fighting, but she's fading quick. She's probably starving. She needs protein. As soon as Heavy gets his answers, she's gettin' fed.

I wrangle her toward the stairs to the basement. We've got a gym set up down there. Nothing fancy. Twitch's old free weights and barbells. A treadmill, all-in-one machine, punching bag. When the addition is finished, we're gonna expand and add a sparring ring, sauna, the works.

For now, it serves our purposes. With the door closed, it's soundproof. Spotty cell phone signal. One way in, one way out.

As soon as I haul her down the stairs, she starts struggling again in earnest, screaming into my palm. She's gonna hurt herself.

"I'll get some rope," Jed says.

"The fuck you will."

She's out of her mind, though. Jerkin' her head back, aimin' to smash my nose, the whites of her eyes flashin'. I drag her into an alcove, away from the bench where Heavy and Grinder are waiting.

"Gimme a minute," I bark at them as she slams a boot into my shin.

For lack of options, I press her against the wall, my chest to her back. I got a hard on—I've had one since I saw her in the middle of the trail, wearin' my shirt—and I know it ain't the time and place, but damned if I can help it. She feels it and makes a strangled yelp.

"Calm down. They're just gonna ask you some questions."

She's got no room to move, but her body's wired taut, and she's tryin' her damnedest to budge me.

She's as bad as the boys get for Sharon when they stay up all night, eating nothin' but crap, and then melt down when it's time for school. Sharon's called me a few times, askin' me to haul Parker's ass into the building. It don't ever come to that. The kid can be reasoned with. Probably 'cause he knows I'll carry him into class over my shoulder like a sack of potatoes.

I never would have pulled that shit as a kid. My old man wouldn't have it. He'd have tanned my hide. But Sharon doesn't approve of "corporal punishment." She says people don't do that no more.

This ain't a kid acting up, though. And if Fay-Lee don't chill the fuck out, I don't how this is gonna go.

Steel Bones has never hurt women, but shit is changing. This ain't the club I patched into when I turned eighteen, my dad at my side. The stakes are multi-million dollars now. Life or death.

The jobs we do now—there's much less risk in the front end. We ain't racking up charges for petty shit like back in the day. Now, if we get popped, it's serious time. Not only for us. The cast of characters we could implicate is growin' every year. If these men don't trust that we handle our business, we all become a liability.

Heavy's made us rich, but he's also made us vulnerable. I believe he will back my call when it comes to this woman who's done lost her mind, but he ain't the only one with skin in the game.

If Fay-Lee knew what Chaos was doin'—if she was helpin' him—I don't know how that plays out. She needs to show she can reason. A person who cannot control themselves is nothing but a threat.

"Come on. Pull it together," I mutter in her ear.

She kicks my foot and whimpers in pain. Steel-toed boots.

"You about done in there?" Heavy shouts.

"Almost." Ah, shit.

If we were somewhere else, I'd give her a shot and a toke. But I don't have my flask on me.

She's not givin' me a choice here. I tighten my grip on her mouth. She's tryin' to bite me.

Fuck. It worked with Parker when he was little.

I reach around, unbutton her shorts. They fall straight down.

Damn. She's not wearing panties. That sweet, taut ass is bare.

This isn't about that. Focus.

She kicks up the volume again, but whatever she's hollering is muffled by my palm.

Here goes nothing.

I back up, bend my knee, and turn her, using one arm to force her over the best I can, freeing her mouth.

Her shrill shriek echoes off the ceiling.

I haul back and smack that ass.

She goes absolutely quiet and still.

A bright red handprint shows up on her creamy skin.

Shit.

I can't tear my eyes away. My hand is huge. The mark spans from her ass crack to her hip.

"What the fuck are you doing?" she gasps.

I smack her again. She squeals, clenches her cheeks tight. "Hey!"

I do it again. Her ass jiggles. Holy shit. I can't believe I'm doin' this. I should stop.

She's still flailing and screaming, though, and it takes all my strength to keep her pressed to my thigh. Fuck. In for a penny, in for a pound.

I crack her again. The whack echoes. She bucks, tries to avoid the blow, but she's got nowhere to go. She's hollering, wordless. She don't sound scared so much anymore as highly indignant.

I lay down four or five more, careful to make an impression, but not use the kind of force that would actually hurt her.

If this don't work, I'm out of ideas.

On the eighth or ninth whack, she starts to calm. Totally silent except for sniffles and an occasional hiccup.

Both globes of her ass are glowing pink.

I rub the handprints, smooth them out. She moans. Her skin's hot to the touch.

"It's all right now, baby. Everything's okay." I set her upright on her feet.

She's breathing heavy. So am I.

She blinks at me with her jaw dropped open. I'm expecting her to be furious, but those big brown eyes are dazed.

"Did I hurt you?" My words catch in my throat. I ain't never done anything like that before. I mean, yeah, I've slapped a woman's ass while we were fucking doggy-style, but this? I watch it in porn, but in real life? No.

"You spanked me," she whispers. She seems as surprised as I am.

"You're calm now," I point out, stepping back.

She squats and tugs up her shorts, casting anxious looks at the doorway to the other room.

"I ain't gonna let anything happen. You have to trust me."

"I don't," she hisses. "I don't trust you." She's flustered

and her fingers keep slipping off the button. I push her hands aside and do it up for her.

She glances up at me under thick black lashes. Her face is as red as her bottom, but she really don't seem mad.

She's unsteady. Scared.

She should be, but I don't like it.

"You need help back there?" Jed hollers.

"Fuck off," I shout back. That asshole is way too eager for this.

Fay-Lee starts trembling all over. Even her chin's wobbling. Ah, hell.

I bend over and snag my butterfly knife from my boot. I flick my wrist back, unsheathe it so she sees it ain't a toy. She gasps.

"You used one of these before?"

Her eyes are as round as saucers. Shit. She thinks I'm gonna stab her.

She slowly shakes her head *no*.

I show her a few times how it opens, how to fold it and hold it by the dull side. I don't think she's following much. Then I hold it out to her, handle first.

"Put it in your pocket. Don't take it out unless you plan on using it."

I'll be able to disarm her before she can undo the latch, but if it makes her feel better, I don't see the harm. Turns out I much prefer her angry to scared.

She nods, somber, and shoves it in her shorts. My chest twinges. She's a brave little thing. Ain't right that someone's let her come to this, all alone.

I gesture to the other room. She walks out, takin' small steps, as if she's headed for an execution.

I try to see things from her perspective. There are six

huge men, stone-faced, arms folded, in a half circle by a bench. Each one looks like a hardened criminal.

Each one *is*, in his way.

Heavy nods to the weight bench. "Sit."

At some point, Nickel joined us. He's the only one pacing. Fay-Lee tracks him, and she jumps when he makes his sudden moves.

If you don't know him, he seems like he's on coke. He's intense. I knew guys like that in the service. PTSD. Hyper-vigilance. Nickel didn't serve, but his upbringing was its own shitshow. He's the only man in his family not incarcerated or dead.

I ain't as worried about Nickel as I am about Jed and Heavy. Nickel's oblivious to it, but if you know him, it's clear he's got a soft spot for the females. Treats 'em like glass. Or like a cottonmouth. Steers clear.

Jed spends a lot of time with the ladies, but he doesn't have much regard for them. Nails and bails. He's ten years older than I am and never had an old lady. Fay-Lee being a female won't earn her any special treatment with him.

And under the fancy talk and gravitas, Heavy is a cold motherfucker. He did Chaos without hesitation. Slit his throat as if he was slaughtering a pig.

My muscles tense. That's not how this is going to go. Fay-Lee was clearly in the wrong place at the wrong time. Along for the ride.

She cowers on the bench, arms hugging her middle, shoulders hunched, and knees pressed tight together. The silence grows thick. Nickel's rubber soles squeak on the floor, somehow amping up the tension.

Heavy slowly, deliberately drags over a metal folding chair. He cracks his jaw and ponderously lowers his bulk. The chair creaks.

Fay-Lee's throat works as she swallows. Her eyes dart all over. She's searching for an escape, but there isn't one.

At least she's got a grip on the hysteria. My palm tingles, remembering. I can't believe I did that. It did the job, but it doesn't sit entirely easy with me.

Heavy clears his throat. "Where did you meet Chaos?"

Her gaze shoots to me, as if she's looking for permission. I nod.

I like her looking to me for the go ahead.

"A rest stop. On 71."

"You know him before that?"

"No."

"Were you hitching?"

"Yeah."

"Where were you coming from?"

"Dalton."

"Georgia?"

"Kentucky."

"Where'd you meet Chaos?"

"I told you. A rest stop. At a picnic table."

"Why'd you leave Dalton?"

"Change of scenery."

"Try again."

"Why does it matter to you?"

Jed gets in her face, peels back his lips so she can see the Steel Bones tattoo inside. "You don't ask the questions, bitch. You answer them."

My chest swells. What did that fucker say?

"You understand?" He grabs her chin.

Hell, no.

I lunge forward, drive my shoulder into him, knocking him onto his ass. I've got my boot raised to crush his larynx when Nickel drives into me from behind, shoving me aside.

Heavy leaps to his feet. The metal chair clatters to the floor.

Jed scrambles to his feet, puffing his chest, arms stretched wide. "What the fuck, man?"

"Touch her again. I'll kill you."

"Have you gone insane?" Jed glances from brother to brother. No one backs him. They're gawping as if they never seen me before.

"You wanna go or what?" I'll settle this now. Not a problem.

Jed doesn't make a move. He knows I can lay his ass out cold in one shot.

Nickel eases away from my side. I suck down a deep breath. I'm good. The red is seeping away, and I'm myself again.

"Back away from her."

Jed spits, but he steps away toward the leg machine. "Who's this gash to you?"

Nickel claps a steadying palm on my shoulder. "Ain't worth it," he murmurs.

Jed sneers. Weak-chinned, wannabe motherfucker. I should drop him on principle; I'll pick which one afterwards.

Heavy gestures for Jed to shut up, and then he turns to me, palms raised. "This was not part of my calculations." He shakes his head, smiling wryly. "Dizzy, my apologies."

What's he apologizing for?

Everyone's staring at me. Fay-Lee's eyes are eating up half her face. I catch my reflection in the mirrored wall.

Oh.

I unclench my fists. I can't do anything about my face, though.

I don't think I've ever looked like this before. Like I'm

about to do murder.

It ain't that I'm unfamiliar with violence. Yeah, I mostly work at the garage. I fill in at The White Van, rousting drunks. But on occasion, if you belong to a club like this, you pull a messy job. And I did do two tours in Iraq.

Still, I'm not one to spar by the bonfire or brawl at the bar. If it's got to be done, I'll do it, but I'd rather be in the garage.

Or I was. My blood's coursing through my veins, and I have to flex my fingers to stop myself from balling them back into fists. If we were alone, I'd happily mash Jed's head into the free weights until it's pulp and bone shards.

"A word?" Heavy gestures to the alcove.

I ain't leaving Fay-Lee here with that asshole.

"She'll be cool, boss," Mikey the prospect pipes up. He plops down on the bench next to Fay-Lee and grins at her. "'Sup?"

She tentatively lifts a shoulder, baffled and tense. "Not much?"

Mikey is a distant cousin on my mom's side. I've known him since he was born. He's almost as skinny as Fay-Lee, but I trust him.

Still. "He doesn't touch her." I point at Jed, and then I glare at the other brothers. "No one touches her."

"Understood." Heavy gestures toward the stairs. I lead the way, up and out into the yard. The cool air hits me, and I take a deep breath. Damn, it was stifling down there.

Heavy leans against the building, takes a pack of cigarettes from his pocket, and shakes one loose for me.

"Nah, man." I quit after my discharge. Quit for good after we had Carson. Hardest thing I ever done.

Heavy's a chipper. I don't understand how a man can smoke one here and there and not get addicted, but he is a man of exceptional will. He flicks his lighter and inhales deep. I still love the smell.

I lean next to him, kick the heel of my boot up on the brick. We stand a while in silence, admiring the woods with the leaves all turned colors.

We've got ourselves a slice of heaven out here. The woods, the fields across the highway, the foothills rising in the distance. Room to spread out. Our grandfathers did well when they pooled their money and bought this acreage after the war.

After a minute or two, Heavy breaks the silence. "We have a problem."

I exhale. "Yeah. I know."

"If she was helping Chaos, she knows things. Even if she wasn't, she can place him here. She's a material witness. Either way, she can be used to bring down this club."

"She's what? Twenty?"

"She's eighteen. We ran her information."

Shit. That's young. Still. "She was in the wrong place at the wrong time."

"Maybe. She's still a liability." I tense. Heavy claps a paw on my shoulder. "Relax. I'm stating facts. You've made yourself clear. She's a risk I guess we're gonna take."

"I don't think she's in on it. Look at her. She's down on her luck."

"Maybe. But we need to ameliorate the risk."

"You're gonna need to speak plain English, my brother."

Heavy went away to college. That's where he came up with the plan that's changing our way of life. He was always wicked smart, but when he came back from Massachusetts, he stopped bothering to hide it.

"We can keep going down this road," he says. "Interrogate her. Put the fear of God in her. Dig up information on her family. Hold that over her head. Send her on her way. We can use the stick."

I don't care for that.

"Or we can use the carrot. No offense, but your woman's stick thin, and she's clearly been roughing it. The weather's turning. She gets along with the other sweetbutts. Maybe we use the carrot. The clubhouse could use a house mouse."

She's not staying here with Jed and a bunch of horny prospects.

Heavy glances at me from the corner of his eye. "You could take her home with you. Place could use a woman's touch."

It could. And my cock definitely perks up at the thought of her bent over the sink, elbow-deep in suds.

But I been down that road. Domesticity. It's all great—mince-meat pie coolin' on the counter, pussy on tap—until your credit cards are maxed out and your woman's talkin' about *self-actualization* all the time like you did something wrong.

Besides, Fay-Lee's too young. The boys would run roughshod over her. Especially if they're gonna be around full time for a while.

I don't need to invite conflict into my home. It's peaceful now.

"If you don't like that plan, we could find somewhere else. Grinder maybe. Or Harper probably wouldn't mind some help around the house."

Grinder would perv on her, and I've seen Harper Ruth with the sweetbutts. Fay-Lee's got spunk, but Harper's a maneater. People eater. Whatever.

"I can't lock her in a room with the boys around. And I gotta work." But maybe I could talk to her. Make her see it's a win-win.

"If this plays out the way I intend, it won't be that kind of thing." Heavy's asking me to trust him. Trust that wily brain of his.

"What's the end game? She can't stay forever." My gut sours. I probably need to eat.

"We'll make friends. She's a friendly girl. We'll find out if she knows anything. Who knows? Maybe we can hook her up with a job at The White Van. She fits in."

Over my dead body. "She ain't dancin'."

"Okay. You call the shots." Heavy's lip twitches.

"What?"

"I don't think I've ever heard you this decisive about anything besides shovelheads."

"Who gives a shit about reliability if it don't sound good?" People got fucked up priorities these days. If you're hung up on reliability, buy a fuckin' station wagon. But yeah. I don't usually show an interest in much besides mechanics.

Heavy chuckles. "Agreed. Let's go back in. I'll lay it out for her." He knocks the cherry of his cigarette off against the brick and pinches the tip. There's an ashtray-trashcan combo by the door. Wall reams anyone who flicks a butt on the ground.

"What if she don't bite?" Unease churns in my chest again.

"I'm a very persuasive man."

I hope so. I have always backed my brothers one hundred percent. I was born and raised in this club. I've never gone against them. I never would.

But for this tiny slip of a girl with big brown eyes and a crooked smile?

My back molars grind, and a jolt of adrenaline shoots through my veins. I ain't thinkin' straight.

This better go like Heavy thinks it will.

5

FAY-LEE

I'm gonna die in a dank basement gym that smells like ball sweat. Jed is probably gonna brain me with a ten-pound weight. He'd enjoy it, too. He's muttering in the corner with Nickel, shooting me nasty looks. He doesn't like that Dizzy made him back off.

He was a lot nicer when I met him with Chaos when we first came to town. We went to some honkytonk bar, and Jed and I played horseshoes out back while Chaos met with some old dude.

Mikey's on his phone next to me watching videos with the sound off, laughing to himself every so often.

Grinder's inspecting the treadmill. He's an older dude, grizzled and barrel-chested, belt holding up his beer belly. I'll go out on a limb and venture a guess that he's not familiar with the machine.

There are two other brothers whose names I don't know, standing sentry at the exit, stone-faced and menacing.

I'm terrified, but I'm also bizarrely calm. My ass is sore. I shift from cheek to cheek, but that doesn't make it better for long. My brain's also foggy.

Dizzy wasn't messing around. He walloped me good. I haven't gotten a whuppin' like that since I got big enough to outrun Mama. I should be livid.

I was hysterical, though. Those men surrounded me, and I got the suffocating feeling. I kept flashing back to the shed. I was out of my mind. Now I'm not. Kind of like I had the hiccups, and he scared them out of me.

Of course, I'm not okay with him doing it.

But okay feels really relative right now. I'm being held hostage, and from the expression on these guys' faces, they aren't just pissed that I've been sneaking in and stealing booze. Somehow, I've fucked up in a serious way.

I rest my hand on the bump the knife makes in my pocket. By the time I get it out and open, they'd have me disarmed, but the gesture was nice.

Dizzy's nice.

Maybe that's not the word for it. Nice guys don't spank your bare ass and kidnap you and whatnot. All I know is I'll feel better when he comes back. When Jed grabbed my face, Dizzy laid him out.

Boom. One hit. On the floor. After that, all the men in the room kind of shuffled back, gave me space.

Shit. What if Heavy took him out to get him out of the way? My heartbeat kicks up. My knee jiggles. Mikey glances over.

"Not much longer," he says.

Dread creeps over me. I really don't want to die. I'm not sure what I want to do with my life, but I want time to decide.

Boots stomp down the steps. My muscles bunch.

Heavy comes in first, ducking under the doorframe. Dizzy's behind him. I exhale the breath I was holding, and my shoulders ease down.

Jed and Nickel move to come over, but Heavy waves them back. He picks up the folding chair and sits.

"Let's start over, Fay-Lee. No questions. Instead, I'm going to tell you what I know."

I look to Dizzy. He's standing to the side, arms folded, face shuttered. He won't meet my eyes. Okay. My jitters swoop to life.

Heavy smiles. It's not the slightest bit reassuring. His canines are crazy sharp. Wolf-like.

"I know you've been squatting. You've been sneaking in with our guests. Helping yourself to food from the kitchen and booze from the bar."

He smiles wider. "I know that despite that, you're probably hungry. Tired. In need of a hot shower. You're a long way from home."

As if on cue, my stomach rumbles.

Where is he going with this?

"You came here with Chaos. Do you know where he went?"

It seems like a genuine question. I shake my head.

"He left you here?"

I shrug.

He waits, head cocked.

"Yes," I croak. I clear my throat. "He ditched me."

Heavy nods his shaggy head. He has the same wiry, black hair and beard as Dizzy, but where Dizzy looks badass, Heavy looks like an extra from a cable TV show about dragons. There're only a few inches and a thirty pounds or so difference between them, but I guess that's the difference between a large man and a giant.

"That's messed up. I'm sorry you ended up in this situation." He waits.

"Thanks?"

He smiles, encouragingly. "I have a proposition for you. Dizzy and I have been talking. We've figured out a solution that will work for everyone."

Dizzy's face doesn't soften at all.

"The way I see it, you owe us for our hospitality. We can't just let folks trespass and steal from us without consequence. Wouldn't look good, would it?"

He waits again. I shake my head.

"It seems to me you owe us. And it turns out that Dizzy here is in need of a house mouse."

Heavy leans back in the chair, clasping his hands over his broad stomach. The chair groans. He cocks his head.

Does this mean they're not gonna kill me?

"What's a house mouse?"

"A woman who cleans. Cooks. Like a maid."

"Like a maid?"

"She's free pussy, too, but mostly cleaning as I understand. I've never had one myself. Grinder, you have, right?" Heavy turns to the older man.

Grinder grunts. "Yup. Danielle bunked with me for a spell. Took care of the dogs. Ate me out of fuckin' house and home. I ate her out, too," he cackles. "We ended up even."

Danielle's a sweetbutt. She's a dancer. And at least thirty years younger than Grinder.

"You know Dizzy has kids. We'd need to be able to trust you around them. We'll need a last name. ID. We'll run a check. Make sure you're solid. It's an opportunity. Get you back on your feet."

They're going to let me out of this basement. I'll be a house mouse. I'll be whatever they want. And as soon as they turn their backs, I'll be gone.

"I don't have ID. Chaos left with all my shit."

"We can work around that. What's your last name, Fay-Lee?"

"Parsons."

"You're good people, aren't you Fay-Lee Parsons? You just found yourself in a bad situation."

I don't know what's happening here. Heavy's black gaze is boring into me. I squirm. I can't help it. I can't tear my eyes from him, though. I'm snared. He's hypnotizing me.

Huh. I thought I was too stubborn for that.

"Yeah." I am a good person, and this situation does suck.

"It'd be good to have a soft bed? Warm food? Rest?"

My chin wobbles. I clench my jaw to make it stop. But he's right.

A bed would be really nice. I'm tough, but my body feels a hundred years old. I could use a break.

"I'll make a few calls. I'm sure you'll check out. You can go home with Dizzy. Deal?"

A flood of relief busts loose in my chest. Yes, I want to go home with Dizzy. Which doesn't make any sense. This whole scenario isn't right. Ten minutes ago, I was in the hot seat. Now I'm a charity case? Something ain't right.

But does it really matter? Heavy's offering me a way out of this basement. I can go along with it long enough to fill my belly.

And a night in a soft bed before I hit the road again wouldn't be the worst.

I don't trust this man. I don't trust any of them. They're working really hard to convince me to go quietly to a second location. I watch missing person shows. You never go to a second location. That's where they kill you.

But what choice do I have?

And they want me to go home with Dizzy. The guy who ten minutes ago was wailing on my ass. I shouldn't agree. It hurts like hell to sit right now, and that's due to him. Why aren't I steaming mad?

I find myself looking up at him. His stone-face falls for a moment, and his eyes seem to want to tell me something. He nods almost imperceptibly.

There's no real reason to trust him. Yeah, he seems to have a possessive streak when it comes to me, but possessive is how all manner of ugliness begins. My sisters love the jealous type. Until they've got to call in every hour, and they get in trouble for going to the male teller's line at the bank.

What's the option though?

"All right," I say.

There's no way these guys are on the up-and-up.

I pray I'm smart enough to bail before whatever trap this is springs shut.

DIZZY HUSTLES me out of the basement right quick. He drags me to the kitchen and bellows for his boys. Takes him more than a few shouts to round 'em up. Then he leads us to his truck and barks at us to get in. He opens the door for me, and he snaps at Carson when he shoves past me to climb over the passenger seat to the back row.

Some of the awful tension seeps from my body. He's not taking me to a second location to kill me with his kids in the truck.

The adrenaline is fading, and now my ass is throbbing in earnest. The scratches on my legs hurt, too. I lift myself gingerly to the passenger seat, and I try to prop myself up by shoving my fists under my thighs. When Dizzy swings into the cab, he notices and frowns.

"When we get home, I'll get you an ice pack. And we'll clean up your legs."

"You could say sorry." I'm feeling a little sorry for myself, to be honest.

I probably shouldn't bait him, but away from the others —and with the kids for protection—I'm getting my courage back.

"You shouldn't have run."

"And what about the other thing?"

He freezes, about to turn the key in the ignition. In the back, Parker and Carson are hollering, fussing at each other over a charging cord.

Dizzy runs his eyes down my body, head to foot. My tummy quivers.

"You hurt?"

I don't know why I tell the truth. "A little. It's not too bad."

His brown eyes darken, and they're glued to me. World War III is breaking out in the back seat, but he's one hundred percent focused on me. Reading my face. Scowling at the cuts on my calves. I feel floaty. *Good.*

Like a first toke or shot, but my brain's not hazy. It's chill.

Carson kicks the back of my seat, and I lurch forward.

Faster than I can follow, Dizzy snatches the charging cable and holds it high in the air. The boys fall silent on a dime. He glares at them in the rearview.

"Carson?"

"Sorry, ma'am," he mutters.

Both boys have their eyes trained on the cable like sharks circling, waiting for the chum.

"Fay-Lee is coming home with us. You two don't give her no trouble." He pauses. "Boys?"

"Yes, sir," they say in unison.

"And if you kick that seat again, you ride in the bed."

Carson's eyes light up. Maybe that wasn't quite the threat he intended.

"You boys understand?"

They mumble vague agreement and shoot me grudging looks as their dad shoves the cord in the glove box and shifts into first. Parker's got his arms crossed and his chin high like a forty-year-old woman unhappy with her landscaping. Carson is very quietly—and very sneakily—kicking the back of my seat. Whenever Dizzy scans the rearview, he freezes. Comically, and very obviously.

He'd be busted if his dad didn't have his eyes glued on me every second he's not watching the road.

I glance in the rearview mirror to avoid his gaze. It makes me squirm. I don't know what to make of it.

Parker's busy shooting me a dirty look. He must blame me that he got his cord taken away.

Hah. No one in my house had a phone before they could pay for it themselves. The little ones were always grubbing mine, getting the screen all greasy and sticky. *Aunt Fay, lemme play the candy game.*

A tiny bud of homesickness unfurls in my chest. I hope their mamas are takin' good care of them. Carol's probably stepped up. She's already got two jobs, but she's got the most sense of any of us.

It wasn't exactly my job to look after the kids. Sure as shit, no one paid me to do it. It was just that if I didn't, no one did. And I tended to be home since the only steady work I ever managed to find was second shift at the Gas-and-Go.

I didn't *want* to leave the little guys, but there were too many for me to look after properly, and since I could always be relied upon to step up, nothing was stopping their mamas from having more.

I still feel guilty, though. But staying would have felt worse.

Dizzy, Parker, Carson, and I ride the next fifteen minutes in silence, the boys sullen, Dizzy seemingly lost in his thoughts when he isn't checking me out from the corner of his eye.

House mouse. I guess that sounds as good as maid or babysitter. It rhymes, so there's that.

I'll give it a day or two. Maybe a week. If the two last names in the backseat simmer down, it could be a nice vacation. I'm not averse to dirty work. I did clean the restrooms at the Gas-and-Go for four years.

Of course, there's the whole "free pussy" thing. Doesn't feel free. Feels like I'm selling it.

I don't want to trade sex for a roof over my head, but at the end of the day, work is work, isn't it?

Could be worse. They could've sent me home with Jed or the angry one.

Dizzy's resting his hand on the stick. I resettle in my seat, letting my knee fall and graze the knuckle of his pinky. His eyes flick down, and his jaw tightens.

He keeps his hand perfectly still. I leave my knee where it is. Little shivers dance whenever we hit a bump and my skin brushes his. The sensation competes with the pain of the thorn scratches until I'm not sure if I hurt or not.

The sun is setting when we turn down a country road, the kind with no line down the middle, and we pull into a long gravel driveway. There's a split-level with white siding and an empty flower bed along the front. There's an attached garage, and next to the house, there's another garage with two bay doors.

There's some kind of sports car with a black cover parked in front of the extra garage.

The grass is trimmed, but there's not a single lawn ornament, only a deflated soccer ball in the middle of the yard.

Dizzy engages the parking brake, and the boys tumble out, racing to the door, hollering again.

I stay put. For some reason, excitement fizzes in my belly.

Dizzy clears his throat and says nothing. We both stare at the house through the windshield, glancing awkwardly at each other. I don't know why he's so nervous. He's the big man who could crush me like a bug. He wasn't uncertain when he was wailing on my ass earlier.

Eventually, he hops out, walks around, boots crunching on the gravel, and he opens my door.

Huh. Did he think I was waiting for him to do it? I wasn't. Sheesh. My cheeks heat. I unbuckle, take his hand, and ease down. My ass is really smarting now. It twinges each time I take a step. Feels like sunburn. The scratches on my legs don't feel too great either. Each cut on its own isn't a huge deal, but together, they make my legs feel sore and raw.

We start for the house, and Dizzy keeps holding my hand.

I let him.

He leads me to the front door. The boys have left it wide open. Heating the neighborhood, Mama would say. Dizzy props it further open for me. His face is very stern. Guarded.

I step inside.

There's a pile of muddy shoes and boots in the foyer, carpeted stairs leading up and down. I bend over to untie my boots. Behind me, Dizzy's doing the same. I place mine neatly side-by-side, toes touching the wall. He leaves his where they fall.

"Kitchen's upstairs," he says.

There's a crash and muffled shouts from the lower level. Dizzy doesn't seem concerned.

I venture up.

This is not what I was expecting.

This is what would happen if someone gave my sister Dee a credit card with no limit and set her loose at a home décor discount store.

At the top of the stairs, there are white canvas panels that read *Live, Laugh, Love.* The theme is continued throughout the living room, expanded upon in stencils above the sofa. *Live Every Moment. Laugh Every Day. Love Beyond Words.* It's stitched on an accent pillow and painted on metal hanging shelves holding fancy candles in jars. That can't be safe, burning candles so close to the wall.

"To your right." Dizzy urges me forward, hand on my lower back.

I feel wrong. Like I'm in someone else's house.

I mean, I know I'm in someone else's house, but I don't feel like I have permission. This is a woman's house. Shit. Is Dizzy married?

He's not wearing a ring. But—shit.

I stop in my steps. "Are you married?"

The question seems to surprise him. "Not anymore."

"You divorced or separated?"

"Divorced."

"When?"

"'Bout four years ago."

I have a lot of questions.

"You got to keep the house?"

He turns his back to me and rummages in a kitchen drawer.

"She moved in with another guy."

"Ouch."

He shrugs. "Made her happy."

He says that matter-of-fact, as if it's a complete explanation.

"Come here." He gestures me to the counter next to the sink. There's a crap ton of dirty dishes. All utensils, cups, and bowls. No plates, pots, or pans. There's one of those ring holders next to the faucet that looks like a butt plug. No ring.

Dizzy's got a box of bandages and a bottle of peroxide set out.

"Come on."

I pad over, hesitant. This is so weird. He's a huge, wild-haired dude in a flannel and grease stained, ripped jeans, and we're in the stereotypical suburban housewife's kitchen. The theme in here is "wine." *Love the Wine You're With. Sip Happens. It's Okay To Wine.*

Dizzy grabs me by the waist and hoists me up to the counter. I squeak.

"Simmer down. I'm gonna clean up your legs."

The counter is cool against the back of my thighs. I cross my arms.

At this height, Dizzy and I are almost eye-level. It's easier to make out his features under all that bushy black beard. He has soft lips. A strong jaw. He's handsome under all that hair.

He dips a cotton ball in peroxide and gently swipes at my scratches. It's cold and fizzy. My lower belly clenches and my nipples stiffen. Crap. I roll my shoulders back so my arms are folded over my tits.

He washed his hands before he started, but he's clearly a working man. His nails are blunt and the beds are torn up. In contrast, my skin is pale and smooth, despite the scratches.

Even though he's been outside and then in that basement gym, he smells like garage. It's a good smell.

"After this, you can take a shower. I'll order pizza." His voice is husky.

My gaze slips down. His pants are tented. He has a hard-on. I wriggle. Is he gonna want sex now? I guess I'm paying for room and board up front.

It might be okay. He's clean enough. And I liked what we did when we met. And how he felt on top of me in the woods. If I have to, I probably can.

He finishes and pats me on the knee. I've got six bandages stuck at random angles from my knees to mid-calf on both legs. Two red hot rods, three purple convertibles, and one tow truck with a goofy grin. He shoves the first aid supplies in a cabinet over my head, not the same drawer they came from.

I kick my heels against the drawers.

He stands in front of me, his body tight, tense.

I chew on my lower lip.

His eyes zone in on my mouth. He lays his big hands on the top of my thighs. I stop kicking the cabinets.

"Thanks," I mumble.

What would it be like if he kissed me? I bet that beard is scratchy.

He tucks a loose strand of hair behind my ear.

It's so quiet, you can hear the clock tick. *It's Wine O'Clock.*

"Are you okay, baby?"

I'm not sure what he's asking, but he makes it sound like a serious question. He waits for me to answer, intent and still. Listening. Like he really wants to know. I can't remember the last time anyone really wanted to know how I was doing. I don't answer right away, nursing the moment out of pure selfishness.

"Fay-Lee?" There's a hint of alarm in his voice.

"Yeah. I'm fine."

I lean forward. He eases closer. His breath puffs warm across my lips. He's gonna kiss me.

Do I want him to?

Two Tasmanian devils come tearing through the doorway, skidding in their socks, knocking into the table. One throws open the refrigerator while the other one cries and grabs his elbow and howls, faking as well as any dude I've ever seen fouled in soccer.

"What's for dinner?" Parker's the one in the fridge.

Carson's the faker. "He pushed me!"

I hop down from the counter and sidle toward the exit.

"Stop." Dizzy doesn't even raise his voice, and they both go silent. "Remember where you are."

Parker backs away from the fridge. Carson drops the crocodile tears.

"I'm ordering pizza." Dizzy slides his phone from his pocket.

"Pepperoni?" Carson's eyes light up. Dizzy raises an eyebrow. Carson's shoulders slump, and he sighs.

"I hate mushrooms," he says.

"You can pick 'em off." Dizzy raises his eyes to me. I pretend like I wasn't sneaking away. "You eat mushrooms?"

"Sure." My stomach growls. Carson snickers.

"Parker, you put these dishes in the dishwasher." Dizzy jerks his chin down the hall. "Bathroom's at the end. Towels are in the closet," he says to me.

As I turn to leave, Parker whines, "Why should I do it? Isn't that what we got *her* for?"

That little shit. I stop in my tracks, mouth open.

"Pardon?" Dizzy beats me to it, voice is completely even, but so ominous, goose bumps break out on my forearms. This kid is gonna get it.

"She's our house mouse, ain't she? That's what Ernestine said. She cleans. Cooks. And wrecks the home."

I have to bite the inside of my cheek not to bust out laughing. I've only been around a week, but I already know all about Grinder's wandering eye and Ernestine's exceptionally high tolerance for male bullshit. If he cheats, and you only blame the other woman, you're missing most of the problem.

Dizzy takes a second himself, trying to get the twitch in his cheek under control. Finally, he says in a voice so stern it sparks jitters in my belly, "She ain't *your* anything. She's *our* guest. Understood?"

"Yes, sir," he bites out, begrudgingly.

Dizzy adds, "You can take out the trash when you're done with the dishes. And then go fold the laundry that's in the dryer."

Parker opens his mouth, and Dizzy holds up his hand. "Remember. Where. You. Are."

Parker clenches his fists. "Yes, sir."

Dizzy nods. "I'm going to the garage. Call me when the pizza gets here." And he bails out the sliding doors to the back deck, calling in the order, and disappears.

Instantly, Parker and Carson's heads swivel to me. Their eyes narrow, and they stalk forward in lockstep, two velociraptors from that movie about the dinosaur park.

They bare their teeth. Both are missing several, so they look like disheveled, pissed off Jack-o-lanterns. I'm taller than they are, but not by much. They've got their dad's height.

I snatch a fancy candleholder shaped like a wine bottle from the table.

"I can take you both. Know that." It's a lie. I outweigh them, but they outnumber me. And my last meal was the dregs of a SoCo bottle.

"We don't want you here."

"Noted. I will not take you on singing adventures through the Austrian Alps."

"What does that even mean?" Parker asks. He's the mastermind. The porky little one keeps eyeing him for cues.

"It's a movie. There's a nun. And a marionette show with goats." I stop talking.

They both stare at me. They've got mud on their faces, in their hair. They're not wearing shoes, but the muck on the hem of their pants is flaking off on the linoleum.

"You're not gonna wreck this home." Carson aims a chubby finger at me.

"I have no intention of doing that."

His face is scrunched up as if he's about to cry. Oh, hell. He's really upset.

"Just so we're on the same page—what do *you* think home-wrecker means?" I ask.

Carson looks to his older brother.

Parker frowns. "You know. Don't be hassling Dad all the time."

"If you can't say anything nice, don't say anything at all," Carson adds.

"Stay out of the downstairs. Unless you're cleaning. You don't mess with our stuff, we won't mess with yours." Parker's warming up.

"Don't be yelling all the time. And crying. And nitpicking." Carson ticks items off on his fingers. "Be cool. Have fun. Don't be stressed out. Don't take things so seriously."

"I can handle that." The boys exchange a look, like *Should we believe this chick*? I'm a little insulted. Kids generally like me. "You know, I have some conditions, too. Since we're laying it all on the table."

I wait. Parker gives me a wary nod.

"I'm not old enough to be your mama. I'm gonna earn my keep, but I'm not cleaning up after you. You make a mess, that's on you."

Parker rolls his eyes. He thinks that is total bullshit.

"If you mess with me, it's war."

"What's that mean?" Parker asks.

"You don't want to find out."

Carson's not even paying attention. "Do you play *Point of Collision*?" he interjects.

"Is that a video game?"

"Yeah."

"No."

"You want to?" Carson offers. Parker shoots him a dirty look.

"After I take a shower, okay."

"You can play winner," Parker says, grudgingly.

"Cool."

The boys exchange glances. Apparently, they're satisfied with our talk. Carson zooms off downstairs, and Parker vaults up on a counter to get a snack cake from a cabinet.

He leaves the door cracked as he races off after his brother. I can't help but peek inside. The knot that's always in my stomach uncoils a little when I see full shelves. Pasta, sauce, canned goods. Lots of open boxes of cereal. There are a few cans of tuna with the pop-tops. I grab them, and two packets of deer jerky.

When I go to take a shower, I hide them in a corner of the linen closet under a stack of towels. The tension in my neck eases. I peel the bandages off carefully. Feels like a waste to trash them, but I've stopped bleeding, and they'll just fall off if they get wet.

I twist the knob as hot as I can take it, and I hop in, spending a whole thirty minutes in the shower, lathering and rinsing until the water begins to turn cool. There's a shit ton of boats and sharks and a sea plane in the tub, but I shove them to the end and enjoy.

"Intergalactic Watermelon" is really an under-rated scent. Plus, it's body wash, shampoo, and conditioner in one.

It's warm, quiet, and no one's banging on the door demanding to be let in so they can take a shit.

I'm all alone, and pizza is on the way.

It's heaven.

AFTER THE SHOWER, I throw my hair up into a ponytail and go looking for some clothes. The master suite is at the end of the hall. I might be able to squeeze into Parker's T-shirts, but Dizzy's clothes are a better bet. Besides, I'm curious.

This dude has layers.

Here in his house, he's like every dad who trudges into the Gas-and-Go for bait or a six-pack. Gruff, take-no-shit. Oblivious. World-weary.

It's hard to believe he's the same guy who demanded to see my pussy. Shivers race down my spine. He was so intense. So *into* it. Not like Rylan was into it—as if he was grabbin' the last doughnut in the box before someone else could get it. With Dizzy, it was more like he couldn't believe his eyes so he refused to blink.

And then later in the woods, and when he cleaned up my leg, he was almost tender. Gentle. I press my hand to my belly to soothe the flutters.

But I can't forget how he was in the basement. Not the spanking. That was—I'm gonna need to think that through later, in the dark, when I'm settled down. But when Jed got in my face, and Dizzy laid him on his ass?

Underneath it all, Dizzy is a dangerous man. He runs with dangerous people, and he knows how to use his fists.

Yeah, in that moment, he was defending me. And that felt a weird kind of good. The flutters in my belly turn to swoops. But I'm not stupid. I don't know my daddy, but I've had a long education in men. If they're the type to use their fists, they can use 'em on you.

It's the basic logic that my sisters can never figure out. If he'll cheat *with* you, he'll cheat *on* you. If he doesn't see his kids by his ex, he'll ghost yours, too. If he spends all his money on himself, he ain't gonna have any left for child support.

That's such reliable logic it's almost math.

I need to tread carefully. Enjoy the shower and central heat, but keep focused. I need cash. Food. Clothes. And I need to get the hell out of here as soon as possible. No one's gonna save me but myself.

With that in mind, I slip into the master suite. I've peeked into the two other rooms on this level. Both obviously belong to the boys. Or a herd of feral raccoons going by the amount of crap on the floors.

This room is—bipolar.

The theme is "beach." That's what it says in block letters over the king-sized bed. *This Way To the Beach*. And there's an arrow pointing what I assume is due east.

There's a teal accent wall, teal curtains, and a teal bench

with teal cushions at the end of the bed. There are huge glass vases filled with shells on both nightstands.

Then it gets weird. There's an armoire—white wood with flip-flop decals on the side—and a wide, low dresser with a mirror. On top of the dresser are a drop cloth and a dismantled mechanism of some kind. Maybe an engine. It's old and rusty. There's a bottle of vinegar, baking soda, steel wool, and a bunch of rags.

And then, between the bed and the door, there are two stacks of cinderblocks with a piece of wood laid across, holding a big screen TV. Underneath are a mess of cables and game consoles. And empty beer bottles.

This must be where the magic happens.

I hear small feet pound somewhere downstairs, and I startle. Enough sightseeing. I need cash. Clothes.

I start with the drawers. In the bedside table, he's got the usual. Lube, lighter, a screwdriver, no cash. There's some jewelry in a tray in the dresser, but it all looks like cheap, costume shit. The armoire's a bust. It's mostly empty. There's a laundry basket next to it with folded clothes. And another laundry basket resting on top with more clothes, not folded.

I check the closet. It's stuffed full with plastic tubs and boxes labeled 12-18 months, 2T-3T. There're also a ton of women's dresses and skirts and blouses. The shoe cubbies are empty, though.

Creepy.

Why didn't Dizzy's ex take her clothes? I check out the dresser drawers. No cash. Most of these drawers are empty, but there's still a whole bunch of yoga pants, T-shirts, and sweaters. I grab a pair of black leggings and a bright pink cable-knit sweater. The leggings are so loose I tie a knot at the waist. The sweater comes down to my knees.

It's weird wearing a strange woman's clothes, but it feels

amazing to get out of that filthy shirt and shorts.

And honestly, how is it different from hand-me-downs? Probably ninety percent of my clothes have gone through at least Carol and Dee.

Now, if I were cash, where would I be? I go to the bed, wedge my hands under the mattress and lift.

Behind me, a throat clears.

I drop the mattress on my fingers and yelp.

Dizzy's standing in the doorway. He fills it, wall-to-wall-to-ceiling. He's wiping his hands with a rag.

"Lookin' for something?"

"The way to the beach? Is it, ah, that way?" I point east.

His lip twitches. I can breathe again.

"Try again." He tucks the rag in his pocket. His shirt's rolled up, exposing muscular, veined forearms. What would they feel like? To wrap my hands around them? Him propped over me?

I shift, squeezing my legs together. What were we talking about? Oh. What I'm up to.

"Would you believe I tried to take a nap? Couldn't sleep. There was something under there. A pea, maybe? I was just checkin'."

Both corners of his lips curl up. "I keep cash in the safe. Safe's in the basement."

"What's the combination?" Hey, worth a try, right?

He chuckles. "You lookin' to run away so soon?"

"Not flat broke, I'm not."

He makes no move to come into the room. Or leave. He's watching me closely, his eyes darkening. Occasionally, they flick to the bed. Oh.

My body comes alive. Flutters. Prickles. Shivers. All of it.

I perch on the edge of the bed. I aim for casual, but I'm awkward as hell. I cross my legs, but the long sweater gets twisted. It takes me a second to tug it loose and smooth things out. He tracks my movements the whole time.

"How come all your ex-wife's clothes are still here?"

"Not all of 'em. She lost weight before we split. She left the clothes that didn't fit no more."

"Why didn't you sell 'em on the internet?"

"Not mine to sell."

"It doesn't bother you, having your ex's stuff all over the place?"

He shrugs. "I'll get to it when I get the time."

"Her name's Sharon, right?"

"Yeah."

I remember from the tattoo. "You carrying a torch for her?"

This conversation is starting to feel treacherous. I know it's none of my business. He doesn't know me, and besides, I'm the house mouse. Not a date.

He's going along with it, though. And as I recross my legs so I can put my weight on my hip—and take it off my tender ass—he follows my every move.

"Nope."

"She was really into decorating, eh?"

He chuffs a laugh. "You could say that."

"She seems like a different sort of person than you."

"That's probably fair."

"How'd you meet?"

"High school."

"Did you go to prom together?" I wanted to go, but I couldn't afford a ticket, and no one asked me.

"Nah. I didn't go to prom. She did."

"You didn't go with her?"

"We were split up at the time."

"On again, off again?"

"Yeah."

"You don't volunteer much in terms of information, do you?"

"You're real curious, ain't you?" His eyes are twinkling.

I switch positions, kneel, take all pressure off my backside. He's utterly focused on me. There's a ruckus coming from the kitchen, but his gaze doesn't leave me for a second.

"You can ask me questions if you want," I offer.

"You wearing panties?"

I shake my head no, bite my bottom lip, playing it up. There's a bulge in his jeans. I'm turning him on. I got my clothes on and he's not touching me, but he wants me. Bad. It's a giddy feeling.

"I like your hair down. Take that rubber band out." Actually, it's a scrunchie I stole from a basket in the bathroom.

He's being real bossy. I should tell him where he can stick it, but for some reason, it doesn't make me mad. It would have coming from Rylan or the few boys I went out with after.

Zings whiz around my belly. I slowly tug my hair loose, combing my fingers through. My scalp tingles.

"Keep it down," he says. There's a clatter from the kitchen. Finally, he shoots a glance over his shoulder. "Pizza's here. Come eat."

He doesn't have to ask me twice. I can smell it now, and I'm starving.

I hop up and follow him down the hall. The boys are already eating, sitting at the small kitchen table, watching the TV on the counter. No plates.

Dizzy takes the chair at the head and grabs a slice.

Well, when in Rome. I help myself. It's all mushroom, half pepperoni. Parker's eaten almost all the pepperoni slices already.

"Carson. Go get Daddy a beer." Dizzy polishes off the crust of his first piece. There are crumbs in his beard. He catches me looking, and he wipes his mouth with the back of his hand. "You want one?"

"Sure."

"Two!" he shouts.

Carson's already in the fridge. He sprints back, sliding the last few feet to the table and slapping the bottles in his dad's hands. Clearly, he's had practice.

I munch as Dizzy cracks open a beer and hands it to me. No one's talking. The TV's blaring. Pro wrestling.

Parker picks the mushrooms off his slice and drops them in the box. Dizzy scoops them up and eats 'em. The boys' chewing is loud and wet.

So this is how it is in a house of men.

Once my brother Robbie left, the only males in the house were my nephews, and they were out-numbered three to one. If this were Mama's house, everyone would be talking at once, laughing, carrying on. At least two kids would be crawling under the table, and there'd be a baby cryin'. Mama would be hollering from the kitchen for someone to come help.

My chest aches. Homesickness is a mind fuck. It can make you miss misery, remember it fondly.

If this were Mama's house, no one would be letting me get a word in edgewise. There wouldn't be enough food to go around. I'd be stressed about Lula tumbling down the stairs in her walker again since no one bothered to put back the baby gate.

I'm not missing anything. And they sure as shit aren't missing me. The shed proved that beyond a shadow of a doubt.

I let myself relax in the chair and take a deep swig of

beer. Even with Parker tearing through the pizza, there's gonna be enough for seconds. There's a whole other box underneath the first. I don't mind wrestling.

Carson goes to help himself to a third pop. That kid's gonna be wired.

As the new house mouse, the good news is there'll be no dishes to wash.

Life's okay.

It's amazing how good you feel with your stomach full of cheese and dough. The whole world takes on a more forgiving light. I yawn. Where am I gonna sleep tonight? If I get the sofa, there'll be plenty of pillows, that's for sure.

What if Dizzy expects me to sleep in his bed? Put out? The thought makes me kind of sad. I shove it aside and let my eyelids drift shut.

"You're tired." Dizzy's gruff voice shakes me from my food coma.

"Yeah," I mumble through another yawn.

"Where's she sleeping?" Parker asks, face pinched. So far, he's my least favorite.

"Well, we got a choice. Carson and you can double up. Or you can take the sofa downstairs."

"Why does she get her own room? That's bullshit," Parker explodes. "Put *her* downstairs."

Dizzy's eyes widen, his expression going terrifyingly dark and still. Carson gasps.

Parker's lips contort all sorts of ways as he tries to suck those words back down. "I mean, she could take the downstairs. Sir."

"Her name's Fay-Lee."

"*Fay-Lee* could take the downstairs."

"Fine. But you can't play your video games all hours if she's down there."

Parker's face is turning purple. "I could just go back to Steve's."

"You can't. Mom and Steve went away for the weekend," Carson offers, mouth full of pizza.

Parker's on the verge of tears. I'd offer to take the sofa so as not to put him out. If he had been the slightest bit nice. Since he hasn't, I'm watching this ride out.

"Why's she need a room?"

"She's a girl," Carson says.

"It ain't fair." Parker glowers.

"You can roll with it for a few days."

"Ain't never a few days, is it?" Does Parker know something I don't? Am I the most recent in a line of house mice? Or is he talking about something else entirely?

Dizzy's jaw tightens, but he's not mad. His brown eyes gentle. "Man has to take what comes."

"That's crap."

"That's life." It's a dickish thing to say, but the way Dizzy says it isn't dismissive. More regretful.

Parker lets out a long-suffering sigh. "I'll take the downstairs." He pushes back from the table and stomps off, all sixty pounds, four-and-a-half feet of him.

Dizzy lowers his head. Carson uses the distraction to nab the mushrooms left in the box.

I attempt to lighten the mood. "If I'm causing trouble, you can always slip me a few hundred. I'll get right out of your hair."

Dizzy looks up. He's bothered, but not by what I said. "That wasn't about him sleepin' downstairs."

"Seemed like it was."

"It wasn't. He don't like shit getting switched up on him. He'll settle down."

"If I find frogs in my bed, I cannot be held responsible

for my actions."

Dizzy's brow knits.

"You didn't see *The Sound of Music* either?"

"That movie with the kid who delivered telegrams on his bike and the dad drove a Mercedes-Benz 540K Cabriolet?"

"Yes?"

"Once when I was a kid. I don't remember it much." He shrugs and stands. "Come on. I'll show you which room. Carson, you break down the boxes, and take 'em out to the trash. Make sure you get the lid back on tight. That raccoon's back."

Carson's eyes light up like it's Christmas morning. "I'll get the BB gun."

"BB ain't gonna kill this raccoon. We'll go down to the tractor supply tomorrow. Get some coyote urine."

"We could get the .22." Carson's not letting this go.

"You plannin' on eatin' racoon? We'll use coyote urine."

Carson finally nods in reluctant agreement. This is a strange conversation.

Dizzy leads me down the hall.

"Aren't I supposed to do the cleaning up? As the house mouse?" I don't want to, but earning my keep is ingrained in me.

"Boys need responsibility. You can do the laundry tomorrow. Ain't none of us can fold worth a damn." Dizzy gestures me through the door next to the master suite.

As soon as I cross the threshold, the smell hits me. Little kid funk. It's as if stickiness were a scent. I'm so tired, though, I can hardly care.

All the leftover adrenaline from earlier in the day seeped away hours ago. My muscles are stiff again. Guess it'll take more than one hot shower to ease the ache of sleeping on the frozen ground for a week.

The twin bed is unmade. I don't see a pillow. There's a flat sheet, but no comforter.

I pick my way through Legos and wadded-up dirty clothes. The only thing I want is to crash on this bed and pass out. I'm not even worried about Dizzy watching me. I'm bone-deep exhausted.

I plop down on the mattress and fall back.

"My door'll be open tonight." He's looming in the doorway, his face turned hard.

"Okay."

"Don't try to sneak out."

"Okay." I'm not going anywhere. This room is toasty warm. The vent is right next to the bed.

"If you run, I can't help you. The club will come after you. They will find you. If they think you're a threat, you'll disappear. Understand?"

His face is tight. Worried. That I'm gonna run? That his club will hunt me down? I am way too tired to sort it out. I'm sure I'll be scared as shit tomorrow, but right now he needs to zip it.

"I won't go anywhere. Just let me sleep." It comes out a grumble. My eyelids are too heavy to keep open. I curl onto my side, tuck my knees to my chest.

Dizzy tromps off down the hall. A minute later, right as I'm drifting off, he comes back. He steps on something, there's a crunch, and he mutters, "Damn it."

Then he covers me with a thick quilt that smells like lavender. I'm too far gone to say thank you, but I offer him a sleepy smile. He traces the scar bisecting my lips with a calloused finger.

"Don't run, Fay-Lee."

"All right."

I fall asleep with the ghost of his touch on my mouth.

WHEN I WAKE UP, the clock on the wall reads almost eleven o'clock. I think. Instead of numbers, there are various makes and models of muscle car. It's forty-five minutes past a Ford Fairlane.

My body is wrung out. The scratches on my legs are sore. My stomach's growling. Last night's dinner must've stretched it out. The knot in Sharon's yoga pants came loose, so my drawers are around my ankles. Thank the Lord the door's closed. I kicked off the quilt in the middle of the night.

Overall, I'm disoriented. Off-kilter. I strain my ears. The house is quiet.

There's a piggy bank shaped like a pit bull on Parker's desk.

Nah. I've not sunk so low as stealing from a kid. Not yet. *The club will come after you. They will find you. If they think you're a threat, you'll disappear.*

I shiver. Yeah. I should've panicked last night. I can't afford to be so tired that I let my guard down. It's broad daylight now. I need to get moving and quit lyin' in bed getting accustomed to the warmth. This isn't home. I'm not safe here.

This is a rock and a hard place situation. With no cash, I don't have the slightest chance of outrunning the club. But if I'm here when they decide I'm a threat? Well, then I'm making it real easy for them, aren't I?

I'm not stupid. There's something else going on here besides me trespassing and taking some food. Someone steals from me, and I beat their ass, take my shit back, and send them on their way. I don't keep them close so I can keep tabs on them.

Maybe they think I saw something. Or maybe this is how they turn women out. I didn't think the club ran whores, but I don't know their whole business.

Yeah, I can't get comfortable. When this turns south, I'm gonna need to be prepared.

I swing my legs over the side of the bed and kick off the saggy pants. The sweater comes to my knees. It'll work as a dress.

I venture out. Dizzy's door is open. The bed's made. He's not in there. I head toward the kitchen. Coffee would be amazing. Someone's playing a video game downstairs. Guess the boys are down there. Why aren't they in school?

There's a coffee maker on the counter, sludge warming in a stained carafe. Three bowls of pinkish-colored cereal milk are lined up on the breakfast bar. Oooh, they've got the sugary stuff. Score.

I make a fresh pot of coffee, and as it's brewing, I riffle through the drawers. Junk, junk, and more junk. No cash. I consider the cereal, but there's bread and a full carton of eggs in the fridge. Oh yeah, baby. I'm makin' French toast. After I squirrel away a few cans of ravioli.

I dash to the bathroom, do my business, and retrieve the tuna I hid in the linen closet. I drop by Parker's room and add my canned goods to the stash I've started under the bed. Then I skip back, my steps light. I whisk the eggs, add milk, and, while I fry up my breakfast, cram three snack cakes down my gullet. Butterscotch crumpets. Delicious.

This is a freakin' great day.

I end up making twelve slices of French toast. Turns out my eyes were bigger than my stomach. French toast gets soggy if you save it for later.

I don't want the kids thinking I'm the maid. I mean, maybe I am supposed to be the maid, but I didn't trade out being Cinderella in Kentucky to be Mary Poppins in western Pennsylvania.

It's a shame to let good food go to waste, though. I lean over the rail to the foyer and holler down to the lower level, "French toast!"

There's a scuffle, and Carson emerges, bounding up the stairs. "French toast?"

I nod at the table.

"Sweet!" He wastes no time, digs right in.

"Your brother gonna want some?"

Carson slides the plate closer and bends his arm around it, guarding it like my nieces and nephews do. "He's out in the garage, workin' with Dad."

"Workin' on what?"

"Bikes."

Guess I could've figured.

I sit down across from the kid. "How come you aren't in school?"

"Teacher work day," he says with a full mouth. "Didn't you hear us leave? We got there, and it was closed."

"Nope. I didn't hear."

"You sleep deep, eh?"

"Sometimes."

He grins at me as he shoves a huge bite dripping with syrup into his mouth.

"Hey. You know the combination to your Dad's safe?" It's worth a try, right?

He blinks at me, chewing. He's got bright blue eyes, sandy blond hair, fair skin, and freckles. He must favor his mother. He's cute. Looks like a chipmunk.

"You fixin' to rob us?"

A feeling not unlike guilt rises in my chest, but I shove it down. "I need money."

He drags the last piece of toast through the syrup, sopping up as much as he can. His nose is wrinkled as if he's considering. "I got five bucks I can let you hold."

"I need more than five bucks."

"Ask Dad for a check."

Well, this is a dead end.

"Can I borrow your phone?" There's always my Hail Mary. If I can remember Carol's phone number, and if it hasn't been turned off again, she *might* bail me out.

"It's dead."

"You kids only have that one charger?"

"There're more. We just don't know where they are."

Carson swipes his fingers across the plate to wipe up the last of the syrup and sticks them in his mouth. "Can I ask you something?" he mumbles.

"Sure."

"What'd you do to make Steel Bones mad at you?"

"Why do you think they're mad at me?"

"Miss Ernestine said no one steals from us and gets away with it."

"She's really salty about some nuts and beef jerky."

"That what you stole?"

"Yeah. And some peanut butter and jelly sandwiches."

"That's crap." He hops up and heads for the fridge. "We can eat whatever we want from the kitchen. Anybody can."

"Not me, I guess."

"You were hungry." His face hardens almost to a glower. Now he looks like his dad. He grabs the milk, unscrews the lid, chugs, and then wipes his mouth with the back of his hand. "That ain't right. If you're hungry, ask me. I'll get you what you want. Nobody'll say anything to me about it."

"I did take some booze from the bar." Since he's being so nice, I feel compelled to be honest.

He shrugs. "I can get you that, too."

"Thanks." Carson is officially my favorite person in this family.

"Want to play *Point of Collision*? You said you'd play last night, but you went to bed."

"Maybe later."

"Cool." He lopes off, heading down to the basement, and he nearly gives me a heart attack when he galumphs back and pokes his head back through the doorway. "Thanks, lady. You make good French toast."

"You're welcome."

Then he's gone, and it's quiet again. Eerily quiet. I pad into the living room and root through the end tables and a fancy antique desk with a rolling cover. Nothing except a half-empty pack of stale Capris. I snag those. I don't really smoke, but they're good for making friends and makin' yourself look legit when you're loitering.

I search through a few closets before I head back for the bedroom. Parker has one of those drawstring backpacks hanging from his desk chair. I commandeer it, shake out a plastic Army guy and a gummy hard candy, and fill it with my food stash. Then I plop back on the bed, at loose ends. I get nervous when I don't have anything to do with myself.

Dizzy did mention the laundry.

I don't *want* to do laundry, but the quiet makes me jumpy. Makes my brain veer toward memories I'm working really hard to block. Walls closing in. My throat raw from screaming.

I haven't seen the washing machine in my travels. There has to be one in a house this nice. I knew a girl in elementary school who had a house like this. I lived for sleepover invitations. I thought her parents were million- aires. The invitations dried up in junior high. The kids who lived in town went to one school and hicks like us went to another.

Her laundry room was in the basement.

I bop on downstairs, fully expecting another theme. Instead, there is anarchy. An overstuffed L-shaped sofa covered in blankets, stuffed animals, and a camouflage sleeping bag. A coffee table with pop cans, deflated bags of chips, a lollipop without a wrapper, candy wrappers.

The floor is a mine field. A race car set with loop-de-loops. Action figures. A castle. Lacrosse sticks. Bright orange plastic rifle. Wooden slingshot. Miniature catapult. A bop bag. Balls. Soccer ball, basketball, tennis balls, ping-pong balls, kickballs, footballs, Nerf balls.

There's a toy chest and bright-colored tubs on racks, but best I can tell, they're empty.

The curtains are pulled tight, and the lights are dim. It takes a second to make out Carson. He's lying on his stomach in the middle of the debris, controller in his hands. He hasn't bothered to move anything, so he's kind of half lying on a board game, his upper body resting on a giant stuffed tortoise.

"You gonna play?" he asks.

"I'll start the laundry first. Is it down here?"

"Yeah, down the hall. When you get back, the other controller is somewhere on the couch. Just dump the other stuff on the floor."

No, I won't. And I ain't cleaning this room.

Not for money.

Not for *nothin'*.

And if the laundry room looks like this, I'm gonna bolt, money or no money. Screw the Steel Bones Motorcycle Club. There are fates worse than death.

But not really.

I sigh. I'm stuck.

When I left Dalton, I swore no more kids, no more constant drudge work, no more takin' care of ungrateful folks who literally would not notice if I died. And here I am. Wading through the debris of Hurricane Unsupervised Kids.

My fingers itch to put it to rights. But I'm not gonna. Sooner or later, Steel Bones is gonna lose interest in me. I'm very forgettable. And the moment they get bored—sooner if I can figure out a way—I'm out of here.

I pick my way through the crap, heading down a narrow corridor. The laundry room is at the end. I breathe a sigh of relief when I flick the light on. There are overflowing hampers, but the clothes are sorted. There's nothing on the floor. There's a stocked shelf with all sorts of detergents.

I check the door to make sure there's no lock before I shut it, blocking out the pew-pew of gunfire and explosions coming from the family room.

This is probably the cleanest room in the house. Thank goodness. The Laundromat in Dalton is filthy. It reeks of cigarettes 'cause the good townspeople figure the county smoking ban can go fuck itself. There are cobwebs in the corners, and Lord help you if your sheets drag the floor as you're folding them.

Up in here, there's a huge front-loading stainless steel washing machine and a perfectly matching dryer. They're almost as tall as I am.

You could do two regular-sized loads in 'em at a time.

There's a load in the dryer. I pop it open—kid's clothes. Psshh. They could've gotten triple this in if they'd tried.

I snag an empty basket and unload. There's a clear table for folding and an ironing board hanging from hooks on the wall.

The room smells like dryer sheets. There are small, high windows that allow in some sunshine. Heat's blasting from the vents, so it's cozy warm. This is my favorite room in the house. All I need is music. Lord, I miss my phone.

I dump the rumpled clothes, shake 'em out, and fold. There's a pair of gray sweats. Probably Parker's. I try 'em on. They hit me mid-calf, but they fit around the waist. Way better than Sharon's fat pants. I also find a long-sleeved raglan T-shirt with red arms and the Bud logo. My boobs are gonna stretch it out, but it covers my midriff.

The folding takes no time at all. I throw in a white load, hoping I add the right amount of detergent. I'm used to powder, not liquid.

I'm reading the bottle when I hear Dizzy's deep voice from the family room.

"That's enough for today, Carson. Go help your brother with the lawn."

There's whining.

A little frisson of fear—or excitement?—zips through my belly. I tug down my T-shirt.

"You seen Fay-Lee?"

There's a mumble.

Then there're footsteps in the hall, and the door opens. He stays there like he did when he found me in his room. Or last night, when I was in bed. He's keeping his distance.

But his dark eyes find me and don't let go. The butterflies in my belly go nuts.

"There you are," he says.

"You lookin' for me?" My insides warm.

"You weren't upstairs."

"You said do the laundry."

"It don't need to be done right away."

"I was bored."

His gaze rakes down my front. My nipples stiffen into points. I went braless the night of the first party, and since Chaos rolled off with my bag, I haven't worn one since. With my A cups, I can get away with it. Not in this shirt, though. The Bud logo isn't conveniently placed.

"Those Parker's clothes?"

"I figure."

"We'll ride into town later. Pick up what you need."

"This works fine."

"I don't want you in boy's clothes."

I swallow. For some reason, my mouth is watering. Dizzy's clearly been working. He's wearing a white, grease-stained T-shirt and ripped jeans. He's pulled his hair back in a ponytail, but strands are springing loose all over the place.

He's bare-footed.

I curl my toes. I am, too.

What was he saying? Oh, yeah. He doesn't want me dressed like a boy.

I guess I should be offended by the heavy-handedness. But there's something about the way he stands on the threshold, won't come a step closer. Makes me want to mess with him.

"Yeah? How do you want to dress me?"

His gaze flicks over his shoulder. He listens for something. Probably Carson. There's silence from the family room.

Dizzy eases in, shuts the door behind him and leans against it. Panic flutters in my chest. I don't need to be scared. I'm fine. If push came to shove, I could fit through the windows.

"I'd put you in something pretty," Dizzy's saying, and I forget about the fear. "Soft."

"You don't like this?" I tug the T-shirt taut.

"No." His voice is gravelly. I love it.

"Should I take it off?"

His jaw tightens. He tenses all over. Does he think he shouldn't be doing this? Because I'm so much younger than he is? Or because I'm a hostage or whatever? Or is it because the kids are outside?

Because he's carrying a torch for his ex?

That thought pisses me off.

I grab the hem of the shirt and pull it over my head. Then I shake out my hair in the best impression of a stripper I can manage. Per usual, I get no bounce. It falls straight to the small of my back.

I'm not a big flasher. Beads on Mardi Gras is a pervert scam, and I'm the only Parsons girl who never went wild.

But I crave this man's eyes on me. I eat it up. It makes me high. I couldn't pass it up any more than I could pass up a buffet. I've been hungry too long. And this is too damn delicious.

My tits ache.

He gobbles them up with his eyes.

"You want to touch them?"

"Put the shirt back on," he growls.

"Why?"

"Do what I say, girl."

My stomach swirls.

"But you love my tits." I cup them, offer them up.

He moves so quickly, I don't have time to react. One minute he's in the doorway, the next he's spinning me, crowding me between his body and the washing machine. The metal is warm against my chest from the hot water.

"I said do what I say."

He draws me back, flush to his chest, and cups my left breast. He molds it, brushing his thumb across the nipple, squeezing, tugging. As if he's milking me. And I know that's weird, but it drives me crazy. I squirm, writhe. His other arm is wrapped around my waist, pinning me to him.

"Do you like that?"

"Yes. Play with the other one." I'm whining. Breathless.

He doesn't make me beg. He switches to my other breast, kneading, drawing my nipple into a stiff, aching point.

I mewl, rocking back into him. My pussy's throbbing, demanding. I never get this out of control. Never go from zero to sixty so quick. There's something about the way he's holding me. I don't need to think. He's calling the shots.

"Do you want to cum, baby?" he murmurs in my ear.

"Yes," I pant. I *need* to cum.

He pushes my upper half into the machine and drags my hips back, shoving the sweats down and delving between my legs. I kick the pants all the way off and brace my arms against the glass door, elbows back.

He's bent around me. I can feel his heat on my back and his rough jeans against my ass and thighs. I try to push up, but he has me pinned.

Besides, I don't really want to get free.

He's wrapped an arm around my waist, and his other hand is spreading my folds. I'm so wet. My cream tickles as it drips down my slit. He strokes with his fingers, teasing my clit, smearing my wetness back from my hole to my bottom. I clench. No one's ever touched me there. *I* haven't touched me there.

"Relax, baby. I ain't gonna hurt you. I'm gonna make you feel good." His voice is raspy and breathless in my ear.

His finger returns to my clit, circling. That hungry wanting busts loose, and I work my hips, helpless, totally covered by his hard body, breathing in his scent. Motor oil and soap.

Then his slippery fingers move back again, and I sidle my legs into a wider stance. His thumb keeps the attention on my clit while his first two fingers ease into my tight hole. It's been a while. Years. I satisfied my curiosity that summer before tenth grade, and I haven't been tempted since.

Until now. This moment. I am so tempted. I want this. More. Dizzy's nibbling my neck, and shivers are shooting everywhere, zinging down my spine.

I love it. I moan.

Then his ring finger's pressing at my bottom. I squeeze tight. I still don't know about that.

"Let me in, baby." He circles, insistent. "It'll feel good. I promise."

I pant, relax for an instant, and he slides in, filling me. I moan. It's so dirty. He has total control of my body. I can't do anything but open for him. Let him do what he wants.

It's strange, and it hurts a little bit, but he's right. It feels good.

My swollen tits are smooshed against the warm glass. The machine vibrates and hums, teasing my aching nipples. Dizzy's at my back, all around me. I'm in his hands, and I'm safe. I'm the center of his attention. It feels amazing.

"You getting close?"

"Yes," I whimper.

"You gonna cum in my hand?"

"Yes." I buck. He takes the cue and pumps his fingers harder.

He nips my neck, his beard tickling my shoulder. Then his soft lips brush my temple, my cheek. He takes my jaw in calloused fingers and turns my head. Kisses me. Sips from my lips. Gently.

Oh.

I like that.

He tastes me again, his beard scratching my chin. He sucks my bottom lip. It's different now. My pussy's fluttering, and I'm on the edge, ready to cum, but these kisses are so sweet. I want more.

He eases his tongue between my lips and licks me, exploring my mouth, almost tentative. I open up. These kisses aren't wet and gross and pushy. They're tender. Perfect.

I always wanted to be kissed this way, but I figured men only did it like this in movies.

I let my brain disconnect and float as he works me into a frenzy with his fingers and soothes me with his mouth. I'm getting higher and higher. Closer and closer. My insides are coiling, stomach muscles tightening.

"Dizzy, I'm gonna cum," I wail.

"Say my name again, baby," he groans against my lips.

"Dizzy!"

And I'm there, tumbling over, my pussy pulsating around his fingers, my asshole constricting so tight I force him out. I go rigid in his arms as I flush hot and break out in sweat. I'm tumbling and then I'm slowing down and then there's random zings popping off inside me like the last fireworks before the drunkest folks turn in.

"There it is." He wraps both arms around me, cuddles me to his chest.

Instantly, I'm hit with a wave of embarrassment. My face burns.

I'm buck naked. He's totally clothed. His finger was in my butt. I stiffen.

He drops a kiss in the crook of my neck.

"Don't move."

He drops me, walks over to the utility sink and washes his hands. I squat, grab the sweats, wriggle them back on.

This is so awkward. What am I doing? I'm not my sisters. I don't get boy crazy and lose my mind.

I need to get out of here. Collect myself.

Dizzy stalks back over. "I said don't move." He snatches my T-shirt off the floor. "Arms up."

I do what he says without thinking. He carefully pulls the shirt over my head, freeing my hair from the neck hole and smoothing it over my shoulder. Then he drops a kiss on my forehead. I keep my eyes on the floor.

"You weirded out?" he asks.

"Yes," I squeak.

"Me, too." My gaze flies up. His eyes are dark, as intent on me as they were before, when he was standing in the doorway, keeping me at arm's length.

He's not smug and self-satisfied like Rylan or those few other boys. Is he feeling unsteady, too?

A strange awareness swirls in my belly. It's like I've known this guy longer than a few days. It's vaguely comforting, but it's also scary as hell.

I think I *get* this guy.

And I don't think this is a case of the big, bad biker taking advantage of the poor, young house mouse.

Dizzy is as shook as I am.

"Go get a shower. We'll have lunch and head into town. I need some coyote urine. We'll stop by the tractor supply after we get you some clothes."

He kisses me again on the forehead, turns, and leaves. Behind me, the washing machine falls silent.

I'm left alone, mind whirling.

It isn't "Was it good for you, baby?" But as far as sweet talk goes, I've heard worse.

6

DIZZY

"This sucks." Parker's got his hands jammed in his pockets, a mulish look on his face. Then again, when don't he?

"Ain't you used to going shopping with your mom?" As I recall, Sharon went all the time.

"She gets clothes in a box now," Carson pipes up. "In the mail. If she don't like it, she sends 'em back." Carson's popping a squat on the department store floor and playing a game on his phone. I don't know why Parker ain't doin' the same.

"Sounds convenient."

"She forgets to mail the boxes back in time, and then she gets pissed." Carson reclines precariously against a dress rack.

We're waiting outside the dressing room in the lady's section. I'm gettin' a lot of looks from the good women of Petty's Mill. A couple smiles, too.

We still gotta go to the tractor supply after this. If Parker keeps up the attitude, he gets to hold the coyote urine on the way home.

Fay-Lee's only been in there a few minutes. She's been bashful since the laundry room. Blushing and stumblin' over her words. I've been touchin' her—handin' her up into the truck, tuckin' stray hairs behind her ear—just to watch her get flustered.

She's pretty as a picture.

I exhale. Corral my thoughts. This ain't the time or place to pop wood.

She was so fuckin' sweet, though. So soft and carried away. There could've been an earthquake, and I bet she would've kept ridin' my hand.

On the ride here, I was catchin' her eye in the rearview every chance I got, just to watch her squirm, until she ended up crackin' the window to get some air, and Parker bitched at her to roll it back up.

I thought he'd be all over campin' in the basement for a few nights. Play video games until all hours. Have his own bathroom he don't have to share with his little brother. I explained this ain't for long.

I rub my chest.

It can't be, right? Fay-Lee's almost a kid herself. Eighteen years old. Fuck. When I was eighteen—well—Sharon and I were hitched, and I'd enlisted.

Eighteen seems younger now, though. And to be honest, Sharon and I had no business settling down when we did. I knocked her up senior year. The pill failed. We lost the baby four months in, but at that point, I'd already proposed, and my folks had helped us make an offer on a house.

Besides, what eighteen-year-old wants a ready-made family? And Fay-Lee's a wild child, everything ahead of her. She's only passing through. Or tryin' to.

I'm sure as soon as she scrapes together enough cash, she's gone. The thought kicks up my adrenaline. She'll look guilty as hell, and as clever as she is, she ain't gonna outsmart Heavy Ruth for long.

I don't think for a minute she had anything to with what Chaos was doin'. She ain't the type. She don't wanna run game, she wants to play one.

Long and short of it is, I don't have no business messin' around with her. It's obvious she's runnin' from something. A charge? An ex?

Don't matter. I'd happily kill any man who tries to take her away from me.

Jesus. I've lost my mind.

There's a rustle from the dressing room, and she steps out, pink circles dotting her cheeks. I straighten.

She's wearing a swingy, pale-blue dress that hits above her knees. She shoots me a shy smile and twirls.

I cough to clear my throat. "Ain't your legs gonna be cold?"

"I'll wear leggings underneath. Do you like it?"

"It's fine." The fabric clings to her tits. She still ain't wearin' a bra. Maybe she's embarrassed to grab 'em with the boys around. I should give her my card and take them out to the truck after this so she can get what she needs.

Parker huffs and rolls his eyes. "We gonna be here all day?"

We are now. "Go try on the next one. The pink."

"This one's seventy-five dollars. It's not on sale."

Is that a lot of money for a dress? Or is that a deal? "Okay."

"Are you sure?"

"I'm sure."

How much is a dress supposed to cost? Don't matter. I laid down a grand for leather saddlebags last week. She can have what she wants.

She waits a second, I guess to see if I change my mind. I don't. She shrugs and heads back in. I turn to Parker.

"What crawled up your ass, boy?"

He smashes his lips together and glares off into the distance as if I ain't talking. He picked that up from his mother.

"You got a problem, spit it out."

"Maybe I don't like wasting the day, standing around."

Carson's gawping at us now, game forgotten.

"You got somewhere you need to be, boy?"

"Anywhere but here."

"People can wait around for your shit, but you can't stand around for someone else?" I don't get this. I bring women around. Not often, but it happens. Parker never acts like this.

Neither boy remembers when their mom and I were together. For them, Steve's always been there. I've always been a weekend dad. Until this past year or so.

"No. I can't." He sticks his nose up the air.

My blood starts flowin'. This child and I are gonna have a thrown down if he don't check himself.

"He's just mad he's missin' that football video game party," Carson pipes up.

Parker huffs and casts his brother an evil glare. Well, guess that's it, then.

"What party?"

"Carl Baker's." Carson's bein' real helpful. He gets to pick the radio station when we get in the truck.

"Who's Carl Baker?"

"He's a kid from school."

"Shut up," Parker mutters, but you can tell, he wants the story told.

"Carl Baker is having a birthday party with video games,

and Parker was supposed to go, but Mom said he couldn't go since she couldn't take him."

"Why can't I take him?"

"She said—" Carson suddenly runs out of steam. He looks to Parker. Parker scowls and stares a hole in the carpet.

I sigh. I'm sure this has something to do with how I'm a greasy gearhead and petty criminal with no redeeming qualities.

"Carl Baker got money?" I ask.

I do, too, now that Steel Bones Construction pays dividends to the patched-in members, but for Sharon, it was always about looks. Back in the day, she wanted me 'cause my tattoos and my cut pissed off her daddy. Eventually, they pissed her off, too.

Irony's a son-of-a-bitch.

"Yeah. They live in Gracy's Corner." Parker toes a loose string in the carpet.

This is bullshit. There's no shame in honest work and dirty hands. What kind of man is he gonna be if he starts believin' other people's opinions of him are worth a damn? That people who live behind gates in big houses are better than other folks?

This is the regret. I don't regret marrying Sharon. I love my boys. Without her, I wouldn't have 'em. Period. And I sure as shit don't regret the divorce. I hate not having my kids all the time, but as the years go on, Sharon has me "watch them" more and more, so the time's fairly even now. I actually have 'em more than fifty percent these days.

But I deeply regret the fucked-up shit they're learning. The Carl Bakers of the world—and their fine, upstanding parents—ain't worth a dime more or less than any other man. Despite what Sharon and Steve think.

"You want to go to this party?"

Parker raises his head. "Yeah."

"You give a shit that I take you lookin' like this?" I watch his face real careful.

He snorts. "You're dressed." That's my boy.

"When is it?"

"Three o'clock."

I check my phone. We can pick up the coyote urine and get him there on time. We need to get a move on, though.

I head into the changing room. No one else's been in or out, so it's easy enough to figure out which curtain Fay-Lee's behind. It's more than a little satisfying to yank the curtain aside and hear her yelp. She pulls a dress up to her bare tits. Like I ain't seen 'em before. Like they ain't burned into my brain.

"What are you doin'?" she hisses. Her cheeks and chest flame bright red. I love it.

"We gotta get goin'." I take out my wallet and hand her my credit card. "Grab some bras and panties and meet us in the truck in twenty minutes."

She's got a speculative gleam in her eyes when she snatches the card. I stalk forward and press her into a mirror. She's yields to me instantly, lets me slip my leg between her thighs. I'm immediately hard.

"You're not in the car in twenty minutes, I'm canceling that card. Then I'm comin' for you."

Her breath quickens, her chest rising and falling. I want to spin her, fuck her from behind, and watch her face in the mirror. But you know—kids.

So I kiss her. I love kissing her. She's surprised every damn time. I look, and her eyes are wide and round and dazed as hell. I don't think she's been kissed much before.

She's not a virgin. I didn't figure she was—kind of girl who parties with bikers—but I eased into her pussy earlier, just in case. She was tight, but she took me easy enough. She ain't experienced, though. For all her sass, when I went for her asshole, she got real flustered.

When she came, that look on her face? Like a revelation? Yeah, she don't know what she's doing. It's crazy, but I love that, too.

"Buy white panties and bras. With lace and shit."

"I'll buy what I want," she sasses.

I spin her, clap my hand on her ass, and head out. It ain't nearly as satisfying when she's wearing leggings.

"White. Lace. Don't test me, woman."

Fay-Lee strolls toward the truck, smirking like the cat that ate the canary, in nineteen minutes and fifty-nine seconds. She struts, a dozen bags dangling off her arms, wrist to shoulder. She must've just piled shit on the counter.

I hate to disappoint her, but I ain't mad.

When we get home and the boys are in bed, I'm gonna make her try on every single thing she bought for me. And then I'm gonna spank her ass again.

I'm fairly sure she'll go along with it. She ain't brought up what happened in the club basement. And she don't seem scared of me. Not going by that smile on her face.

I grab the bags and stick 'em in the bed, batten 'em down with the cargo net. She's climbed into the cab before I get the chance to hand her up. I'm gonna need to break her of that habit. Men open doors for women. Parker and Carson need to learn right.

My step's light as I hop in. The boys are in the back, earbuds already in, playing on those damn phones.

If it were up to me, they wouldn't have 'em, but Sharon

insists that she be able to reach them at any time. As far as I can tell, she don't call or text, but I'm gonna respect her wishes. I considered givin' them limits, but it's like that damn mess downstairs.

I put my foot down, and then I got a deadline on a mod, or one of them gets sick, or I get sick, and they're glued back on the fucking things. The house is wrecked. And I'm too damn tired to fuss.

And then there're moments like this, when I'm almost grateful for the damn things.

"Card?" I hold out my hand.

"What card?" She blinks all innocent, but she can't hide her wonky smile.

"You think you're cute, don't you?"

"I know I am."

"I just want you to know, that's ten."

"Ten what?"

"You'll find out tonight. It *was* five. Now it's ten."

Her eyes grow wide. She squirms in her seat. She knows what I'm talking about.

The muscles in my stomach draw tight with excitement. Her ass was so perfect, glowing rosy red, bouncing under my hand. I need to see it again. Feel that rush. I know it's kinky. But not, *really* kinky, right?

If she didn't like it, she'd act different. Wouldn't she? She'd be keepin' her head down. Acting skittish. She wouldn't bait me and sass me. Right? Still, it ain't fun if she's not into it.

"You need, like, a word?" I clear my throat. Keep my eyes on the road. My mouth is dry.

"A word?"

"You know. If you don't like it. If shit goes too far."

She shifts. Props her feet up on the dash.

"Feet down." That's an easy way to break your legs in a fender bender.

She huffs, but she drops them back to the floor. "Banana."

"Banana?"

"You got a problem with my safe word?"

"Nope."

"I changed my mind. I want rutabaga."

"You can't change your mind."

"Rutabaga!"

"Nope."

"What about falafel?"

"You hungry?"

"A little bit."

"There's a protein bar in the glove box."

"Gross. I'm not that hungry."

"Suit yourself."

"I will." She stares straight ahead, a smile playing at the corner of her lips.

We're quiet for a while. She turns on the radio, flips from station to station.

As we pass through the gate at Gracy's Corner, the bougiest address in town—which ain't sayin' much for this part of the world—she holds up my credit card.

"You want this?"

"You keep it. Don't charge more than three thousand at one time. It'll trigger the fraud detection."

"Are you shitting me?"

"If I don't know exactly where you are, I cancel it. Besides, whatever you bought will tell me exactly where you are."

"And then you come for me."

"And then I come for you. You better hope I find you first and not the club."

She swallows, and then she licks those pouty lips with that little scar.

I got to think about the mod I'm working on to cool things down before we get to the Baker's house. Right as I'm pulling up, I get a call from Mikey the prospect. Heavy's called church in an hour.

This don't bode well.

Mikey don't say what it's about. I tell him to let Heavy know if it lasts longer than an hour, I'm gonna have to bail early to pick up Parker.

I have enough time to meet the Bakers—I make a point of it—and get to the clubhouse before an hour is up. Carson races off to the playground Wall built in the yard out of old tires. Fay-Lee's more uncertain. She clings to my side.

I like it. But she obviously can't come to church.

Thankfully, she sees some of the sweetbutts she's been hanging out with at the bar. Without a "See you later," she skips over to Story. Story's young and hot, but she ain't really a sweetbutt. Nickel sees to that, even though he won't touch her. She's chewin' the fat with Danielle and Jo-Beth from The White Van. Danielle can cause trouble, but Jo-Beth has uncommonly good sense.

Crista Holt is behind the bar, pouring drinks. She gives me a dip of the chin. Fay-Lee will be fine.

The way gossip flies around this place, everyone should know she's off limits, but we get a fair amount of hang arounds. And there are some brothers who'll take their chance if a woman ain't wearin' a cut that reads *Property Of*. Jed, for one. That asshole was fixin' to pop Fay-Lee in the face back when we caught her, and he's the kind who don't know the difference between hating a woman and wanting to fuck her.

I'm the last to enter church, but there're plenty of empty seats. *Spank the Devil* is next weekend up in Stonecut County, and a lot of brothers left early to camp and go huntin' before the rally. We barely have a quorum.

Heavy brought this quorum shit back with him from college. His pop ran things different. If there were a goodly number of brothers, we proceeded. If not, we drank until a few more men showed up.

Club charter requires ten patched-in members to bring a motion, and Heavy goes by the letter of the law. He's sitting at the head of the table, Grinder to his right, Pig Iron to his left. Gus and Boots are sitting at the foot with Eighty. Lots of old-timers here. Camping in the mountains in November is a younger brother's game.

Jed is here, though. He ain't into roughing it. Creech, our resident tattoo artist, is next to him, talking to Cue. Big George rounds out the number.

"Good," Heavy says when he sees me. "This pertains to you. Where's your house mouse?"

"In the commons. At the bar."

"Good. We need to keep a close eye on her."

Unease settles in my stomach. "Why?"

"Creech here had a few drinks at Twiggy's last night." Twiggy's is a honkytonk near the county line. Watered down drafts and hillbillies, mostly.

"Yeah?"

"The bartender's a friend. I did his ink." Creech leans back in his chair, indolent, earlobes dangling. Dude has the biggest gauges I've ever seen. You could hit a golf ball through 'em. Bullet has tried. "He says Chaos was there. The

day before that big party in September. He was meetin'
someone."

Creech pauses. Waits for someone to ask him "Who?"
He's got a flair for the dramatic.

I don't say shit. Neither does anyone else until Boots
hollers, "Well, did you forget who the fuck he met?"

"Rab Daugherty."

The president of the Rebel Raiders. Shit.

"Was Fay-Lee there?" Adrenaline surges through my
veins.

"My boy Dan didn't notice a woman."

"That doesn't mean she wasn't there." Jed shoots me a
sly look. "Place gets crowded."

Bullshit. Ain't never been more than a dozen people in
there, any time I've been. Even when there's a game on.

"Did Dan the bartender hear what they talked about?"
I ask.

Creech shakes his head. "He said they were real cozy in a
booth. Heads together."

"Fuckin' blown job," Grinder declares.

"Fuckin' blown job," a couple brothers echo.

It's the reason that the Rebel Raiders and Steel Bones
have been feuding since '93. We used to be one happy club.
Then it all fell apart.

"If Slip hadn't asked Stones Johnson to take that load for
him, we wouldn't be in this situation today," Eighty says,
gettin' warmed up. This is one of the old-timers' favorite
topics of conversation.

"If Stones Johnson hadn't let that boy of his drive, they
would've never gotten pulled over on Route 29," Gus opines.
"Boy had a lead foot."

"Stones should've taken the River Road. Cops ain't never
on the River Road." Boots adds.

"If whoever had fucking planted those Kalashnikovs under the cigarettes had done a better fucking job, Sheriff Do-Gooder would've never found 'em." Eighty hawks and spits in an empty beer can.

Sheriff Do-Gooder is Senator Do-Gooder now. The bust was a huge deal, made the papers and the nightly news. He rode the publicity all the way to Washington, D.C.

"That's dumb as shit," Cue Ball scoffs. "Stones would still have been busted for the cigarettes. What you think the cops are gonna do with three pallets of name-brand smokes? Leave 'em in the truck when it goes up for auction? You can't hide shit in a cargo container."

"The question is who put them guns in that vehicle." Gus leans back and strokes his chin.

"I still say Stones did it himself. He saw an opportunity, and he went into business for himself." Eighty's a proponent of the "inside job" theory.

Grinder's a true believer in the "government conspiracy" theory. "Sheriff Fuck-nuts planted those guns. You gotta ask yourself. Who stands to benefit? Stones is in jail. Fuck-nuts is on C-SPAN. Who came out on top, eh?"

I don't know the answer to that, but I know the clubs lost. Steel Bones and Rebel Raiders.

Stones and his oldest kid Knocker got twenty-year bids. Stones died on the inside. His other boys—Inch and Dutchy —blacked out their Steel Bones ink and founded the Rebel Raiders with Rab and Book Daugherty.

We could have lived in peace, but then when Stones died, Dutchy went crazy and brained Heavy's little brother Hobs with a baseball bat. Now, there can be no peace. Only lulls in a two-decade war. It'd be worse if the Raiders were organized. Besides the Johnsons and the Daughertys, they don't have much heart for the fight. They're busy dealing meth and brawling.

"We may never know." Gus leans back in his chair, lighting up a smoke.

"No." Heavy doesn't raise his voice, but it still rings out, and every man listens. "We will know. As the man says, 'My righteousness draws near speedily. My arm will bring justice to the nations.'"

"Leviticus?" Grinder guesses.

"Isaiah."

It's a particular habit of Heavy's to quote Scripture. His mother, Miss Linda, was always thumpin' her Bible. She was a passionate woman, may she rest in peace.

"Does that mean we're gonna go after the Raiders. Put 'em all down? It's past time." Jed is bloodthirsty for a man who's never had to take a life, as far as I know.

"'For everything there is a season.'" Heavy answers.

"If we're goin' to war, it's gonna have to wait until next week. I ain't missin' *Spank the Devil*." Cue Ball's got his priorities.

"We're not gonna make a move until the time is right." Heavy says. "And Mando from Los Insurrectos is bringing me up an 81' custom from Nogales. No one's missing *Spank the Devil*."

Thank the Lord and Spank the Devil is one of the biggest rallies on the East Coast. It's always the weekend before Thanksgiving, and it's always a wild ride. Sharon's managed to time her emergencies, so I haven't been able to go the past three years.

"So we're gonna do nothing? It's clear the Raiders are trying to fuck with our business." Big George says. "There's no innocent reason Chaos was looking at those blueprints. He either knows or suspects something."

This spy shit with Chaos is crazy, though. "Rab Daugherty is no criminal mastermind. If he was gonna come for us, it'd be with a gun." It ain't like the Raiders at all.

"No, he's not," Heavy agrees. "But Knocker Johnson is."

And that's the truth. In a club like this, everybody gets one thing. I know engines. Creech does tattoos. Cue eats pussy. Knocker Johnson was the smartest man anyone knew.

Until Heavy came into his own.

But that's what everyone knows about Knocker. He had a Willie G special, and he was fuckin' brilliant. He was older than me, but until he went away, we worshipped the guy. He was insane.

"Knocker's got to be comin' up for parole soon," Pig Iron muses.

"Next month." Heavy taps his fingers on the wood table.

"It look good?"

"No. They're gonna make him serve out his sentence. But he's only got four years left."

"You think Knocker's behind this?" Pig Iron asks.

"You think Rab Daugherty or Chaos had the idea to go after those blueprints?" Heavy raises his eyebrows.

I do not. Doesn't seem like anyone else wants to argue the point.

"So what do we do? Chaos knew about the blueprints, so that means the Raiders likely know enough to get the Feds interested if they were so inclined. Or the Raiders can make trouble with our clients. We don't know if she realizes it, but Dizzy's house mouse has shit on us, too. We got a lot of exposure here." Pig Iron looks to Heavy.

"I say you let me take that skinny bitch back to the basement. Alone. I'll make her talk." Jed makes sure to eye fuck me while he says it. From all the way over on the other side of the table. Pussy.

"We can go any time you want," I remind him.

This wannabe badass. He thinks he can bait me. I ain't uncertain about the size of my dick like he is. He ain't takin' Fay-Lee nowhere. I will be takin' him to school, though. If not today, soon.

"Come on over here. We'll see who the skinny bitch is."

Heavy holds up a hand. "Now is not the time. I have a different idea. Pig Iron, when are you going up to SCI Wayne next?"

"I was thinkin' I'd drop by on the way back from *Spank*."

"Push that date up. Go on your way there. Ask Scrap what he hears about Knocker."

"They ain't in the same block. Knocker's up the hill in medium security."

Heavy nods. "Tell Scrap to let it be known that we will fill up the commissary, or bank account, of anyone who has information on our friend. Make sure the guards hear, too. I want to know who visits him. Who he calls. Who calls him."

"We just gonna ignore the fact that we have a source of information prancing around out there in the commons?" Jed sniffs.

I push back from the table and make my chair screech just to watch him jump. It's gonna be so unsatisfying to beat his ass. He's such a poser.

Heavy gives me a slight shake of the head. I raise an eyebrow.

"Pig Iron," Heavy says. "Would you be okay with us taking Deb somewhere to get her to talk?

"You can't shut her up." Pig Iron chuckles. "But I believe you're trying to make a point. So, no. You can't touch my old lady."

"The skank's been here a hot second. She ain't Dizzy's old lady." Jed must have developed a death wish.

"I'll ask Nickel if he's cool with us takin' Story down to the basement next time I see him. When he's got questions, I'll refer him to you." Pig Iron claps Jed on the back. "You're wrong, young blood. And you're racking up the ass-whuppins. Don't mistake Dizzy's restraint for weakness. I been huntin' with the man many times. He waits for his shot."

It ain't a lie.

Heavy bangs a fist on the table. "So if there're no objections, I propose we release funds not to exceed ten thousand dollars to shake the trees up at SCI Wayne and see what we can find out about Knocker Johnson. Dizzy talks to his mouse. Finds out what she knows."

"Motion seconded," Grinder says.

"All in favor."

There's a smattering of "ayes" and an "I need a beer" from Boots.

"Motion carries."

We file out. I notice that Heavy and Grinder wave Jed ahead. They're only saving him time. We're gonna have it out. I don't know why he has a hate-boner for my woman, but he's gonna learn he doesn't speak her name.

My woman.

Shit. I can't think that way. She's over a decade younger than I am. She's pretty and bright and happy. If I claim her, what's stoppin' shit from going down the same way it did with Sharon?

Maybe it'll be good for a while. Maybe we make it official. Have a baby or two. And then she grows up. She wants more. A class at the community college. A promotion. A dude who cuts his hair and wears a suit.

And then I'm a weekend dad again, alone in a house full of shit I didn't buy. But it'd be worse. 'Cause I've known Fay-

Lee only a few days, and I can't stand it when I don't know where she is. What's that feel like in a few months? Years?

It's a fuckin' mistake even thinkin' down that road. She's more girl than woman. As evidenced by the fact that she did not stay where I put her. When I come back to the commons, she's coming down the stairs from the bunks.

That—coupled with my bleak thoughts—riles me up.

"What were you doin' up there?"

She blinks, surprised. "I was looking for something I lost."

"What?"

People are staring. I ain't bothering to keep my voice down. My temper's rising. Jed talked all that shit, and I was frosty. But this girl makes me worry for a second, and my blood's hot.

"You're not the boss of me." She raises her chin.

Wrong. "Oh, I am."

She gets an ornery look, and her gaze darts left and right. She's gonna bolt. I grit my teeth so I don't grin, my grumpiness evaporating.

I hope she does. My dick perks to life. I'm gonna give her a head start, and then I'm gonna catch her, throw her over my shoulder, and—

"What's for dinner?" Carson comes racing down the hall and skids to a stop, slamming into my thigh. Oof. This kid's getting meat on him.

Fay-Lee breaks into a wide, lop-sided smile.

She's gonna regret that tonight.

"I don't know. What's for dinner, house mouse?"

That dims her smile. My stomach sinks. I want it back.

"There's mac and cheese in the cabinet. You could make that," she sasses. "I like it made with milk, not water."

"Who makes it with water?" Carson turns up his nose.

Fay-Lee bristles. "You've never been out of milk?"

But you can just tell it wasn't a matter of being out of milk. How hard was it where she came from? I assumed she was naturally thin, but I'm curious to see what happens when I feed her.

"Let's go get Parker. I'll make dinner."

I want my woman nice and full. I'm gonna wear her out tonight. She's gonna need her strength. She's gonna tell me why she was wandering around the clubhouse all by herself. And I'm gonna love makin' her tell me.

7

FAY-LEE

I searched the clubhouse top to bottom for my phone. It's definitely gone. No one has seen it. The only places I didn't check were the occupied rooms upstairs, and it's probably not there. The longer I'm here, the more I realize that Steel Bones is sitting pretty. None of the brothers would be interested in a crappy prepaid phone.

As we drive to pick up Parker, nerves start swirling in my stomach. If my phone's well and truly gone, I don't have a Plan B. I don't know anyone's number by heart except my Gram's, and she passed three years ago.

What were the guys meeting about? It seemed like serious business. Prospects were posted at the door, and no one dared walk past. People who wanted to go out to the yard went out the front and circled around back.

They couldn't have been talking about me, again, could they? I thought it was settled. I took the deal. I'm the house mouse, and I pretend that they're not acting really weird.

A reasonable reaction to catching me squatting would be to have the sweetbutts beat my ass and send me on my way. But they decided to keep me close. Like I got something they want. Or I know something I shouldn't.

It's hot in the cab, and somehow, Carson smells like wet dog. He's got his earbuds in, cackling and snorting randomly. I think he's watching cartoons. I roll down the window. I need fresh air.

It's only six o'clock, but the sun's going down. The gust whipping in the window is deliciously cold. I stick a hand out to ride the wind and let the chill numb my fingertips.

Dizzy shoots me a quizzical look, and I turn to meet his eye.

"Am I in trouble?" I ask.

He searches my face. "I ain't gonna let anyone hurt you."

Shit. That's not a "no."

"Does someone want to hurt me?"

"No, baby. Just—" He works his jaw, focusing back on the road. "If you know something, you got to tell me. There ain't nothin' I can't handle. But you gotta tell me."

"Tell you what?"

He thinks a long minute. "If Chaos asked you to do something. Take something. I ain't mad. You didn't know us then. You were in a hard way. But you gotta tell me now."

"He didn't ask me to do anything."

"You can tell me the truth, Fay-Lee."

My face heats. I'm not a liar. "If you're accusing me of something, spit it out."

He tightens his grip on the steering wheel. "Goddamn."

"They think I stole from them? More than some food?"

Is this a trap? Did they let me go with Dizzy so they could watch me, see if I led them back to whatever it is they think I stole? Like I'm a fuckin' pirate who buried some booty?

"Calm down," Dizzy says.

"I am calm."

"Your knee's tapping."

"I didn't steal anything." Besides the food. And booze. And a few bucks I lifted off folks who'd passed out.

We pull up at Carl Baker's big ol' house, and I've got my arms crossed tight, and I'm glaring out the window. Dizzy tries to catch my eye. I hike up my chin.

He sighs.

"Be right back."

He's in there a long time. Long enough that the truck cab cools. I didn't think to buy a jacket when I sprinted through the store earlier like Supermarket Spree. That was a missed opportunity. Carson's playing on his phone, passing gas in the back like an old dog. It's so cold that I deal with it. Breathe through my mouth.

When they come back, Parker wrenches open the back door, hops in, and slams it shut. Dizzy hauls himself up, head low, as if the weight of the world is on his shoulders.

"What happened?" Carson's phone is off, and he's all ears. An asteroid could have hit this car on the ride here, and I swear he wouldn't have noticed, but now, he's fully present.

"Nothing," Parker mutters.

"Not your business," Dizzy says.

The atmosphere in the cab gets even more tense. We drive about a mile in total, stewing silence, until we turn down the road to home and Parker breaks, blowing up.

"I didn't call him a pussy!" He tries to keep it cool, but in no time, he's shouting in earnest, face bright purple. "I said Smith is a pussy, and he *is* a pussy! I didn't pick 'em. I wouldn't pick a pussy to play! And I sure as shit wouldn't be a pussy and tell my daddy about it, if someone did call me a pussy, which I didn't!"

The snort slips out before I can stop it. And then a snicker.

Dizzy frowns at me, but Carson's giggling now, and I can't stop. Soon, we're both howling, and Parker's baring his teeth, clenching his fists. Carson better watch out. He's in range.

Dizzy pulls into the driveway. Parker lunges for the door-knob, and Dizzy engages the locks with a snick.

"No one goes nowhere."

Shivers zip down my spine. It's a voice you can't ignore. Some primitive part of me whimpers and bares her neck.

We all simmer down. I'm only a little scared. I don't *think* he's going to lose his temper. He hasn't yet. But the nerves are delicious. Like at the top of the Ferris wheel at the carnival.

Dizzy gazes into the rearview. "Look at me, boy."

Parker raises his chin the minimum acceptable amount. His black hair's sticking up at all angles, and his young face is hard and mean. He's the one who resembles his daddy, but they have such different temperaments.

Dizzy starts, "It ain't about calling him a pussy or not. You disrespected that man's house. He invited you as his son's guest, and you disrespected his home. You apologize for that."

"We were in Carl's bedroom! No one heard but us. Carl's brother was saying way worse shit."

"Don't matter."

"Carl's a goddamn snitch."

"Don't matter."

"I should've just told his dad I didn't say it." Parker hunches over.

"Then you'd be a liar, wouldn't you?" Dizzy lets his head fall back against the headrest. "Listen. Carson, you listen, too. There are three things to learn here. One. You disrespect a man in his own house—I don't care if you meant to or not—you apologize. A man's home is his castle."

Carson nods sagely, as if he's heard this before, and it doesn't get more true. I wouldn't know. I do know that a woman's home is more or less a motel for ingrates, in my experience. Don't know about a man's house. Until Dizzy's, I never been in one.

"Two. Better to be embarrassed or wrong than to be a liar. You know what Grandma always said— 'The Lord hates a liar.'"

I agree. There's worse things to be than a liar, I suppose, but there's nothin' worse that's more common.

"I didn't lie." Parker's barely holding back tears. I wouldn't want to disappoint this man, either. I'd hate to look small to him.

"I know you didn't." Dizzy unbuckles his seat belt and unlocks the truck.

"What's the third thing?" Carson asks.

Dizzy shakes his head as if he nearly forgot. "Don't be friends with a snitch."

Amen.

Everyone piles from the car.

"Are we not gonna talk about how messed up it is to call people pussies?" I call after them, but the boys are already to the door, and Dizzy's getting my shopping bags.

Strangely, Parker's crappy playdate has calmed me down. Or maybe it was Dizzy's lecture. Mama never took up with a man who had much time for kids, so it's weird to see it up close. Parenting or whatever.

"You comin'?" Dizzy's laden down with bags, and he's holding the door open for me with his foot.

"Yup." I scurry in, and as I pass him, he wallops my butt, bags swinging.

"That's one," he says. "Nine to go."

Little shivers skitter all over my skin. It didn't hurt at all. But I see he hasn't forgotten.

Is he really gonna spank me again?

He did before, but I was out of my mind. If there was much pain, it didn't really register. Afterwards, I was sore for a few hours, but there was so much else to worry about.

And I kind of liked the soreness. After I gave it up to Rylan Dorset in the field behind his house, three whole months after I let him get to first base, I ached for a day or two. He was in the wind; he'd gotten what he wanted, and I think he was pissed he'd had to work as hard he had for it.

I didn't much care that he was done with me. It's wasn't love; it was curiosity. But I did like that ache between my legs. It made me feel different. Like I'd done something. Something had happened to me, and that meant I was real.

It was kind of the same with my sore bottom. I checked it out in the bathroom mirror when I was taking my shower. My butt cheeks were pink, but it was subtle. No one else would've been able to tell. But I could.

I admired my ass for minutes, from all angles. It felt like I was doing something I shouldn't have been doing. Like the rush when you slip a nail polish into your pocket at the pharmacy or pop a grape in your mouth at the grocery store.

I come from a line of women who make very dubious choices when it comes to men, but none of them would let a man spank 'em willingly. My sisters would all think I'm sick to be looking forward to Dizzy maybe doing it again.

I want him to. I want to see what it's like when I'm not upset.

"You rest a while if you want while I make dinner," Dizzy

hollers at me from the kitchen. I realize I'm standing in the foyer, one boot off, lost in thought. The kids already have that video game on downstairs.

"I'll see about the laundry," I call back. I go down, wade through the disaster, and put in the dark load. I restart the white load in the dryer.

At the laundromat in Dalton, if the load didn't dry all the way during the first cycle, or if I got distracted and it somehow got cold and wrinkled in the machine, then that was that. But I'm seeing the upside of owning your own machine—and not being the one who pays the electric bill. You just turn the darn thing on again.

Rich people and their second chances. I shake my head and start refolding a basket of towels so they're in thirds the way I like.

"Dinner!" Dizzy bellows down the stairs not much later.

Carson races into the laundry room and repeats, "Dinner!" Then he sprints away.

As I make my way up, Parker's sulking on the sofa picking apart a Nerf ball. I ain't cleaning that.

"You comin'?" I ask.

He gives a long-suffering sigh and drags his butt up the stairs behind me. Must be tough. Food on the table. Your own room. Hell, your own level of the house. Every toy you can imagine. Birthday parties. A dad.

We all sit at the table, same seats as last night, and the TV tuned to the same station. MMA this time instead of wrestling. And Dizzy's set the table. There's a bowl and spoon in front of everyone, and a stainless-steel pot of macaroni and cheese sitting on a dish towel in the middle.

We're gettin' fancy.

Even when times were the absolute toughest, if Mama was makin' dinner, there were always serving dishes. Before we inherited Gram's wedding china, we used a set Mama picked up at a yard sale. We all have our vanities, I guess.

"Carson—" Dizzy barks, but the boy's already in the fridge, getting two beers and two pops.

Dizzy unscrews my top for me while the boys fight over the serving spoon. Soon enough, we're all settled and chowing down.

The mac and cheese is even better than the kind you can make with milk. This is the kind where there's cheese in a foil pouch. You don't add anything.

It's so creamy good.

I get anxious when Parker and Carson finish before me and go for seconds, but turns out, there's a whole other pot on the stove. We all get as much as we can eat.

There's no conversation. Parker's still out of sorts, and Carson's glued to the TV.

Dizzy's watching me. My mouth. When I finish my beer, he has Carson get me a pop. Guess I'm cut off at one.

I'm watching him, too. He'll get a dab of cheese in his beard, and then he'll wipe his mouth with a worn handkerchief. I've noticed he keeps one in his pocket.

It's funny. Carson and Parker can both sit in their chairs with their heels on the seat and their knees tucked to their chests. Dizzy hardly fits in his. His muscular thighs spill past the sides, and his broad chest totally hides the back of the chair. Only my chair fits just right.

I'm Goldilocks.

Soon enough, both pots are empty. Parker's eyeing the dirty dishes and casting me grudging glances. I was thinking about offering to clean up, but not now.

"I'll see to these," Dizzy says, pushing back from the table. "Boys, you want to order a movie?"

"Seriously?" Carson's stoked.

"You know the passcode. Don't pick nothin' your mom is gonna fuss at me about."

That is putting a great deal of trust in a seven-year-old.

"Pick one of them superhero movies that you haven't seen," he suggests.

"We've seen 'em all," Parker grumps.

"Then watch one again."

Carson has no problem with this. He races off, and I guess Parker realizes he better beat his brother to the remote if he wants any kind of say in the decision-making, 'cause he shakes off his moping and flies off, hot on his tail.

Dizzy turns his attention to me. "We got three solid hours if they pick the last one that came out. The one where they time travel." He listens for the movie music to blare, and then he smiles, wicked as sin. "You. Go to my bedroom. Take off your pants. Bend over the side of the bed and wait for me."

I swallow. Instantly, my pussy creams.

Is he serious?

He jerks his chin toward the master suite. "No panties."

I don't even have any panties except the ones I bought today, still in the bag with the tags on.

Am I going to do this?

I slowly push back from the table and stand.

It's wrong, isn't it? Kinky. I shouldn't want this. He shouldn't want to do this to me.

I look at him. His gaze is even and sure. There's a twinkle in his brown eyes. This is a game. I have a safe word. *Banana.* Or *falafel.* I'm not sure where we came down on that.

But it's also not a game. I'm broke, friendless, and I'm in some kind of trouble with his MC. He's older than me; he's got a ton more money than I do. Really, he could do whatever he wants. I'd probably take it for a few more nights of a warm bed and a full belly.

I chew on my lip as I walk slowly down the hall.

I did rack up nine hundred dollars in clothes on his credit card in twenty minutes. It surprised the shit out of me how easy it is to spend that much money.

He could always return the clothes.

I *was* being a brat.

Excitement's thrumming in my belly. My body wants this. Not the pain. But what comes with it. That blissed-out state. That feeling of being tethered down by a cord that can't break. Secured.

I don't think he'd *really* hurt me. But what if he doesn't know his own strength? What if it's okay, and then it's not? What if I say stop, and he doesn't? What if I say *banana*, and he laughs?

Even the fear is a mind fuck. On the one hand, it's ratcheting up my anxiety higher and higher. On the other, it's amping up the wild nerves swooping in my belly. Making my nipples ache for his touch.

I linger at the door to Parker's room. I bet if I just went to bed, Dizzy would drop it. And he might never try it again.

Or he'd drag me out and do it anyway, and that would ruin everything, too, 'cause I'd be out the door the very next second he turned his back. There's nothing that makes me think he'd force me, but that's the whole thing with men, isn't it?

Carol didn't think Dan would leave her.

Dee didn't think Reggie would ever hit her.

Keira didn't think Brian was using again.

Kayden didn't think Chad could possibly be the one taking cash from her purse.

And every man Mama ever brought home surprised the

crap out of her each time he cheated or snuck into one of our rooms or pawned the TV.

Trusting men makes you stupid. Trusting *anyone* makes you stupid. 'Cause wasn't Kayden steppin' out on Chad? Wasn't Keira drinking herself into a stupor as soon as she got home from work?

Now I'm standing in the middle of the hallway like an idiot, head full of garbage.

I wish I could turn it off.

"Go into my bedroom, Fay-Lee." Dizzy's voice is deep. Calm.

So I do.

As soon as I shut the door—after checking again that it doesn't lock—butterflies tear through my belly. I flick on a bedside lamp. I don't think I could do this with the overhead lights on.

I tug off my sweatpants and drop them in a hamper. I see that Dizzy's lined up the shopping bags on the bench at the foot of the bed. I count them. Twelve. Damn, I did some damage.

I walk to the bed, super aware that I'm naked from the waist down. I'm only wearing a new button-up plaid shirt that I bought at the store. With each step, my pussy lips slide against each other. I'm sopping wet.

He's gonna be able to tell. My inner thighs are getting slick, too.

I bend over and lay my upper body across his dark green comforter. It clashes terribly with all the teal, but it smells like him. Spicy but reassuring.

I position myself so I'm facing the disassembled engine on the dresser. I arch my back, stretch. It feels good.

I shift my hips. My slit opens. I don't have one of those

pretty shaved pussies with puffy lips. I've been on the road too long, and I've got folds and a clit that peeks out.

My nipples are hard, chafing against my shirt, and my ass is getting cold.

Every second I wait, my breath grows shallower, and my nerves go crazier and crazier. I'm nearly crawling out of my skin.

It's totally quiet in the room. My head is a different story. It's like it cracked open and everything fell out in a jumble. I don't know where to begin sorting it all out.

I'm alone.

Vulnerable.

Aching.

Scared.

When the door snicks open, I startle. Dizzy slips in, and then he kicks the stacked laundry baskets in front of the door. It wouldn't stop an intruder, but it'd give us enough time to get decent if the kids needed something.

Shit.

What if the kids need something?

"Are they gonna—uh—interrupt?" I stand.

"Nope. We ain't gonna hear from them for hours. They hate bedtime. They ain't gonna come up until I call 'em."

"Are you sure?"

"Yup."

He moves to stand behind me and grabs my waist, rotating me gently and urging me to bend back over with his heavy palm on my back. I let him move me. He makes a hum of pure appreciation as he pushes my shirt up as high as it'll go, and his fingers trip down my spine. I warm head to toe.

"Spread your legs." He steps back for a better view.

I flashback to the room at the clubhouse as I edge my feet apart, opening myself to his gaze.

He didn't touch me that day. He's definitely gonna touch me now. Are we gonna fuck after? Are we gonna kiss? I really want to kiss some more. I glance over my shoulder, try to read his face.

"Eyes straight ahead," he orders.

I obey. My hair falls in a dark curtain around my face like blinders blocking him out. He bends over me, gathers it gently, and then drapes it over one shoulder. I'm not hidden now. He can see my face. I can catch his movements in the periphery.

Tingles dance across my skin.

"Now put your hands on your ass. Spread your cheeks."

No way. I can't. He'll see my asshole. And how wet I am.

"You just earned yourself another one. Spread, Fay-Lee."

I gulp, lean forward and rest my chest on the comforter, and grab my ass. He groans. "Wider."

I pull forward, squeezing my eyes shut. He can see everything. And the way I'm pulsing, he can probably see my channel contracting on air, hungry for cock.

He approaches, slowly. I can sense him. Hear him. But I can't see him. He clicks on the TV and turns up the volume. Some car show.

I tense, brace myself for a smack.

Instead he eases my hands back to the bed and cups my ass, rubbing, pressing his thumbs into the base of my spine, massaging away the fading ache from sleeping on the ground.

I moan. It feels amazing.

"I'm gonna make you feel good, baby," he whispers, like it's a secret. "In the end, you're gonna cum so hard."

My hearts falls, just a little. Does that mean he's not gonna spank me?

And then his hand falls on my ass. Hard. Really, really hard. I yelp. My hand flies back. He catches it mid-air, returns it to the comforter.

"You get another one for that. Don't move. Take it like a good girl."

My pussy spasms. My left ass cheek burns, and I'm bracing for an impact, and every second of anticipation cranks the dial on my excitement.

Crack.

I sway. "Hey!" He hit me on the same cheek! Unfair.

"That's two more. You don't say 'hey.' You're not the one in charge here."

He nails me two more times on the exact same cheek. It's beyond a burn now. It hurts. My eyes are tingling. Am I gonna cry? I never cry.

He lays down another wallop on my right side. Somehow this one's worse. I gasp.

"You were naughty, weren't you?"

He grabs my ass, digs his fingers into the hot flesh. Ouch, ouch, ouch. I cry out. "Yes!"

"You pulled a stunt, didn't you?"

He wallops me, and I buck my hips, try to escape his hand, but it's too big, and it hurts. It steals my breath it hurts so bad. Crack. Crack. He rains blows on the tender flesh at the top of my thighs, and then he slaps my pussy.

"You were bad, weren't you?"

"Yes," I sob. Tears are dribbling down my cheeks, salty on my lips, soaking the comforter.

"You racked up nine hundred bucks in twenty minutes, didn't you, naughty girl?"

Whack. Whack. Whack.

I can't say yes. I can only blubber into the bed sheets. My brain is on the fritz.

I could say *banana*.

I could say *stop*.

I could stand up and walk away.

I could kick him in the balls.

But I don't want to do any of that. I want more.

I'm better than fine. My ass is on fire, but I'm floating. Everything's okay. I don't have to worry about anything at all.

It's been way more than ten. Or twelve. He keeps going, and every so often he stops, massages my ass, and that hurts worse, but then he slips his fingers into my pussy, smearing my cream over my folds.

He holds his fingers to my mouth. "Open up. Suck."

I do, tasting myself, his calloused finger rasping against my tongue. It's earthy. Tangy. All of a sudden, everything becomes hyper-real. Like someone switched the room to high def.

"You're a dirty girl, aren't you?" he growls. "My perfect, dirty girl."

He lands three final, sinus-clearing claps to my lower cheeks, and then my legs give out, and I sag against the bed.

Instantly, he's on his knees behind me, drawing me into his lap, cradling me in his strong arms. His beard tickles my neck. I'm sniffling. He wipes my eyes with the sleeve of his flannel shirt.

"You're so beautiful," he murmurs in my ear as he rocks me, pressing kisses to my temple. "You took that so good, didn't you, baby?"

His praise wraps around me, warms me. I love this.

"You're okay." His fingers skim across my skin as if he's reassuring himself. "You're okay."

His cock is hard and poking me in the back. Are we going to fuck now? I feel like a rag doll, but my pussy's still swollen and needy. My ass is truly beginning to burn.

I wriggle to prop myself on a hip, searching relief. He chuckles, his massive chest vibrating against my back.

"We're not done yet."

"No?" My voice sounds drowsy, even though I'm wide-awake.

"No." He reaches behind him. "Here. Drink this." He holds a bottle of cold water to my lips. I gulp it down. I didn't know I was so thirsty.

I perk up a little, blink. The room comes a bit more into focus. I sigh and stretch my arms overhead. I feel so calm. Almost weightless. But it's not scary at all.

"Now you're gonna show me what I bought."

"Huh?"

"Yup. You're gonna try on every outfit you bought with that nine hundred dollars. We'll see if you can keep 'em."

"What if I say no?"

He chuckles. "I don't know. Call it a night, I guess. We could watch a movie. Your ass has had enough."

It has? The pain is a dull throbbing. I can hardly stand the feel of the denim of Dizzy's pants on my tender skin, but love the feel of his arms around me, so I only squirm, I don't fight to get up.

I also love the way he holds me as if I'm the most precious thing in the world, and how he's as infatuated with staring at me now as he was when he had a lot more to see.

"You want to watch a movie, baby?" He rubs his rough hands up and down my arms.

No. I want to see what happens next. I shake my head, brushing his beard back and forth.

"All right, then. Alley-oop." He rises, lifting me with him, and then he sets me on my feet. "Go model my new clothes for me."

He jerks his chin toward the bags and settles himself against the headboard, legs spread, a wild-haired outlaw well-pleased with himself. I can see the bottoms of his huge bare feet.

He's a picture. Torn, faded jeans. Thighs like tree trunks. Broad shoulders, massive biceps. Green plaid flannel that's been washed a thousand times. Thick, wavy black hair and beard. Dancing brown eyes. I bet some women look at him and want to clean him up. Comb and cut his hair. Buy him a crisp new shirt.

I love the way he looks. Like a mountain man or a lumberjack. He looks like he works hard, and he knows what he's doing.

He winks at me. I roll my eyes.

I rummage in the bag, pulling out a bulky burnt orange sweater with leaves around the hem. I thought it was festive, considering the season. My third-grade teacher wore sweaters like this all the time. I tug my T-shirt over my head, and slip the sweater on, checking Dizzy from the corner of my eye. He's watching.

The TV is on behind me, but his gaze tracks my every move.

I consider bottoms. Jeans are out. I don't want anything to touch my sore ass. I slip on a cute pleated skirt I bought in dark brown.

"Okay. Show me."

Dizzy cracks open a beer he must have brought with him and takes a sip.

I feel silly. "You can see it."

"Twirl." He gestures with his bottle. "Do like those models do."

"I feel stupid."

"You look pretty as hell. Show me. If I like it, you can keep it."

I think he'll let me keep all this anyway. He's teasing. His lips are curved up. He's enjoying himself.

He's so much more at ease. Way more relaxed than I've ever seen him. Me, too. Did the spanking do that for him? Like it did for me?

I don't know anything about this. I saw that movie with Dee. The one with the red room and the whips. That girl didn't look like she was having much fun. Except for the helicopter ride. She seemed to dig that.

I cock a hip, rest my hands on my waist, and sashay in a circle. The skin on my ass feels tight, twinging each time I take a step. I bet it's red.

"Do you like it?" I ask. My face heats. I glance at him from under my eyelashes. I'm not used to being the center of attention. Not at all.

"Do you?"

"Yeah." It's cozy. It reminds me of back to school time. I always loved the day after Labor Day. Breakfast and lunch five days a week. Air conditioning. And my teachers always liked me. I think it was my lop-sided smile. People often take a shine to me because of it. I think that's why Chaos agreed to give me a ride.

"Put it in the keep pile, then. Next."

I'm warming to this game.

I sort through the bag, looking specifically for a dress I grabbed at the very last moment. It was on a rack of home-coming gowns. All I saw was a poofy, electric-blue skirt and rhinestones, and I snagged it.

"How about this?" I hold it to my front.

Dizzy raises an eyebrow.

I take off the sweater and skirt, fold them carefully, and set them on the bench at the foot of the bed. Goose bumps rise all over my body. I'm naked, and he's staring.

My nipples stiffen to achy points. My pussy throbs. I really like him watching me.

He takes a sip of beer with his soft lips. I loved kissing him in the laundry room. I hope he kisses me again. To be honest, there's not much I don't love about him.

I lower the dress over my head. My hair's a mess at this point, so many wisps and flyaways. The dress is slinky. Spaghetti straps. Plunging neckline. And so many sparkles. It hits me high on the thigh, and poofs out almost to my waist. It's awful.

"Do you like it?" I smoosh my upper arms together, try to create some cleavage, and fail miserably. I do duck face to complete the effect.

"I hate it."

"Well, I wanna keep it."

I don't know where this sass is coming from. Back home, you got what you got. If you decided to be a brat, you got slapped upside the head. I never bothered pouting. It didn't help. If Mama didn't have the money—and she never had the money—that was that.

I heard plenty of pouting once I got the job at the Gas-and-Go, that's for sure. *Fay-Lee, lend me five dollars. Fay-Lee, let me put ten bucks in the tank. Tell your boss you must've miscounted someone's change.* I never picked up the habit myself, though.

"You serious?" Dizzy asks.

"Yeah." I smooth my hand down the sparkles. It's the kind of fabric that feels flammable. Truthfully, it's hideous, but it reminds me of Carol's prom dress. She used to let us play dress-up with it before she traded it at a swap. It was the fanciest thing I'd ever worn. Well, until now.

He lifts a shoulder. "You ain't gonna wear it outside of the house."

"So says you."

"So says me." His lips curl. "Put it in the keep pile, then, if you like it."

He can't be serious. This dress is hideous. I wait a second, but he doesn't say anything, so I put it with the sweater and skirt. I check the tag before I look through the next bag. Two hundred and forty-seven dollars. Holy crap. That's way too much for a joke.

"You don't look at the tags. I worry about that. Not you."

Oh, I love this game.

He deserves a reward.

Even though my ass burns. Why aren't I upset about that? I'm not. Not at all.

I really want to see what it looks like. I dig through two bags until I find what I want. I only bought one. They aren't practical.

It's a white lace thong. There's a matching lace bra, too, with a tiny bow and a rose bud between the cups. I hold them up.

Dizzy grins, as happy as I've seen him. "That's what I'm talkin' about."

I pull on the bra and hook the clasps. Then I slip on the panties.

Dizzy swirls his index finger. I turn where I stand, pausing when I catch sight of my ass in the mirror above the dresser. It's rosy red, especially against the white lace. I crane my neck. There are red fingerprints on the very tops of my thighs.

"You like what I did to you, baby?" His voice is low. Growly.

My belly swoops. Already, I've soaked the panties.

"Yeah." I know it's wrong. I'm not supposed to be proud of my red bottom. It doesn't make sense. But that's as close a word as I can think of to describe what I'm feeling. *Proud.*

And that's messed up, isn't it?

"What are you thinkin'? What put that frown on my pretty girl's face?"

Dizzy misses nothing.

I turn away from the mirror. "I don't know. Are we—are we supposed to be doing this?"

He tenses, his jaw tightening. "Do you want to stop?"

"No. But—" I come prop a knee on the foot of the bed. "This isn't what people normally do. Right?"

"Guess not." He's frowning. Shit. I ruined the moment. "What do *you* think?"

I gnaw at my bottom lip. "I don't want to stop. I like it. But all my sisters, all my girlfriends—they'd lose their minds if they knew."

He glances past me to the door, and his jaw tenses. "We don't have to do anything. You can keep all the clothes. I wasn't actually gonna take any back anyway. We can watch a movie."

He's disappointed, but he's tryin' damn hard not to let it show on his face.

"I don't want to watch a movie."

His eyes return to mine. I can't hold his gaze. I keep sneaking peeks at the huge cock tenting his jeans.

"What do you want, baby?" he asks.

I check the door. There's no lock. Just two laundry baskets. I can leave whenever I want. There are windows, too. Three big ones with heavy teal curtains and white sheers.

And Dizzy, sitting against the headboard.

My pussy's achy.

I want him.

He's hard. There's a bulge in his jeans. A big one.

"You wanna fuck, baby? You want me to make you feel good?"

I nod.

He leans over and grabs a foil packet from the bedside table. Then he unzips his pants. His cock springs out, ruddy, thick, and veiny. He wasn't wearing underwear. He slides his jeans down a few inches, not much. Now I can see the dark thatch of hair at the root of his cock.

He's way bigger than Rylan Dorset and those couple of boys I experimented with in high school. Longer. Thicker.

My breathing goes shallow.

He rips the packet open and unrolls a rubber down his cock.

I don't know if he'll fit.

But I wanna try. I wriggle my thong off and kick it in the direction of the hamper.

"Come here."

I kneel all the way on the bed. His eyes are glued on me. On my face.

I shuffle forward on my knees until I'm beside him. He cups my neck, draws me in. Kisses me. I melt.

"Here we go." He places his hands around my waist and lifts me until I straddle him. His cock is hot against my lower belly. If I want him inside me, I need to rise up and take him. Do it myself.

His fingers skate up my back. He unhooks the bra and

pulls it free. Then he cups my breast. He's so big, all of me is in his hand.

"Gimme this," he says, and I arch my back. He drops his head and takes my tit in his mouth. He sucks and draws, lapping my nipple with his raspy tongue. It's so good. Hot and wet and demanding.

The best part is how *serious* he is. He's not trying to warm me up. He's devouring me. It's like feasting on my tits is even better for him than it is for me.

That's how all this is. Whatever feels good to me seems to rev his engine twice as much. As if there's a direct connection between my pleasure and his satisfaction. It's crazy.

He suckles, tongues my nipples until I'm whimpering, grinding down, sliding my pussy along his cock, smearing the condom with my cream. I want more.

His hand rests flat against the small of my back, and he turns his attention to my other tit, sucking hard, tugging until I cry out, releasing it with a pop.

This is torture. And I can stop it.

He gives my tits a break and brushes kisses along my jaw, gathering my hair and holding it in a ponytail with one fist. "Ride my cock, baby," he rumbles in my ear. "Come on."

My clit throbs. I grind, but he stays frustratingly still, his lips gentle, even though he's panting as if he's in pain. He kisses my scar. The tip of my nose.

If I want it, I have to take it.

And I want it. I really do. For the first time in my life.

I grab him by the root and wrap my fingers around his girth. Even through the rubber, he's hot to the touch. I rise up on my knees. He's so big; that's not gonna do it. I have to kind of squat over his lap.

I don't know how to do this. I'm fumbling, and then his

hand is on mine, aiming, and I feel him press at my entry. He's huge. I don't take him automatically. He's too much.

The fingers of my other hand find my clit, and I rub furiously as I spread my thighs, tilting and wiggling. I want him inside me. I buck and rock, working myself down, inch by inch, impaling my pussy on his thick cock. He grunts, his face contorted, his eyes desperate. He's sweating, and he smells like musk and man.

I want to touch his bare skin. I want to rake my tits through the wiry hair on his chest. I unbutton his shirt, frantic, and he helps me, tossing it onto the floor, peeling off his white undershirt. And then my palms find his rock-hard shoulders, and I hold on as I take more of him, moaning as he stretches me.

"I'm so full," I moan.

"Does it feel good?" he growls, breathless.

"Yes."

Oh Lord, it feels so good.

His stomach muscles are bunched tight, the strain showing on his face. He's letting me set the pace, and it's costing him.

Finally, I take him all the way, and he breaks. He bucks, fucking into me, lifting me and drilling my pussy. I'm on top, but he's in control. Every stroke is the best feeling, and I want it, every inch, I want him to use me, slam me down onto his cock over and over, and make me take it.

There's the wet, sticky sound of slapping, and it's so dirty. And hot. I'm gonna cum.

My pussy's spasming, pure pleasure coiling in my belly tighter and tighter, a wave looming, ready to wash me away. I can hardly play with my clit, he's pounding me so hard. My hair has fallen in our faces, tangled in his beard.

"Does this feel good, baby?"

"Yes," I sob.

He grabs my tender ass, digging in, lifting me and slamming me down as he pistons, faster and faster. It hurts, and it makes everything feel even better. I don't want him to ever stop, and I can't bear a single second more.

"You're taking my cock like a good girl, aren't you?"

"Yes," I gasp.

"Ride my cock harder, dirty girl. Take it all. Come on." He's grunting in my ear, his quick breaths hot on my neck, and I'm coming, waves of pleasure cresting through me, my belly tightening, and I throw my arms around his neck, holding tight as I shake and tremble, shoving my face into my upper arm to stifle my screams, my mind blown to pieces.

He drills into me once, twice, bottoming out as he swallows a triumphant shout. Then he wraps me in his arms, pressing me to his sweaty chest. His heart pounds against my bare tits.

We catch our breath together, skin to skin.

Eventually, as the air begins to feel chilly, he eases me to the bed and tucks me beside him under the covers. I can't move my legs. Or form words.

He goes to the bathroom, cleans up quickly, and when he comes back to bed, he brings my water bottle. He crawls in beside me, but over the covers, lounging on his side, all self-satisfied.

"Drink. Finish it." He holds it to my mouth. I gulp it down. I'm parched.

He smooths my hair out of my face and smiles.

"Hey, beautiful girl."

"Hey."

He lost his pants in the bathroom. He's completely naked now, tan, ripped. Gorgeous.

He stretches out beside me and cups my jaw. "Are you okay?"

I hum. It's a happy sound.

"Go to sleep now."

I'm almost there.

But what about the boys? What if they find me in their dad's room?

That breaks through my post-sex fog. I struggle to sit. Dizzy shakes his head and splays a heavy hand on my chest. "Go to sleep."

"What about the kids? I should go back to Parker's room."

"Nope. My woman sleeps in my bed."

"Your woman?" A burst of warmth, so bright I can hardly believe it, explodes in my chest. I'm Dizzy's woman?

"You doubt it? Fuck. If I need to prove it again, you gotta give me a few minutes. I ain't twenty years old no more."

He chuckles and sprawls back on the pillows, switching the channel to a different car show.

"You need food?"

I yawn. For first time in my life, I don't think I could eat. "No."

"Warm enough?"

Yes, between my still-burning ass and the human heater next to me. "I'm okay."

"Go to sleep." He sips his beer.

My eyes drift shut, and I curl up against his side, his arm curved around me.

I feel safe.

Cared for.

I know life is never this easy.

But I'm gonna leave worrying about it for morning.

8

DIZZY

When I was a kid, I knew I wanted a Shovelhead for my first bike. My first ride was a chopper, a rebuild that Big George guided me through. A beautiful ride. I laid her down in an early ice storm when I came back from my first deployment, and she wasn't salvageable. My next bike was a Shovelhead, too.

But when Parker came along and I needed a truck, I didn't know what I wanted beyond American-made.

Dad and I went up to Baldwin, on the state line, where there's a strip of dealerships and no sales tax. We started at the first place we came to. We'd narrowed it down to three different models beforehand.

The minute I sat behind the wheel of my truck, I knew it was the one. Dad insisted we test-drive it and take the other models for a spin. To be sure. But I was sure. I went along with it. Dad was good company. Funny as shit. But we could've called it a day and gone fishing. I was sold the minute I slid into the driver's seat.

The closest feeling I can compare it to is when I held Parker for the first time. And Carson. They were mine.

So is this girl curled up beside me, snoring softly, nestled under my arm. I know that ain't the way it's supposed to be. Shit, there are whole magazines for folks who need all the specs and reviews before they even go to test-drive a vehicle. But I know. Fay-Lee belongs to me.

It's gonna hurt like a bitch when she decides she wants to leave.

I kiss her on the forehead and ease out of bed. I need to check on the boys, get them ready for bed. If I let 'em, they'll stay up all night.

Parker can come back up to his room. Fay-Lee is stayin' in my bed. No sense in him bunking downstairs for another night.

I grab another beer and some chips on my way to the lower level. I'm starving. What I really want is meat. I thought I had some deer jerky left, but I search the shelves and can't find it. Carson must've finished it off. Oh, well. It was good. Can't blame him.

I find the boys watching the end of this movie from the 80s that they've seen a hundred times. It's about a cat and a dog, and they get lost or something. Maybe there's a hurricane. I've sat through it enough, but I never paid much attention.

"What happened to the action flick?"

"We seen it before."

"You've seen this before."

"Yeah." Carson scooches to make room for me. I plop down between them, kick a few toys off the coffee table so I can prop up my feet. This room is a fucking disaster. I'm gonna have to take away dirt bikes again until they clean it up.

I pop the chips, and both boys' hands dive in.

"After this, it's bedtime."

"Okay, Dad." Carson's eyes are drooping. He's the one who'll pass out wherever. Parker's like me. A light sleeper.

We watch in silence. By the time the credits roll, Carson is conked out with his head on my lap. Parker is wide-awake, his face set in a scowl. He's still pissed. That boy carries a grudge just like his mama.

"You gonna tell me what crawled up your ass?"

He shrugs. He wants me to try a little harder before he'll give up the goods. So much like his mama.

"You can sleep in your bed tonight."

He's surprised. "Fay-Lee gonna sleep down here?"

"She's sleeping in my bed."

"She your girlfriend now?" This news has distracted him from his pouting. The gears in his brain are turning.

"Somethin' like that."

He's quiet a minute. He's really thinkin'. "Does this mean she'll be here a while?"

"I hope so, but she's her own woman. She might have plans she wants to get back to." I rub my chest.

"If she's here a while, would she get a job?"

"She could if she wanted. I'd rather her work around the house, but that's up to her."

"If she decided to stay home, could I come live with you?"

Whoa. Did not see that coming. "Why do you ask that, bud?"

I'm playing for time. I know Parker gets real hinky when it's time to go back to Steve's. It can't be easy livin' with one foot in one place, the other somewhere else. It sucks. Carson rolls with it a lot better.

"If I lived here, we could finish the rebuilds a lot quicker."

True. Parker and I rebuild old dirt bikes we find on the

internet and donate them to local families who have kids who want to ride and can't afford it. It's a great way to teach him about engines. We've done 2-strokes, 4-strokes, you name it.

"We ain't under a deadline."

"But if Carson and I stayed here, we could do all sorts of stuff more. Like, um—Like just be here. With you. At Steve's place, we're alone all the time."

I school my face. Make sure he can't see the ugliness I got inside when it comes to this.

My dad never said a bad word about my mother in his life. I distinctly remember her driving him insane, bitchin' about him getting grease on the towels or her carpet, and he'd get so pissed. He'd stomp out to the garage, bang shit around for a few hours. Then he'd come in for dinner and kiss her. She'd have made his favorite—fried chicken or cobbler—and that was the end of it.

Sharon and I ain't together, but I want my boys to understand that's how it goes. Behind closed doors, shit gets real. But around other people, a man treats his woman with respect. Full stop.

So I don't say what I'm thinkin' about his mother. Instead, I say, "Your mom says she's got a work thing. In a little bit, y'all are gonna be staying with me for a few weeks while she's out of town."

"I'm not talking about a few weeks. I mean, like, for real."

I sigh, grit my teeth. "Your mom and I have a setup. You know that."

"Mom won't care." His voice is bitter.

"Why do you say that?"

I ain't thick. I know he's noticed how things have been going. A few hours turning into a few days. A weekend turning into a week. Sharon's doing well for herself, and selling houses takes a lot of time. The hours ain't regular. I try not to judge.

But she was so damn hot to make sure I didn't get no more visitation than the minimum when we first split, though. I try not to dwell on it. But every time she asks me to "watch" my own kids—when back then, she swore to the judge I was a piece of shit—it's a raw wound.

"She's always showing houses. If someone's home, it's Steve, and he don't want us around."

Fuck. I wasn't prepared for a heavy conversation when I came down. I probably should have been. Parker's clearly been working himself up to this for a while.

"Yeah? He always seems like a friendly guy."

Steve's a dick. Smiles like a used car salesman and talks like a sports announcer. *Play one game at a time, right? Slam dunk. Got to keep your eye on the ball.*

He always comes across as smug to me, as if he's proud of himself for fuckin' my wife. But he's got it twisted. As soon as she gave it up to him, I didn't want her no more. Truth be told, it was a relief. I'd been mostly hanging around for the boys for a while before she stepped out.

"Steve's fake as shit."

I can't argue with that. Hold up. Exactly how fake is Steve's nice guy routine?

"He don't hit you or nothin'?" I'll put him in the ground.

"No. He huffs around, bitchin' all the time about how we make a mess and cost him so much money."

Bullshit. Sharon gets way more than the court-ordered support. And anytime she asks, I write a check. The mess, though. Steve's got a point.

"You kids are terrible at cleaning up after yourselves."

"I know. But he's such a dick about it. He hates us."

I shove a handful of chips in my mouth. I got no idea what Steve thinks about my kids. I know if I follow my inclination—pay him a visit tomorrow, remind him who the fuck he's dealing with—it ain't gonna play out the way I want.

"You talk to him about this?" I hedge.

Parker snorts. "Yeah, I asked him why he hates us so much."

Fair. It was a stupid question.

"What about your mother? What does she say?"

"She says clean up your shit and stay out of his way. Then she says she's got to get back to work. That's what I'm sayin'. We may as well be here. The bikes are here."

"What does Carson think?"

"Carson thinks Steve doesn't like him 'cause he's fat."

"Carson ain't fat." He's got a little baby chub left on him, but wait until he has his first growth spurt. He's gonna be a linebacker. I was the same way. "Why's Carson think that?"

"'Cause it's true. Steve makes him eat egg white omelets for breakfast. Calls him husky all the time."

The fuck?

"Carson thought he meant husky like the dog, so he didn't mind. Then I told him what it meant."

"You really needed to do that?"

Parker's lip sneaks up. "Guess not."

Yeah, Steve and I are gonna have a conversation. He's a gym rat. Tans. Got himself veneers. The whole shebang. But I still got at least fifty pounds of muscle on him and no compunction about makin' him get his teeth done again.

"I asked Mom. She said we can't live here during the week 'cause there's no one to watch us after school while you're at work. If Fay-Lee stays, she can watch us."

That's what Sharon said? She probably was sayin' what first came to mind. Sharon loves her kids. She'd never agree to change the custody arrangement. 'Course she did just ask me to take 'em for a month or so. And she don't seem to notice that it's a pretty even split now. But I'm only "watching" them for her when I take 'em extra days.

I sigh. I don't know what to say. "I'll talk to Steve."

"He's gonna tell you what you want to hear, and then keep bein' a dick to us."

"You think so?"

"That's what he always does."

This is a fuckin' mess. I'm happy Parker's speakin' his mind, though.

"I'll talk to your mom then."

"You're just gonna piss her off, and it'll make everything worse. I told you I talked to her. She basically said it's our fault."

"I'll sort it out." Somehow.

"It's okay." Parker tilts his head back and rests it on the couch, the weight of the world on his thin shoulders. I fuckin' hate this. It's not what I wanted for him or Carson.

"I'll take care of it."

Parker grabs some chips from the bag. "I told Steve if he calls Carson 'husky' again, I'm gonna punch him in the face."

That's my boy. "What did he say?"

"Gave me a lecture. Told Mom. She took my phone."

"He call Carson husky again?"

"Nope." Parker grins. First smile I've seen from him today.

We polish off the chips, and then I carry Carson up to bed, Parker behind me. I wake Carson up long enough to brush his teeth, and then I tuck them both in. Parker's getting too old for the whole bedtime routine, but he lets me do it sometimes.

After the boys are down, I check that the doors are locked and turn out the lights. I grab another water in case Fay-Lee wakes up thirsty.

I fully intend to fuck her a few more times before morning.

When I get back to the bedroom, she's still asleep, same position, curled up like a shrimp. The only part of her sticking out of the covers is a mess of shiny black hair and her cute nose. She stirs when I slip under the sheets.

"Dizzy?"

"Hush, baby. Go back to sleep."

Instead she snuggles into me, kissing my chest. I fold her in my arms. She fits so perfect, and she smells so good. Like watermelon.

"Dizzy?"

"Yeah?"

"Can I ask you something?"

My stomach knots. In my experience, it don't ever go well when a woman asks that. "Of course."

"Can we ride dirt bikes tomorrow?"

I fuckin' love this girl. I laugh, roll her over on her back, kiss the corner of her sweet, tilted mouth. "Not tomorrow. I got work. But we'll go next chance we get."

And then I fuck her nice and slow until she cums on my cock, face smothered in my chest as she cries out my name. Until she leaves, I'm gonna enjoy the hell out of her. The most perfect woman in God's whole creation.

We have three perfect weeks. The kids go back and forth between me and their mom a few times. Fay-Lee and I fall into a pattern. She makes dinner and forces me to watch some show about people who always dress nice and have really long conversations in fuckin' living rooms.

I make excuses to come in the house during the day when I'm supposed to be workin'. I fuck her in the kitchen. The shower. On the living room floor. She convinces me to let her braid my beard, and I make her wear her hair down.

The kids and her take to each other. She bakes brownies from a box and things like that for dessert when they're over, and they're always bringing shit over from their mom's to show her. Then there was a prank war that was goin' for some time until I called it off 'cause my truck got dinged in the cross fire. Took the cost of buffing it out from Fay-Lee's ass.

It's been nice. Easy.

Then, before sunrise on a Saturday morning, a wild animal wakes me up. Claws slice my shoulder and a sharp kick lands in my ribs. It's right before dawn, and the room's light enough so I can see the comforter flailing, but I can't make out what's goin' on. There's a weird keening sound from under the covers.

Did the raccoon get in?

Fuck.

I leap out of bed, grabbing the baseball bat I keep behind the night table.

I hurl the covers, bat raised. Fay-Lee sits straight up, gasping for air, eyes as big as saucers. There's no raccoon. Only her.

My heart's pounding. I crane my neck to check my side. She drew blood.

Her lungs are heaving, and I can see her heart beating in her chest. She's so damn thin.

"Jesus, Fay-Lee." I drop the bat and go to her, pull her

into my lap, hold her as tight as I can. She's shaking like a leaf. "Did you have a nightmare, baby?"

That was some PTSD shit. I struggled for a while after my second deployment. Dreams. Trouble concentrating. Still happens, sometimes. Time has been good for me, though. Dulled the edges. Other guys I served with, it don't go that way.

"What happened, huh?" I rub her back, rock a little.

"I had a bad dream." Her voice is so weak. Distant.

"You want to tell me about it?"

"Nope. Not right now." She scrubs her bleary eyes.

"Okay, baby." I ain't gonna press right now. Later, I will. If someone hurt her, they ain't never gonna have the opportunity again.

God, she's so small. Defenseless. She was all alone after we took care of Chaos. The brothers are decent men—mostly—but we get all kinds of hang arounds. And before she rolled into town . . . I can't think about. Gives me fuckin' indigestion.

"You want to go back to bed? Are you hungry?"

"I want to take a shower."

"Okay."

"And then I want to eat."

"All right."

"I want to make pancakes."

I grin into her hair, breathe her in to calm my racing heart. "More than fine by me."

"And then I want to go dirt bike riding." I said we could go a while back, but with one thing and another, we haven't gone yet.

"Whatever your heart desires." She wiggles in my lap, and I figure she's gonna get up, but she surprises me. She reaches down and grabs my dick. It leaps to attention.

"Please," she whines, brown eyes wide and needy. "Make me feel good first?"

"Yes, ma'am." She strokes me, and I'm rock hard in seconds. She's already climbing me, ready to shove me in her pussy. She ain't wet enough, though.

She's scared, and tryin' to distract herself. She's not worried that she's gonna hurt herself. That's not all right.

I hoist her by the bottom, and lay her down on her back, legs dangling over the bed. "I got a better idea. Put your heels here on the edge."

I wish I could take a picture of her expression. Her eyes light up, and that smile curls. She knows what I'm thinkin', and she's more than down with it. She don't waste time gettin' in position.

Now I see some cream. I'm gonna lap it up. I sink to the carpet, spread her wider with my hands and leave them resting on her knees. I flatten my tongue, start at her asshole, and lick all the way up to her clit, slow and steady.

She reaches for me, but she can't quite grab whatever she's aimin' for, so she rests her hands on mine, twines our fingers as if she's tryin' to hold me in place. I'm not going nowhere.

I stiffen my tongue and spear her hole. She has a powerful taste. Tart. Delicious. She's definitely been fucked recently. Last night, in fact. Twice. She's swollen, too. From *my* cock. I love it. I eat it up and listen to her pants turn into moans and pretty pleas.

"Dizzy, don't stop. Please, don't stop."

I can keep going as long as she needs. I suck her clit, tease it. She raises her hips, shoves her wet pussy into my beard, demanding as hell.

She wants it so bad and that drives me crazy.

She's whining, tugging on my hands. "I want cock, Dizzy. Give me cock."

I ain't gonna say no to that. I flip her over and thrust, reaching between us to circle her clit, keep it popped out of its little hood.

This pussy is mine. This girl is mine. I cum with her clenching around me like a vise, neck twisted so she can catch my lips.

Later, she makes an entire box of pancake mix worth of pancakes. She uses up all the eggs. And she eats her fair share. So does Carson, of course. Parker and I max out after one stack each.

She's sitting with one leg tucked under, swinging the other. She's trying to spare her ass. I wailed on her good last night. No reason except she asked.

There were no handprints this morning, but the apples of her bottom were pink. Next time, I wanna leave marks.

Maybe she needs to get it for wasting pancake mix.

Nah. I don't want to discourage her from eating. She still chows down like she's making up for lost time.

I should probably give it a break anyway. She's been game these past weeks, but I don't wanna push too hard 'cause I'm so into what we do.

Ever since we got the internet when I was in high school, I always search the same videos. I ain't into the chains and ropes and ball gags. I like when the girl gets her ass reddened. The way her pussy looks peeking through red cheeks. The bending over. That's the best part. And the squirming and squealing and dancing on her toes.

I don't know. Some men like to look at jizz drippin' out of a woman's pussy. Some men like tits. I like a red ass.

Sharon would never go for it, and I never pressed it. Part of what makes it so hot is the woman's got to be into it, too. I tried gettin' it going with a few women since the divorce, but no real interest. Not like Fay-Lee.

With her, it feels like a game. You know the difference when someone really wants to play versus someone's goin' along for whatever reason? Fay-Lee wants to play. And that makes her a fuckin' rarity. I don't want to bend her over, and she thinks "This again?"

Besides, she and I do have bigger fish to fry. My ghost girl's still keeping her secrets, and with the club already suspicious, the sooner she trusts me with them, the better I can keep her safe.

I don't want to wake up with a raccoon in my bed again.

Bad enough we've still got the one out back.

9

FAY-LEE

After breakfast, we ride out to the clubhouse. Dizzy keeps bikes in the garage there, and there are tons of spares. Dizzy hooks me up with a 150f, and he brought along the protective gear he bought Parker for Christmas. It fits, but it's tight.

Parker glares at me when I come out of a corner of the garage wearing it. Honestly, when I asked to go riding, I had it in my head that it'd be like back in Dalton. My brother Robbie had a bike, and we'd go out to the fields at the end of our street and ride. No helmets or pads. I should have figured on the gear. The kids were all geared up when I ran into them on the trails that day I got busted.

"Is that the chest protector you were goin' to give me for Christmas?" Parker scowls at his dad.

"Yup." Dizzy doesn't look the least bit abashed.

"This mean I can get the better one I showed you?"

"Guess it does."

Parker smiles. Darn. Kid's face totally changes. "Sweet."

Carson's already geared up and revving his engine in the

yard. He's big for his age, so you tend to forget how overall tiny he is until you see him on the bike. It's adorable.

There's no one else around outside. It's early yet. From my week of squatting, I know that on the weekends, no one stirs much before noon.

The weather's damn near perfect. Sixty degrees. Sky so blue it's hard to believe it's real. A hint of woodstove in the air.

Dizzy rolls my bike outside and holds it steady while I mount and check it out. It's got more bells and whistles than Robbie's, but the basics are the same.

"You know how to ride, right?"

I raise an eyebrow and smirk.

He grins. He's backlit by the sun, all wild dark hair and beard and sparkling eyes.

He checks my chinstrap, tests my helmet. It's on tight.

I lower myself to the seat. Oh, shit. This was not my best idea. I'm not that sore, but in an hour? I might need to ride back standing on the foot pegs. Last night was intense. Dizzy wanted to stop, but I begged for more. He's more cautious than I am. Always checking in and searching shit on the internet to make sure he's not gonna hurt me. I love it, but in the moment, I just want him to keep goin'.

"Follow me," Dizzy orders, heading for his own bike. "Not the boys. They know the trails."

"Yes, sir. Follow the boys. Gotcha." I salute.

I expect a swat, but I get a scratchy-bearded, smooshed-up, through-the-open-visor-of-my-helmet kiss instead.

"Smart ass." He hops on his bike—no helmet, I guess 'cause his hair won't fit in and he's invincible—and we head out to the tree line.

We ride for an hour, the boys racing ahead and then circling back on side trails, showing off. Dizzy does a fair amount of showing off, too. We reach the bottom of the low mountain—a foothill, really—that looms a few miles west of the clubhouse.

There's a stream running through a gully before the trail disappears up a sharp bank. A downed tree lies in a clearing, covered in moss and surrounded by beer bottles. Dizzy gestures for me to pull off. The boys' bikes are already here, but they're nowhere to be seen. Probably climbing the boulders that rise on the other side of the water.

I dismount, bend, and stretch, and Dizzy does the same beside me. Oddly enough, my ass is numb. I tug off my helmet and shake out my hair. The cool breeze soothes my hot scalp.

Dizzy rests a cold water bottle against my shoulder. "Drink."

I grab it and guzzle it down. I'm parched.

It's so gorgeous out here. The leaves are fluttering to the ground in slow motion like red and yellow confetti, and it's quiet except for the occasional howl or crack or hoot in the woods.

There's a soothing bigness to it all. An openness.

I don't know what New York City will be like, exactly, but it won't be like this at all. It's a sucky thought.

"What's that?" Dizzy runs his thumb along my frowning bottom lip. "You hurtin'?"

I shake my head and lope off to check out the stream. I don't want to think about how this is temporary. And it is, right? I'm the house mouse. Free pussy and maid service in exchange for room and board. That's the deal. Isn't it?

No matter how comfortable it is, how natural it feels.

I can't stay here. This can't be for real. He's a dad with a real job and a house and responsibilities. I'm—Well, I don't have any of that. He might be into me now, but how long is that gonna last?

This isn't a fairy tale. In real life, Cinderella is underemployed, and the prince isn't gonna want to support her indefinitely when he's got bills of his own.

Something inside me turns mean and grumpy. I kick some rocks in the steam, make a splash. It doesn't make me feel much better.

There's a crunch as Dizzy comes up behind me. He stops a few feet back. I ignore him.

He shuffles his boots.

I squat and root through pebbles for a nice flat one to skip.

He coughs.

My nails are long again now. Grit sticks under them.

"Fay-Lee."

I can't find a good skipping stone. They're all round or lumpy. I grab a handful of pebbles and roll them in my palm.

"Fay-Lee."

I squeeze and let the pebbles dribble from my clenched fist, bit by bit.

And then Dizzy's crouching next to me. In terms of size, it's like a silverback gorilla sidled up and popped a squat. He gives me space, but he's still imposing as hell. Makes me feel even more ornery.

I start tracing my initials in bubble letters in the dirt.

He sighs. "The boys' mother did this."

He's bringing up his ex? Now?

"She wasn't so childish about it, but she did the same thing. She'd get mad, wouldn't say why. I was supposed to guess. But I'm shit at guessin'."

Oh. My shoulders slump. That *is* what I'm doing, I guess.

"You tell me what's wrong, I'll fix it. If what we're doin' is too much for you, we can slow down. If somethin's happening that you don't want, it stops."

A lump swells in my throat.

That's literally never been the way life has gone for me *ever*. If something was wrong, I had to fix it myself or deal. If I didn't like something, I could suck it up. There were a dozen other mouths to feed, and most were younger or sick or in a bad way.

Nothing in me believes him—that's not the way the world works—but the words have such a wonderful ring to them. I want him to say it again, but I can't think of how to get him to repeat himself. So I try the truth.

I glance up and meet his eyes. "I like it here. I don't want to leave."

His brow furrows. "I don't want you to leave. Why are you thinkin' about leaving?"

"Well, I can't stay forever. I mean, I need a job. Stuff. My own place."

His face falls. "Okay." He stares at the stream trickling past, carrying tiny elm leaf boats. "What job do you want?"

"I don't know. I worked at the Gas-and-Go where I'm from."

"You want to work at a gas station?"

"No, I don't *want* to work at a gas station. I mean, it was all right for what it was. Not many jobs in Dalton."

He tries to run a hand through his hair, but it's majorly tangled after the ride. "Okay. So what stuff do you need? You mean like makeup?"

"Yeah, I guess. And food and all the other things a person needs."

"You've got all the food you need. You want something, we can stop by the grocery store on the way home."

This conversation is getting stranger by the minute. It's like a dubbed movie where the voiceover doesn't quite match the actor's lips.

"There's enough food at the house. But I can't live off you forever, right?"

"You ain't livin' off me."

I roll my eyes. "I am. I don't really have a choice—y'all didn't give me one, either—but I am."

"Is that why you're letting me fuck you?" His body's rigid. If I pushed him, he'd topple over. Timber. I'd never do it, though. Well, yeah I would. When we're playing. But we're not playing now.

"I like what we do. I want it."

His shoulders lower, and his muscles relax.

"I have no idea what that says about me, but I don't really care, either."

Rylan Dorset and those other boys were more a chore than a good time. My sisters had me convinced I needed a boyfriend, and to get a boyfriend in Dalton, you have to put out. They were wrong on all accounts.

The spanking hurts, and that sucks. But everything else I *love*. The anticipation. The weird headspace after the tenth or eleventh smack. Afterwards, when he holds me and fusses over me. And I love that he wants it so bad.

People *always* want something from me. My nieces and nephews want a few bucks or a snack or help unscrewing something or finding a lost blankie. Mama and my sisters are pretty much the same. They need to borrow twenty bucks until the EBT deposit, or they need me to watch the kids, or they need to borrow my makeup or my high-heeled shoes.

It's a *taking* kind of wanting.

Not a powerful kind of wanting.

I let Dizzy do things to me—things I'm growing to crave —and right after, I suspect he'd do whatever I asked him to do. It's a heady feeling. A rush. This enormous, wild man wrapped around my finger.

Hold up. "Do you mean that? You don't want me to leave?"

"No," he says immediately. "I mean, yeah. I don't want you to leave. I want you to stay. With me. And Parker and Carson. Not just until shit is settled with the club. But as long as you want."

"For the free sex and maid service?"

"Nah. For the hassle and the smart mouth." His lip curls up at the corner. "You're my woman. I told you so."

"You can't mean it. We hardly know each other."

He sits flat on the ground, knees bent, and grabs a stick to draw swirls in the mud.

"You've got nothing to say to that?" I sink to my butt, too, and cross my legs. I take my own stick and mess with his swirls, give them ears and tails.

"I got no reasons, girl. It's just the way it is."

"What would you do if I left?"

"Chase you. Bring you home."

"What if you really get to know me, and you decide you can't stand me?"

"It's a definite possibility."

I slap him, and he chuckles.

"This is crazy."

"I ain't bothered. You really want a job?"

Do I? In my head, I get off the bus in New York City, and I'm looking up at all the skyscrapers like they do in the movies. Maybe twirling around with a suitcase in my hands. I didn't get much beyond that.

I kind of figured I'd waitress since I'm friendly, and I'd be able to sneak leftovers. I wasn't stoked about it, though.

"I guess I should get one."

"You don't have to. You can stay home. Take care of the house and the kids."

I shudder. Ugh. Not interested. I've been doing that as long as I can remember. I don't want more of the same.

"No. I want a real job. Then I can pay towards rent."

"The house is paid off."

"Well, groceries then."

"Your money is your own. I do all right. You can buy yourself more sparkly blue dresses."

I'm not sure why I'm arguing. Any of my sisters would have their hand jammed in his pocket long before this point.

"I got my high school diploma. What kinds of jobs are there around here?"

"What do you want to do?"

"I don't know." If I had a choice, what would I do? I've never had choices. Not in Dalton. Not when I had no reliable transportation. "I like people."

"You get on well with the women at the club, don't you?"

"I like Story and Crista."

"Not Harper." He's teasing me.

"I don't like lawyers."

"Smart."

"Yes, I am." I rest my head on his shoulder and tilt to ease the pressure on my butt cheeks. The ground is hard. "I wouldn't mind an office job. Or a job in a store. Where you work with people, and it's okay to chat."

"I got an idea."

"Yeah, what?"

"Lemme talk to Big George. I don't want to get your hopes up if it don't pan out."

"You're gonna help me get a job?"

"Yeah."

There are shouts in the distance. Carson. But it's rambunctious, not cause for alarm. Sounds like the boys are heading back this way.

"Okay. I'll stay. What will the boys say?"

"They seem to like you fine."

"They do? Parker doesn't seem too happy."

Dizzy lumbers to his feet and stretches his back. "He's got some shit goin' on. Don't have to do with you. He likes you fine."

"Could have fooled me."

Dizzy snorts. "I brought a woman named Faith home about two years ago. They didn't take to each other. Parker told me he'd sleep out in the garage 'til she was gone. I do believe he would have done it."

"There they are." I catch flashes of neon green through the trees. They come tumbling into the clearing, ruddy-cheeked and laughing, talking over each other. Apparently, they caught a salamander, and it got away.

They're happy in a way that my sisters' kids never are. Confident. Carefree.

They want us all to race back to the clubhouse, but Dizzy says I'm not a good enough rider. He may be right. He tells the boys they can race each other, but they stay with us, circling and looping and waiting in the trail when they get too far ahead.

They want to go to a place called Duck's Diner for lunch, and Dizzy agrees like it's not a thing. We only get sandwiches, and it still costs thirty bucks with tip.

Afterward, we stop by the kid's elementary school and let them run off some more energy on the playground. Parker's a brand-new kid. In the outdoors and sunshine, he's finally shaking off whatever's been weighing him down. When I show them how I can flip over the monkey bars, he even flashes me a shy smile, identical to his daddy's.

That kid's got big worries. I recognize the slump in his shoulders. It's a cryin' shame. He has everything he could possibly need, and still, the world's messin' with his mind somehow. It ain't fair, but it sure is how life goes.

Dizzy and I are sitting side-by-side, and I'm tucked as close to him as I can get. I've got my arms wrapped around my knees, and he's manspreading with his arm resting on the back of the bench.

We're alone except for two mothers with their little girls. The girls steer clear of Parker and Carson, sticking to the swings, and their mothers steer clear of us. They've got their heads together, casting Dizzy dirty looks.

Could be 'cause even without his cut and his ride, he's every inch an outlaw biker. But I guess it could also be 'cause he's so much older than me. These past few weeks, we've stayed home or gone to the clubhouse. We haven't been in public together much at all.

"They're talking shit about us." I jerk my chin toward the women. Dizzy's had his eyes on either the boys or me. I don't think he noticed.

He sniffs. "They're talkin' shit about me."

"They should find somethin' better to do."

"Let 'em have their fun." Dizzy stretches his legs and raises his face to soak in the sun. Then he winds his arm under my braid and drapes it around my neck.

One lady takes this as an affront. Her nose goes straight in the air, and she folds her arms tighter, giving us her back. The other lady glares.

"That bitch needs to mind her own business."

"You need to mind yours."

"What?" I squirm in indignation, try to wriggle loose, but he holds on and chuckles.

"Who gives a shit what Lori McClure and her friend think?"

"You know those women?"

"Lori's kid is in Parker's class. They been together since pre-K."

I'd forgotten it's a small town. Dalton was the same. Everybody knew everybody, but half the people acted like they didn't. Folk will be snobs, even if it's people in twenty-year-old beaters pretending they don't see folks hitchin' rides.

"Not very friendly, is she?"

"I wouldn't expect so. I think she bought her house from my ex. They talk."

"What's that mean?"

"That means my ex don't have much nice to say about me."

On the one hand, I'm not surprised that divorced people don't like each other, but my stomach still sours. A crazy ex is a red flag. I learned that from my sisters. Nine times out of ten, the man drove 'em crazy.

"Why is that?"

Dizzy sucks his cheek. "I'm a biker. I hang around with criminals. I don't got ambition."

"You don't have ambition? You're a mechanic."

"Yup. That's what I always wanted to do. And I don't never want to do anything else."

I don't see how that's problematic.

Dizzy frowns at my confusion, huffing a sigh as he tucks a flyaway behind my ear. "Sharon and I started in the same place, but we went different directions. That happens long enough, one person looks at the other and don't understand them no more. It's human nature."

"That's bullshit. Mechanic is a real good job."

"I agree. But that's life. One day you'll decide for sure what you want to do, and you'll head that way. The people in your rearview won't mean the same to you anymore. It ain't a bad thing. It is what it is."

He turns to watch Carson dangle from the rock wall, his face closed off. He resettles his arm, resting his forearms on his thighs.

I get what he's saying. I've heard people say similar shit before, generally when they're trying to justify doing what they please. Dee's changed her life so many times, she's outgrown everyone in Dalton at least twice.

I ain't against self-improvement, but I think I'm fine the way I am. I've only got complaints about my circumstances. I've done what's needed doin', though. I'm on my way. To where, I'm not so sure anymore.

"I already did what I wanted to do," I say.

"Yeah?" He keeps his eye on Carson. "What's that?"

"Leave Dalton."

His gaze returns to me, serious and intent.

"Why'd you want to leave Dalton?"

A rawness expands in my chest. I can't name it, but it fills me up. God, I've been waiting for someone to ask me that question. So far, no one has. I didn't give anyone the chance to ask when I left. I skedaddled before dawn one day when I was finally strong enough, and I figured they'd notice eventually. Or not. I didn't owe any of them anything.

Chaos was fixated on his own business. I was lucky he agreed to give me a ride. He didn't ask me shit but for a blow job one night, and then he passed out before I had to come up with an answer.

I never told the ladies at the clubhouse. I needed them for cover, so I kept it light. No one wants to hang out with a downer. And my story is a downer.

But I've wanted to tell. I've wanted so bad for someone to care enough to ask.

Dizzy's body is tensing beside me every second I don't speak. I think if there were a villain in my story, he'd go after him. I hold that thought tight, pack it away to take it out and admire it later.

"The house I grew up in is like the old lady who lived in a shoe. Mama has six kids, and except for Robbie who left for Florida, all of us live at home. I mean, we've all moved out at some point, but shit falls through. And Mama's house is big. She got it from my Gram when she passed. I've got—"

I take a second to make sure my counts right. Folks are always coming and going.

"Three nephews and four nieces who live with us. Dee's oldest lives with her baby daddy's parents, and Carol's oldest moved in with her boyfriend."

I pause for breath. Dizzy's following. Listening. It's heady, having this huge, scary man hanging on my every word.

"So it's crowded. Hectic. Everyone doubles up. Or triples up."

"You wanted space." It's a question.

I shake my head. "I was accustomed to it. I don't . . . didn't know another way." Not until the week camping alone under the stars. Now that I'm forgetting what it feels like to freeze to death, it might be one of my top memories of all time.

"Anyway, we have a shed out back. No windows. It's made of corrugated metal on a concrete slab. We keep the push mower in it, busted bikes, stuff like that. There's a padlock on the door 'cause of the mower."

Dizzy's jaw tics under his beard. If I were any further from him, I wouldn't be able to tell. I love that tic. I barely resist reaching out and touching it. To make sure it's real. But I got to get this out.

"Kayden's boy needed a tire for a secondhand 10-speed a neighbor gave him. I thought there was one on Dee's old bike. I went to check the shed. I was in the back, rummaging behind some boxes. Someone didn't realize I was in there and locked the door. By the time I hollered, they were gone."

Dizzy sucks in a breath.

"No one noticed I was gone for over two days. It was September. There was a heat wave. I almost died from dehydration."

"Fuck." He tugs me so I'm sitting on his lap, so he can hold me. The ladies across the playground recoil.

I see what he means. I don't care what they think. I like where I am, these steady arms, the heat of this solid chest.

"I was missing for fifty-three hours. I was in what the doctors called hypovolemic shock when they found me. They had to call an ambulance and everything."

A thought occurs to me. "That bill's gonna be a doozy. Gonna be tough for them to collect." I smile, bitter. "They were real nice at the hospital. The paramedics were dicks, though. They thought I had OD'd out there. No one has much patience for junkies anymore in Dalton."

Dizzy's grip tightens. His arms are so strong. He could've gotten out of that shed. I hold up a hand, examine my fingers. I ripped out most of my nails trying to claw my way out. I couldn't get the metal to give an inch.

"I took care of all those kids. Their boyfriend's kids even. I made food. Patched up boo boos. Washed clothes. Tied shoes. I shared a goddamn room with Keira. She slept like a baby, didn't even ask where I was. No one noticed I was gone for more than two days. They only found me 'cause my nephew got sick of waitin' for me to show up with a tire and came lookin' for one himself."

"Jesus Christ."

"Yeah. As soon as I was discharged and I got my strength back, I left."

"I'm so fuckin' sorry, baby."

And he's not just saying that. He's so stiff his biceps are twitching. I glance up at him. His expression is stern like he gets when he's had words with the boys. Like he's hiding what he's feeling in order to take care of business.

I cuddle closer, breathe in the smell of oil and a hint of the hot sauce he put on his sandwich at lunch.

I love this man.

I don't care if it's too soon, and he's too old, and I'm on thin ice with his club. I know my mind.

"I hear what you're sayin' about folks moving in different directions, and I'm sure that's true and all for them, but that's not how I see things," I say.

"No?"

"Nope. I almost died alone in a hot metal box. I know what matters."

"What is that?"

"That someone will come looking for you if you're missing."

He growls. Literally growls. "You deserve more than just that."

That's such a huge idea that I don't have room for it in my head. I wrestle free from his gorilla arms and hop up. "Anything more than that is gravy."

I smile as big as I can 'cause I can't stand the sadness in

his brown eyes. And then I sprint off toward Carson. I'm gonna show that boy how to climb a rock wall. He's goin' about it all wrong.

The sun is way high overhead. It's the very last minutes of a fall afternoon when every squeak and shout echoes in the brisk air. Breathing is easy.

Dizzy's right. Who cares about the ladies clucking their tongues and scrolling through their phones, pretending not to watch everything we do?

It's a beautiful day. I'm alive, fed, and warm.

I clamber up beside Carson, and I chase him across a swinging bridge. We shriek and laugh, and Parker can't help but join in the fun.

Dizzy sits on the bench, dark eyes hooded, keeping watch on the three of us, the scary, wild-haired biker who thinks I deserve more.

My man.

AFTER THE PLAYGROUND, we came home. I was gonna make myself useful, but Dizzy told me to get on the sofa. He ordered subs, and all four of us watched an old western from the 60s until the boys fell asleep.

I don't know how the guys told the actors apart, and the plot meandered worse than *In the Arms of Love*, but I like horses, and Parker poked fun at the hokey dialogue under his breath the whole time, cracking me up.

When we went to bed, Dizzy fucked me real slow and thorough. No kinky stuff. It was still good.

The next day was even better. We spent the morning in the garage. Parker showed me how to replace brake pads, and we dropped off one he finished to some folks who live down on the flat. Then we visited Boots, an old-timer from the club, and went fishing off his pier.

And now it's Monday, and it's a bit of a downer.

After Dizzy took the boys to school, he disappeared into the garage. I cleaned up breakfast, started a load of laundry, and took the opportunity to add a few cans of soup to my food stash in the back of Dizzy's closet. I know I don't need it, but I like having it. Just in case.

Anyway, all that took less than an hour, and then I was bored. I watched game shows for a while, but I was restless.

I'm used to constant noise, constant demands. I hated it, but I'm accustomed to a hustle and bustle, and I can't get used to the quiet. My nerves get jangly as hell.

I was all excited to make Dizzy lunch, but he beat me to it. He'd scarfed down some leftover Chinese and was wiping the crumbs from his beard by the time I made my way upstairs from folding a load of sheets.

"I was gonna make you lunch." I pause in the doorway, lean on the frame, and pout.

"Don't have time. I got to get this done before I pick the kids up from school."

"I thought they were at their mother's this week?"

"She called. Her boss asked her to do some prep work for that big job she's got coming up. She asked me to take 'em for the rest of this week."

Good. The house could use their background noise. It's too creepy without it. And I'm getting really bored.

"Can I watch you work?"

Dizzy finally gives me his full attention. He was gulping down a glass of tap water.

"You'd be bored."

"I'm already bored."

He studies my face. I don't know what he's looking for.

He should be able to tell from the way I organized the mugs on the counter from biggest to smallest that I'm tellin' the truth.

"You can't. I'm workin' on a new mod."

"And what? It's top secret?"

He stares at me evenly. "Why don't you watch TV?"

"I already watched TV."

"Did you run out?"

"I want to watch you work."

He raises his brows. "No."

Then, he sets his glass on the counter next to the empty Chinese cartons and heads for the door. The sink's an inch to the right. The trash can's right under the counter, for that matter.

He slides open the door.

"You just gonna leave your trash on the counter for me to clean up?"

Oh, my Lord. I sound like my mother. I don't even really care. "Are your arms broke or just your manners?"

Dizzy stops mid-step and turns back to me and cocks his head.

"I said it." I suck my cheek and raise my eyebrows right back.

And he grins so wide, I can see his back teeth. He eyes the clock and shrugs a shoulder. "I guess I got a few minutes, naughty girl."

And then he starts for me. Oh.

Shit.

I bolt, shrieking. Down the stairs, out the front door, around the house. I haven't totally lost my mind. I don't want him to catch me in the middle of the road and have the neighbors call the cops. Houses are spread out here in the country, but sound carries.

He catches me on the deck stairs in the back of the house. I have a half-formed plan to get back inside and lock him out, but he grabs me mid-step. My legs flail.

"Let me down!"

Instead, he holds me tight to his chest and bends forward until my boobs are pressed against the wood stairs.

"You asked for it, baby." All I can see are the utility tubs under the deck through the gap between stairs, but I can tell he's fiddling with his belt.

Uh, oh. I don't know if I'm ready for this yet. We looked at it together on his phone, and it turned me on, but I don't know if I want this in reality.

It's not like me to start shit I can't finish, though.

Should I say *banana falafel*?

But then I wouldn't know what's gonna happen.

He must feel the fight leave my body. He rises, no longer pinning me down with his chest.

"Hold on to the steps, naughty girl." He cracks his belt. Blood surges to my pussy, making me swollen and needy. I whimper, and I grab the edge of the step, screwing my eyes shut. If it's too bad, I can safe word. Or say stop. He will. I've tested him.

He stands tall, tugging my yoga pants down to trap my ankles. I'm wearing a new pair, black with a teal stripe down the side, and a matching crop top with three-quarter sleeves. It was fine for the house, but outside in November, my bare midriff is puckered with goose bumps. The rest of me is, too. My spine and scalp are tingling, the hairs prickling on the back of my neck.

This is gonna hurt. I can't wait.

He rubs my ass, one cheek and then the other. Then he slaps them experimentally. It hardly stings. It's a warm up. I moan.

He slips his rough fingers into my slit. I'm sopping wet. He gathers my cream and strokes down my bare thighs, sending shivers dancing across my skin.

"Are you allowed to tell me what to do, naughty girl?" He trails his belt, whisper soft, up my thighs along the trail he just traced.

"No," I answer, breathless. I can't help but arch my back, bare my throbbing pussy to him. I'm so turned on. The anticipation stretches, plays on my body like a physical touch.

He spanks me a few times, and I let myself cry out. "It hurts!"

"It's gonna hurt worse," he growls, his hand roaming, slipping through my juices, teasing my clit, and then petting my ass before he swats me a few more times. "You've been bad, haven't you?"

"Yes," I moan.

"You're sorry, aren't you?"

"Yes," I pant.

"You're gonna count. If I don't hear you, you're gonna get it again. If you move your hands, you're gonna get more. Understand?"

"Yes." I want him to do it. I need him to do it. I know it's gonna hurt, but I'll explode if he doesn't.

Crack. The leather swishes through the air. I yelp. It burns. A sharper pain than his hand, but not too bad. I can take it. He's definitely holding way back.

The air whistles again. Crack. I shriek. That one had a little more bite.

"I said count baby. How many times are you gonna get number one?"

"One!" I holler.

He chuckles, dark and low. His fingers stroke a line down my ass. He's admiring his handiwork.

And then there's a whoosh as he swings his arm, and a line of fire crosses both cheeks. I clench. "Two!" I gasp.

"Three more. Unclench your ass."

"I can't." I'm still trying to catch my breath from the last one.

"Don't tell me no. That's two more." He lays the belt on me again and again.

"Three. Four. Five." I'm squirming now, dipping my hips to avoid the blows, but it's useless. Pain blossoms, searing, rushing my brain and drowning out everything but this moment. I squeeze the stairs with all my strength. "Six. Seven."

And I collapse, sobbing, the wood rough on my cheek. I can't keep my hips raised anymore. I'm done in and floating away. But then strong hands lift me, hold me up, and Dizzy slams his hard, bare cock into me as his fingers find my clit. I kick off my pants so I can spread wide for him. Oh, Lord, he's so hot, he's thrusting so hard, he's so much to take.

I'm a ragdoll. My ass is on fire, but my hungry pussy feels so good. He's groaning louder, and he's hotter, closer than ever before, and—oh, fuck.

The condom.

I mumble, meaning to remind him, but I can't find my words. He props me upright and drills me, forcing deep inside me, stretching me, making me take all of him.

"That's right, naughty girl. Take this cock." He pounds me, and I can't worry. I don't remember how. All I can do is go along for the ride. He'll make sure it's okay.

I'm coming before I realize it, shaking, crying out, and then another wave crashes over me, and I'm coming again, harder, and it keeps going and going as Dizzy drives into me, faster and faster, and then he pulls out and cums in hot spurts up my back.

I dangle in his arms, boneless.

He's breathing hard, but his muscles aren't quivering at all, and his grip is strong and sure.

He presses a kiss to my temple. "We need to get you on the pill."

I nod my head, gasping down air. Damn straight. "No babies."

"We'll get you to the doctor. I'll make the call." He sets me gently on my feet and trails his fingers over my burning ass. He groans in appreciation. "You okay?"

I crane my neck, check out the damage. It hurts worse than the spanking, for sure, but it's a bearable pain. Mostly stinging. The stripes from the belt are hot, the skin raised and pink.

"You didn't break the skin."

"Nah. It's an old belt. Worn edges."

We both stare at my ass, him stroking alongside the raised welts.

"Kind of wild," he says.

"Yeah."

I shake my head clear and try to bend over to tug up my pants, but I'm too wobbly. He helps me out, easing my panties over my sore ass. The pants are too rough, so I kick them off. He scoops them up, and then turns me, wrapping me in his arms and peppering my face with kisses. His beard tickles. I wriggle, and he holds me closer, trapping my palms against his chest.

There's a sharp twinge. "Ouch." Oh, damn. I have a splinter in the mound of my thumb from holding onto the stair. It's bleeding. Dizzy notices it the same time I do. His dopey smile disappears.

"Damn it."

He lifts me into his arms and carries me up the stairs as if it's nothing. I squeal, but I don't fight him. I don't think my brain's reconnected to my legs, yet. I'm lost in this yummy, hazy fog. My limbs are weak, and I'm yawning.

It's like when you spend a whole day at the river, swimming, and then you lay out in the sun. That kind of perfect peace and exhaustion.

When we get to the kitchen, Dizzy leans me against the counter. Thank goodness he doesn't set me on it. My ass would not take kindly to granite right now. He takes out his trusty first aid kit, removes the splinter, pours some hydrogen peroxide over it, and slaps a bandage on. I get the purple convertible this time.

When he's done, he nips the tip of my index finger and then kisses it. I giggle. I'm as content as I've ever been, and the unsettled feeling from the morning is gone.

He pours me some tap water. "Drink."

I hate room temperature water, but my mouth is dry. I chug, and he refills the glass.

"You want to take a nap or watch TV?"

"TV."

He carries me downstairs, knocks some action figures off the sofa, and sets me down. I curl up on my side. Actually, I'm probably gonna take a nap.

He covers me with a camouflage comforter.

"After I get the boys from school, we can go somewhere. I'll be done with work by then."

"Why can't I watch you?" I mumble though a yawn, although I'm no longer interested.

"It's top secret," he says, smoothing my hair. "I could tell you, but I'd have to kill you."

He grabs the remote and sets it beside me, and then he

tromps upstairs. I sigh, snuffle under the covers, and sink into a deep, dreamless sleep. Safe. Satiated. Warm.

I wake up to a flood of light and an angry woman poking me with a plastic sword.

"Where are my kids?"

I bolt straight up, flailing, my legs tangled in the comforter. My top has worked its way up past my boobs. I yank it down as I kick at the blanket.

The woman steps back, scowling so nasty I can't make out anything except for hot pink lipstick, an angled bob, and expensive highlights.

This has gotta be Sharon.

"Where's Dwayne?" she snaps.

"Dwayne?" Oh, she means Dizzy.

She sneers, raking her gaze over me. "Oh, for Christ's sake. Who are you?"

I finally get loose from the blanket and swing my legs over the side of the couch. My ass is sore. My brain's slow. I scrub the crust from my eyes.

Sharon stands in the middle of the unholy toy mess, judging and finding everything sorely wanting. She scans the room, and everything she sees turns her face sourer. A half-eaten bag of chips on the floor. Coffee rings on the end table. Me.

"Don't tell me you're the maid," she sniffs.

She pushes a dirty, balled-up sock away from her with the toe of a shiny beige high heel. She's dressed like a lady who works in a bank. Ruffle-waisted tan pantsuit with a thin braided belt. Chunky hot-pink beaded necklace and matching bracelets. Big sunglasses with rhinestones on the sides propped on top of her head.

We don't have women like this in Dalton, but I've seen

them on TV. Stressed-out women who get paid to yell at each other.

"Not the maid, no."

Her eyes catch on the scratches on my bare legs. Yeah, I'm not sure what Dizzy did with my pants.

Her lip turns up, disgusted. "Seriously? Are you even eighteen?"

"Sure am, ma'am. Are you Parker and Carson's grandma?"

I make sure to smile as big as I possibly can.

She sucks her teeth, and her eyes go cold and calculating. "Oh. You're one of those club whores, aren't you? Honey, you are too young to be fucking men twice your age for a place to stay."

Dizzy's not twice my age. Not quite.

"I appreciate your sincere concern for my well-being, but I assure you, I'm fine."

She shakes her head. "I'm sure you are. This is a new low for Dwayne. He lets you around my kids?"

"Haven't bitten 'em yet. I'm house-trained."

"You think you're funny, don't you?"

I shrug a shoulder. I wish there were bottoms nearby I could pull on. If I have to fight this bitch, I'd like to be wearing pants when I do it.

Luckily, she's decided I'm not worth the time. She whips out her phone and dials.

"Where are you?" she demands, turning her back to me.

There's a deep rumble from the other end of the line. Dizzy.

"I'm at the house. Something came up. I'm back in town for a few days. I figured you'd have picked up the kids by now, or I'd have gone to the school."

She rests her high heel on top of a soccer ball and rolls it back and forth.

"Yeah. I met her. We'll have a conversation about it when you get here. How far out are you?"

More low rumbling. She says, "Okay."

And then she turns back to me, and I swear, it's exactly like the scene in that dinosaur movie when the raptor finds the kids hiding under the table. Like she can already taste the meat.

Her blue eyes glint, and there's no natural light in this basement.

"Let's try this again." She flashes her white teeth. "I'm Sharon. Parker and Carson's mother."

She says it like *Thomas Edison, inventor of the lightbulb* or *George Washington, father of our country*. Sharon, mother of Parker and Carson.

But if she's offering an olive branch, I shouldn't be critical.

"I'm Fay-Lee."

She blinks. Then she raises her eyebrows. And waits.

"Parsons." Folder of laundry. Eater of pizza.

"Fay-Lee Parsons," she repeats. "And are you living here?"

"Yeah. For now."

"For now," she echoes, pursing her lips. "And are you and Dwayne in . . . some kind of relationship?"

Good question. Not gonna touch it.

I try a diversion. "Parker and Carson are great kids." I smile and try really hard to sound sincere. They *are* great. It's just what I really want to say to this woman is "Fuck off."

"Yes. They are." She's not diverted. From the look on her face, she's doing complicated math in her head. Maybe how much force it'd take to launch me into space.

She doesn't care for me one bit, but based on the snide way she says "Dwayne," I don't think it's 'cause she's carrying a torch for her ex.

"Listen. We got off on the wrong foot." She pauses. I nod. "It's just—You're *so* young, honey. I was your age once. I know the allure of the 'bad boy.' But there's no future in it." She puts on the fakest sympathetic face. "Do you need some money? To get home?"

I didn't ever think my pride would stop me from taking cash. "No, thanks. I'm good."

"Oh, but honey, you're *not*. I'm sure this is not what your mother wants for you. You deserve better."

I bet her mother didn't want her messing around with Dizzy. And going by the pantsuit and the fancy phone, I think I understand what she means by "better."

I get the angle she's trying to play. It's like when Shiloh fell for Maddox on *In the Arms of Love*. Miranda thought she'd saved Shiloh from the mob when she adopted her, and it killed her to watch her daughter fall for the Capo of the Fortunetti Syndicate. Miranda guilted Shiloh to come home, playing the "you deserve better" card.

The only problem is that this is real life. My mother doesn't want things for me. She wants things *from* me. And as for what I deserve?

Life isn't about what you "deserve." It's about what you can get and manage to hold on to.

Right now, I've got Dizzy. And I'm not letting go for this bitch.

"*Honey*, with all due respect, I don't need your advice."

She sighs. "Well, don't say I didn't warn you. I guess we all have to learn the hard way."

She heads for the stairs, and then she pauses, her foot

on the first step. Yeah, she has a flare for the dramatic. She turns, her face smug, as if a thought has occurred to her.

"Oh. Fair warning, sweetie. You don't want to get too comfortable. You're not the first half-naked skank I've found in this house. I'd think you all would take a hint from the décor, but maybe that's why he picks 'em so young. You don't question it."

I try so hard not to rise to the bait, but I'm only human. "Question what?"

She rounds her heavily-lined eyes. "Why we've been divorced for years, and Dwayne's kept the house exactly like I decorated it. Are my clothes still in the closet?" She trills a mean laugh. "I bet they are. I would even bet he's still holding on to my wedding ring. Check my jewelry box. I'm sure it's in there."

She shakes her head. "You might think you're special, but you're not. You're being used, and you're going to end up cast off and traded in for a newer model while Dwayne waits for me to come back. You should go home. Go back to school. Make something of yourself. This is a dead end. *Honey.*"

And she exits, swishing her frilly, pantsuited ass as she goes. I hear the screen door slam and the crunch of Dizzy's truck pulling up.

Ugh.

My stomach aches.

Muffled voices filter in from the driveway.

I dash upstairs to the master bedroom, tug open the top dresser drawer, and dig through the jewelry. I'd thought it was all plastic and beads. I force my shaking hands to steady and go through it piece by piece. There. At the bottom, tangled in a beaded necklace. A thin gold band, sized for a woman.

A car door slams. I don't have time to unknot the necklace. I dash to the closet and shove it into my backpack stash just as the front door slams.

"Fay-Lee?"

Shit. I can't deal with this right now. I peel off my crop top and panties as I shout, "I'm taking a shower!"

I scoot to the bathroom, turn the knob and hop right in, shivering as the water blasts freezing cold from the showerhead. It heats quickly enough, but my teeth are already chattering. I cuddle my arms to my breasts, my brain whirling.

Sharon's a bitch.

Maybe she's jealous. There's a kind of woman who doesn't want a man anymore, but also doesn't want anyone else to have him, either. Or maybe she doesn't want to compete with anyone for his cash. Or she could just look at me and think I'm trash. It happened all the time back in Dalton.

Everybody thought the Parsons house was pretty much a brothel, and that made me a whore, regardless of the fact everyone knew I worked at the Gas-and-Go and was broke as shit.

Maybe Sharon doesn't want me around her kids, although she didn't seem worried about them.

It doesn't really matter. Sharon sucks—that's a given— but is she right?

Is Dizzy waiting for her to come back?

For Christ's sake, Fay-Lee. I slap the side of my head. He's kept the house like a shrine to her, and her wedding ring is still in the drawer.

I'm not this stupid. If this were Dee or Keira, I'd be rollin' my eyes so hard, they'd pop from my head.

I'm a house mouse. *Free pussy.*

He's even talked about when I figure out what I want to do with myself and head off to live my life. Yeah, he talks sweet about how I'm his woman, and he wants me to stay as long as I want, but those are just words, aren't they? And I swallowed 'em hook, line, and sinker, too, didn't I? I let him do whatever he wanted to me. I bent over for it.

I'm so stupid. And I should know better.

Brian Foster called Dee his fiancée for *months*, but he never left his wife for her. That guy Darren had a whole story about a house he was gonna buy for Keira in North Carolina and a job his cousin was gonna get her. Keira didn't get the job or the house, but she got another baby.

This is *exactly* what it looks like.

I'm trading sex for room and board. I'm a whore.

I angle my head so the hot water burns my scalp and sets my ass on fire.

I'm not saying it's something I swore I'd never do. I guess I just figured that I'd realize what I was doing when I did it.

I rub my chest. It aches. And I want to puke.

There's a knock on the door.

"Fay-Lee?"

I ignore him. The shower's on. Let him think I can't hear him.

What do I do?

I hock the ring. Go back to Plan A. New York City.

I'll need a ride into town. I could walk. It's not that far, but I'm not sure of the way. No cell phone means no directions.

My eyes are prickling, and I feel bone weary. I don't want to go to New York City. I want to crawl into bed and have a long cry. I want things to be different. I want to go back to this morning when Sharon hadn't gleefully popped my stupid, shiny bubble.

Bang. Bang. "Fay-Lee?"

The door's unlocked. I double-checked that on my way in. If he wants in, nothing's stopping him.

"*Fay-Lee.*" This time, it's an order. I shudder, turning the water off. I grab a towel, wrapping it tight. I don't want to talk to him naked.

Dizzy busts through the door. Guess he thought I'd locked it.

"What are you doing?"

"Taking a shower." I wipe off the mirror with my hand, avoiding eye contact. Come on, dude. Take a hint.

"What did she say?"

"Doesn't matter." I grab another towel and squeeze my hair dry. I'm freezing. My skin's covered in goose bumps.

He growls in exasperation and reaches for me, grabs a handful of towel and compels me forward with his huge hand on my back.

I jerk and whirl, rip the towel free of his grasp and clutch it to my chest, turning until my back is to the sink.

"No." I point my finger at him. "*Banana.*"

He freezes. We're no more than a foot apart. He dominates the small room, wild hair, clunky black boots, grease-stained coveralls.

His chest is rising and falling as he eyes me warily. He slowly raises his hands, palms up. "Okay. You're the boss."

I'm trembling. I fold my arms to try to stop the shaking.

He searches the bathroom until he sees the toilet. He lowers the lid and slowly sits. It's ridiculous. One broad shoulder brushes the wall, the other is halfway in the tub. Even seated, we're almost eye-to-eye.

He carefully rests his hands on his thighs. "You're upset."

He's using the same tone of voice as he does when

Carson unleashes a wild, breathless jumbled-up story and Dizzy's trying to figure out what happened.

I nod, curt, struggling to hold it together. Be adult about it.

"Sharon said something that upset you."

"Are you still in love with her?" It spills out.

"No."

"Why do you still have all her stuff around then?"

He exhales. "I ain't got a good reason. I just always had something better to do than redecorate."

I grit my teeth. I want to ask about the ring, but if I mention it, he'll know I have it. That's my ticket out of here.

"Baby, you have to tell me what's goin' on in that head of yours."

"How many house mouses have you had before me?"

"None."

"But there've been lots of other women. Younger women."

"I've hooked up with women since I got divorced. Some were younger." He says it like he's waiting for me to get to the point.

He's gonna be waiting a long time.

I don't have a point. At least not one that makes sense. I've only got questions I don't dare ask.

Am I special? Am I different? Do you love me?

Am I a sad and stupid fool, falling for a man's bullshit despite a lifetime of firsthand education?

I got my pride. I will never, ever ask.

Dizzy scrubs his face. Then he raises his head and pierces me with his dark brown eyes. "What do you need, baby? You got to tell me. I can't give it to you if I don't know what it is."

What do I need?

That's a ridiculous question. How do I answer? Unconditional love. Safety. To be the most important person in the world to someone.

A billion dollars, three wishes, and a unicorn that shits rainbows.

A home.

Him.

I hug my arms hard against my chest.

It's a terrifying thing, to know I'm this weak. That at heart, I'm a sucker, like every other woman in my family.

"Do you want to redo the kitchen or something?" Dizzy's forehead is wrinkled, and his grip tightens on his thighs. He's getting frustrated.

"I don't want to redo the kitchen."

He huffs and tilts his head back, staring woefully at the ceiling. "Do you want *me* to redo the kitchen?"

"The kitchen is fine."

"Goddamn it," he mutters. Then he thinks of something. He digs in his pocket and takes out his phone.

"Here." He holds it out. "*Here.*" He shakes it.

I take it. "Who am I supposed to call?"

"Check it. Check my messages. There's nothin' between Sharon and me but the kids."

I recognize this move. Brian pulled it with Dee all the time. It turned out he had his wife in his contacts as *Mom.*

Still. I'm not gonna miss the opportunity.

"What's your password?"

"I don't have one."

"You don't have a password?" I swipe. No, he does not. He doesn't even have a picture of his kids as wallpaper. It's the blue factory default background.

I pull up the text messages. George. Heavy. Parker. Carson. Cue.

Sharon.

I tap.

Coming back earlier than I thought. Will text when I'm an hour out to let you know if I can get them from school.

Ok.

Remember I'm gonna need you to register P and C for the winter session and both boys are gonna need new cleats. Three hundred should do it. Cash would be better. Send it in the app.

Ok.

School called and Carson has a fever. I need you to pick him up. I'm showing a house. Can you take him to the ped if he needs to go? I've got a closing later.

Ok.

It goes on and on. Ok. Ok. Ok.

That woman's workin' him like he's on payroll.

I glance up. He's watching me, dark eyes hooded. He's leaning forward on his forearms.

Out of curiosity, I open his pictures. I scroll down, going back months, then years. He has hundreds of pictures of engine parts and motorcycles interspersed with Parker and Carson, generally on their dirt bikes or posing by a vehicle. No women.

Except three pictures. Taken when we went riding. Me.

I'm squatting by a stream, gazing into the distance. The sun's shining on my face. My eyes are closed.

I hold the screen up to him.

"Why'd you take these?"

He squints and then lifts a shoulder. "You're beautiful."

My lower lip quivers. He keeps his gaze trained on me, serious, deliberately calm. He's listening.

"I don't wanna be a whore." I blink back the tears. I'm not gonna cry, wet, cold, and naked in a bathroom.

His face falls. "Baby. You're not a whore. Is that what she said?"

"If I'm gonna be a whore, I want to at least *decide* to be one."

"Shit." He plunges his fingers in his hair. For a second, it looks like he's gonna come for me, but he must think better of it. "You are not a whore." He holds out a hand. "Come here."

He leaves it there, extended, calloused palm up, waiting. "Come on, baby."

I don't know what to do.

"Come here."

"Why?"

"'Cause you belong here. And you know it."

"How can I know?"

"Am I wrong?" It's a quiet question. Simple.

He's not.

I hesitantly reach for him.

His hand envelops mine, and he drags me to stand between his legs. The towel drops. He wraps his strong arms around me and squeezes tight. His beard bristles against my collarbone, and he presses soft kisses in the divot where they meet.

Eventually, he eases up an inch and cradles my cheek.

"I'll talk to her. She ain't gonna say shit to you again. Okay?"

It's not about Sharon. She's a piece of work, but she's not anywhere near the meanest bitch I've ever dealt with. She should meet Stephanie, my old manager at the Gas-and-Go.

But I don't know how to explain the feelings crashing into each other inside me like possessed bumper cars of emotion.

The grief I'd been holding off while I worried about food

and the cold, it's broken through and hit me in a wave. My family's messed up, but I always thought that push-come-to-shove, they loved me. They just don't know how to show it.

That wasn't the case.

My family might care, but the feeling is shallow as shit. And it hurts, knowing you're not worth looking for.

And here's this man, offering me everything, and how do I trust him? I can't.

But I want to—*so, so* bad.

I have sympathy for my sisters that I never had before. It's not weakness to believe in a man. It's surrender. You can only stay out in the cold so long before warmth is irresistible.

I don't know if Dizzy's serious, or if I'm one more in a line of half-naked chicks buying into his bullshit 'cause she's too damn tired. I'm rollin' the dice, and it doesn't feel like a safe bet, not at all. Not because Dizzy seems like a liar, but because I know how the world works.

But he's right here. Patient and quiet. Waiting for me to make the next move. And I'm not made of stone.

I nestle closer to him and nuzzle my nose in the crook of his neck. I inhale, soap and gasoline and his off-brand shampoo.

I can feel the tension leave his body.

"You want to go out to dinner, baby? We can go to Broyce's. Get steaks."

"Okay."

First, he carries me into the bedroom and makes love to me, tender and sweet, his eyes dark and unreadable. He whispers in my ear.

Beautiful.

That's it, baby.

Open for me.

I've got you.

It's okay.

He knows this thing we have is fragile and balanced precariously, and it won't take much to knock it over and send it crashing to the ground.

But not tonight.

And if I'm lucky, not tomorrow, either.

THE NEXT FEW days are peaceful. Nice, even though the house is dead quiet without the boys. Dizzy spends most of the days in the forbidden garage, working on his secret project, bopping over to the house every few hours to check on me.

The only thing he asks me to do is put together a grocery order for pick up. I can't believe that's a thing. You go on the internet, pick what you want, someone packs it up for you, and you go get it. Bernice at the Compare-n-Shop won't even hit her light if a price tag is missing. You can go back and get another one with a sticker on it your damn self.

Even though Dizzy doesn't ask, I scrub down the kitchen. Then I get bored, and I clean the bathroom. After *In the Arms of Love*, I'm at loose ends, so I start organizing the lower level. When the boys come back over, I'm gonna take Carson up on that five bucks he said I could hold. I've earned it.

At night—and at lunch and on his breaks from work— Dizzy and I fuck. Dirty, sweet, kinky, fast, slow. And then he hauls my exhausted body onto his chest, and he turns on wrestling or racing. He strokes my hair or rubs my back, and if I'm inclined to talk, he listens.

He's easy. I didn't know men came in that variety. If he's fed and fucked, and if I came hard, he's good.

He misses his kids, though. Every so often, I find him in one of the boys' rooms, straightening up. But it's more like he needs to be in there, around their things. I watched him pick up a matchbox car. He spun the wheels, held it up and squinted into the teensy, tiny windows. Then he polished it up on the hem of his shirt and set it carefully on a shelf.

Dizzy and the kids text each other. It's adorable. Dizzy sends them pictures of vehicles. Parker sends Dizzy videos of him playing his games, and Carson sends terribly-executed selfies, always during times he should be in class and from places he has no business being. Dizzy doesn't seem to notice. He always replies with the thumbs up emoji.

My dad bailed when I was few months old. He was an addict. He disappeared one day. No one in Dalton's heard from him since. Based on what happened to me in the shed, I wonder if Mama even bothered looking for him.

I think Dizzy's a good dad. That's a mixed-up feeling, too. I love the way he cares about the boys. But it's kind of emotionally awful, too, getting a front row seat to what you missed. It's totally fucked up envyin' a kid 'cause he has what you didn't.

Maybe that's why I'm out of sorts. Or maybe it's the weather. It's been gray and gusty. Pretty soon it'll be winter. I'll have even fewer choices if this situation goes south.

It's after lunch, and I'm unloading the dishwasher when there's a growl of engines in the front drive. My heart leaps to my throat. I've got no reason to be spooked, but a voice in my head whispers, "This is it."

It's the same feeling as when I tried to open the shed door, and I realized that snick and rattle I heard hadn't been my imagination.

Boots hit the gravel. Dizzy calls out a greeting from the garage.

I hustle to the living room and peek out the picture window. Three bikes. Heavy. Jed. Nickel.

Their faces are hard. Dizzy joins them, wiping his hands on his dark blue coveralls.

The men dismount, and they gather. Heavy's doin' the talkin'. Dizzy folds his arms, sets his jaw, and glances at the house.

Shit.

What's goin' on?

Dizzy's face is grim. He's shaking his head no and widening his stance. Something's wrong.

I scramble for my stash, fishing out the butterfly knife and the ring. I jam them in my pocket. I'm wearing skinny jeans, sneakers, and a pale blue hoodie. It's cut too tight for me to hide a can or two of food in the pouch. Damn, damn, damn.

The front door opens. "Fay-Lee! Can you come out here?" Dizzy's voice is stern, but calm.

This can't be about me squatting at the clubhouse. Three of them wouldn't come out here for that.

But I don't think it was ever just about me stealing some food and trespassing on their property. I didn't quite understand back then, but hanging with Dizzy, it's clear. These guys are businessmen. They aren't lookin' for drama like the bikers I knew back in Dalton.

They wouldn't have hustled me into a basement to interrogate me over a missing can opener. Not with the kind of cash they're flashin'.

My eyes burn, and my pulse kicks up a notch. Fuck them. I didn't do anything wrong. Not *really* wrong.

"Fay-Lee? You hear me?" Dizzy hollers.

"Yeah. Coming."

I fight the overwhelming urge to run. Dizzy won't let anything happen to me. I think.

I blink until the prickling in my eyes goes away and take a deep breath as I head downstairs, hands shoved in my pockets. My jeans are tight, and I don't want them to see the knife bulge.

When I get out front, the men spread, pivoting to face me. Sweat breaks out behind my knees. These are scary men, and they don't look happy.

Dizzy's expression is inscrutable. I've never seen him like this. He's stiff and sober, the way he was in the framed pics of him in his Marine Corp uniform.

"How are you doing, Fay-Lee?" Heavy asks. He peers down at me from on high. I swear, he reminds me of a character in Parker's video game. You just know he makes a crunching sound whenever he walks, no matter what he's walking on.

"Um. Good?" I look to Dizzy. He's glaring at Jed.

Heavy shifts until he's in my line of sight. "Dizzy treatin' you well?"

Dizzy's temple pulses. Tension radiates from his squared shoulders.

"Yeah."

"We got a question for you, Fay-Lee."

"Okay."

He holds up my phone. I can't help but reach for it, but he pulls it back.

"Where'd you find it?" I ask.

Heavy holds it high, out of reach. Like we're playing keep-away. What is this?

"Harper said you were looking for this at the clubhouse."

"Yeah. I lost it at that first party I was at."

"Dizzy says you didn't mention losing a phone." Heavy raises his thick eyebrows. The resemblance between him and Dizzy is uncanny. But if this were a fairy tale, Heavy's the beast version, and Dizzy's the man once the spell wears off.

"I guess I didn't."

"Why is that?"

"I don't know. It didn't come up. Can I have it please?" I hold out my palm.

Heavy makes no move to hand it over. "This is your last chance, Fay-Lee. If there's something you need to tell us, now is the time."

What do they want from me? Dizzy's no help. He won't meet my eye. He's at my side, glowering at the others.

"I don't know what you want."

Heavy flips open the phone. "Put in the passcode."

"Why?"

Heavy appeals to Dizzy with a silent glance.

Dizzy snarls. "Do it, Fay-Lee."

Shivers zip down my spine. Is he mad at me? I don't think so. I think that tone of voice was meant for Heavy.

I take the phone and type in 1–2–3–4. Heavy's got a reputation as a genius, but he can't be that smart.

Shit. I have a ton of texts and missed calls. I go to check, but Heavy grabs the phone back. He taps and scrolls, his mouth turning down.

Then he holds the phone up for the others to see.

It's a text. It's from a guy named Rab I met when I first came to town. He's a biker from another club. Chaos hung out with him while Jed and I played horseshoes at a bar outside town. Afterwards, we all did shots and danced to the jukebox. I vaguely remember drunkenly adding him to my contacts. He said he owned a tattoo parlor, and he'd give me a discount.

The text reads *where is chaos bitch?*

Nickel cracks his neck and skewers me with a death stare. "I told you."

"This don't mean nothin'," Dizzy says.

"Brother—" Heavy shakes his head. "She's got dozens of messages from Rab." He hands me the phone. I start scrolling.

where's chaos?

what you done with him bitch?

pick up the phone you dumb hore.

"I didn't do anything to Chaos. He left me. I don't know where he is."

Heavy doesn't even acknowledge what I'm saying.

"She's got to answer for herself," Heavy says to Dizzy. "We need to know."

"*I* talk to her. No one else." Dizzy steps forward until he's blocking me from the others.

What do they think I did? My heartbeat breaks into a gallop.

"You're too close, Diz," Heavy says. "You got to let us handle her."

"The fuck I do." Dizzy puffs his chest. Nickel balls his fists, his black eyes glowing with unholy glee. That dude is insane. And Heavy's huge. Jed's kind of doughy, but he makes three against one.

I can't let them fight.

"What do you want to know?" I pipe up, my voice wobbling.

"Don't say nothin'," Dizzy warns.

"I don't have anything to hide." As it leaves my mouth, I realize it's the exact thing every guilty person says.

"What did I say, woman?" Dizzy shifts on his feet. Nickel bares his teeth. They're gonna fight.

There's a long moment when the men glare at each other, shaking out their arms, fingers twitching. A showdown in the driveway.

Then a neighbor drives by, honks, and waves.

Heavy sighs and shakes his head. "Dizzy, let's take a minute. Walk with me." He jerks his head toward the garage.

Dizzy doesn't budge.

"No one will touch her. You have my word. We need to talk, brother."

Finally, Dizzy gives a curt nod. Heavy, Nickel, and him head off and go into the garage, stone-faced. I'm left alone with Jed.

"What's happening?"

This guy was an asshole to me in the basement, but he was nice the first time we met. He's like most of the men my sisters date. Buzz cut. Clean-shaven. Showered, new boots, nice jeans, and bad teeth.

Jed pivots so his back is to the garage. He pulls a gun from his waistband.

Oh, fuck.

My hands fly up, and I open my mouth to scream.

"Shut up and put your damn hands down."

"Put that gun away."

He isn't aiming at me, but still, blood swooshes in my ears. What the fuck is going on?

"Hands *down*." He waves the gun at me. I drop my arms.

"Now, listen. I don't have time to explain this twice. This is your lucky day. Right now, Heavy's over there convincing Dizzy to let us kill you."

I swallow a whimper. Dizzy wouldn't agree to that. Never.

"I bet you're thinkin' he's your man, and it ain't gonna go down like that. How long you been spreadin' your legs for him, girl?"

He waits for me to answer, but my mouth is bone dry, and my brain's disconnected from my voice box. The gun is dangling between us. His finger is on the trigger.

"A few weeks? A month? I don't see no ring. I don't see no cut that says *Property Of*. I see a runaway who no one would miss if she disappeared."

The words are a direct hit. I sway from the impact.

"Let me explain how an MC works. You hear Heavy call him 'brother?' That's what we are. Brothers. And blood is thicker than water. It might take Heavy a little talkin', but Dizzy's gonna hand you over. We're gonna take you back to the basement. And you ain't comin' out this time."

I stifle a moan. Every nerve in my body shouts at me to run, but there's nowhere to go. The gun has me pinned on the spot.

"Now, I know you got nothin' to do with this. But Heavy don't know that. Dizzy don't know that. What's on your phone is mighty fuckin' incriminating."

Incriminating *what*? Do they think I did something to Chaos?

"But like I said. This is your lucky day. You're gonna run. Start hitchin' as soon as you hit the main road. I'll give you as long as I can. Then I'm gonna fire this gun. I'm gonna say you grabbed for my piece, we grappled, it went off, and you ran that way." He points into the woods across the street.

What? This is crazy. Dizzy will talk sense into Heavy. I didn't do anything.

Jed's studying my face, and he's growing more impatient by the second. Finally, he shakes his head.

"You dumb bitch. Don't you get it? Chaos was stealing

from us. Steel Bones killed him. And you're the only one who can put him at the clubhouse. You're a material witness to murder, and if the Feds get ahold of you, your testimony could prove racketeering. You could put the entire club behind bars for life. Put a needle in Heavy's arm."

I'm shaking my head. I'd never rat.

Jed keeps going. "And that guy Rab who's texting you? He knows somethin' happened to Chaos, and he knows you were the last to see him alive."

Jed glances toward the garage. They're still in there.

"Dizzy might love your pussy, but you really think he'd risk all his brothers' lives for you? You think he'd risk jail for you? Risk his kids growin' up fatherless? For some gash he's been bangin' a month or two?"

Oh, God. I'm gonna puke. I fight down a wave of nausea. I don't have time to panic. I can lose it later. They could come out at any minute.

Dizzy. My heart cracks.

It was too good to be true. Of course, it was.

I spin on the ball of my foot and sprint down the drive, pumping my arms. The cold November air burns my lungs. As I turn onto the main road, I skid on loose gravel, almost fall to me knees, but my forward momentum keeps me barreling ahead.

I don't want to die.

I'm not gonna die.

I escaped that shed, and I'm gettin' out of this alive, too.

I run, and when I can't anymore, I jog. After a mile or so, a gunshot rings out behind me, a sharp crack muffled by the low gray clouds. I push harder.

I lift my knees, and I keep going. Faster. Faster. I didn't survive two days without water in a heat wave to get run down on the side of a rural highway in nowhere Pennsylvania.

Sweat rolls down my face, stinging my eyes. A motorcycle engine growls behind me, closing in, and I reach in my pocket for the knife, knowing it's useless against a gun, but I'm not going down easy.

A bike pulls off onto the shoulder ahead of me. There's a man I've never seen before. He's wearing a denim cut with the red-and-white Rebel Raiders' insignia. He's got a paunch, a gray, braided ponytail and beard, and a red Willie Nelson bandana headband.

He grins. "Hey, sweet stuff. Jed called me. You need a ride?"

He shuffles forward on his hog. It's gonna be a tight squeeze.

"Can you take me to the pawnshop?"

"How 'bout I take you to my place? Lay low for a spell?"

Ugh. No.

"I need cash. I got to get to the pawnshop."

His brow furrows, but eventually he nods. "All right. Don't think it's open, though. Saddle up."

I hop on, and we peel off, my Mama's voice rattling in my head about the devil you know versus the devil you don't. For the life of me, I can't remember which is worse, but if I have a choice between going with this guy and watching Dizzy choose to hand me over to his club, I'll pick this guy every time.

I can deal with a broken heart. Broken dreams. It hurts, as if my chest has been sliced open, but I'll endure it.

But I can't handle more concrete proof that ultimately, I mean nothing to anyone in this world. There's an orneriness that kept me alive in that hundred and five degree shed. It gave me the courage to leave Dalton. Maybe it's survival instinct. Maybe it's grace. I don't really know, but it's damn clear about one thing.

You can't trust anyone but yourself.

And now Dizzy doesn't have to choose between his club and me. It's like that cat in the box we learned about in Mrs. Flynn's physics class. Schrödinger's cat. Until you open the box, the cat's not alive or dead.

As the wind whips my hair into knots and numbs my cheeks, I'm in that space. Dizzy didn't choose me. And he didn't betray me, either.

It's a cold place to be, but I'm not stuck. I'm flyin' forward.

Heavy's between me and the door. Any second now, there's gonna be an epic showdown where I use my tool cabinet to bulldoze his gigantic ass out of the way. Nickel can get a piece, too, if he steps into it.

"Listen." Heavy raises his palms. "It looks bad."

"Don't give a shit how it looks."

Heavy could have shown me Fay-Lee snappin' pictures of blueprints with one of them James Bond cameras, and it wouldn't make no difference. She's mine. She done somethin' wrong, I'll make sure she don't again, but no one else gets to lay a hand on her. Ever.

"She clearly knows Rab. She lied about it."

"Did you ask her if she knew Rab?" I ask.

Heavy scoffs. But it ain't a stupid question.

"Did you?" I direct the question to Nickel. He shrugs. Dude's a single-use tool. He kills shit. Questioning shit ain't in his wheelhouse.

"I don't think 'bitch' and 'whore' means you're on good terms with a person," I point out.

When I find Rab Daugherty, he's dead. That's a given, regardless.

"She wouldn't be on good terms with the man if she was supposed to deliver blueprints and decided to shack up with you instead." Heavy's using his "reasonable" voice on me. He picked it up in college. He sure as shit didn't talk that way when he was a scrub tryin' to sweet talk me into fixin' his ride.

I snort. "Fay-Lee ain't got nothin' to her name but the clothes on her back. Lord knows she went through my house with a fine-tooth comb, lookin' for loose change. She moved all my shit around. She ain't sittin' on a payday."

"Maybe she's getting paid on delivery. Maybe they turned her out, and she's doin' it for a man."

My nails dig into my palms. No. She's mine. No one's takin' her from me. If there's a man, it don't matter. He's dead.

"You're too close. Let us take her to the clubhouse. Talk to her. When we find out what we need to know, you're the first call. If she needs to be put down, we can do it quick. Painless."

I shake my head, my lips peeling back in a bitter grimace. "No."

"Dizzy, you got to be reasonable."

"You ain't gonna fuckin' touch her. And she ain't goin' nowhere. You want to ask her anything, you can do it at the kitchen table."

Heavy exhales slowly, stomps over to stare down at the project I'm working on. It's still in pieces. Ain't nothin' to see. "Dizzy, you have to think about the club."

I hold my peace, his words echoing in my head. *Put her down.* He don't get to fuckin' look at her again.

"Think it through," he argues. "If Rab's involved, the

Rebel Raiders sent Chaos for the blueprints. That means the Rebel Raiders know there's somethin' going on with the buildings. They want to destroy us. Somehow, they stumbled on the way to do it. Now that Chaos is missing, they have confirmation they're on the right track. But they got no moves left. They tipped their hand. It's a dead end. Except for the house mouse."

"Her name's Fay-Lee."

"She can put Chaos at the clubhouse the night he disappears. They collect one or two other pieces of evidence, they have us over a barrel. Blackmail. The Feds. She could put a RICO charge on every man in this club."

"She ain't gonna say shit."

"You've known her a few weeks. I seen her ribs, man. All the Raiders need to do is offer her a few hundred."

"You can keep talkin' all you want, college boy. You ain't goin' near her."

"You're not seeing clearly." He raises his voice, lets it boom. I remember when he was a pimply beanpole with an unhealthy infatuation with that card game where you roll dice. This master of the universe shit might work on civilians, but I ain't impressed.

"You understood back at the clubhouse that day when we found her. You think I changed my mind? She's mine. You can talk to her inside the house with me right there, or you can fuck off."

"You're not makin' sense. We're your brothers. We're *family*."

I nod. That is true. But *he* don't get it.

"Yeah, we're family. You gonna ask for my ride when you're drunk? You gonna ask me to hand over my kids? Family don't ask for that shit. And you're president, you're not God. You don't get to decide what's mine or not mine.

She belongs to me. You want to come for her you go through me. End of story."

I fold my arms and raise an eyebrow. Nickel shifts from leg to leg, eyeballin' us.

And then a shot rings out. Close. Jesus. Fay-Lee.

I sprint, Heavy on my heels.

There's Jed, pistol smoking.

No Fay-Lee.

"What the fuck happened?" Heavy roars.

Jed points across the street. I grab him by the collar. "Did you shoot her? Is she hurt?"

"She grabbed my gun. She ain't hurt, man. She shot the ground. She got the jump on me. She ran. That way." He jerks his weak chin at the woods.

Shit. Shit.

I run, heart crashing in my chest. Nickel, Heavy, and Jed are on my heels.

"Spread out!" Heavy shouts.

She was scared. She didn't trust me to handle it. Goddamn it.

"No one hurts her!" I roar. "Jed, put your fuckin' piece away!"

We crash through the undergrowth. You can run for a yard or so, but then thickets and gulches slow you down. The terrain favors a smaller person like her. I can't hear her. Heavy's busting through the woods like a stampeding elephant, sending birds squawking into the air.

"Baby, come back," I shout. "It's okay. No one's gonna hurt you."

A crow caws angrily, and there's a violent flapping of wings from a towering maple.

My heart's stuck in my throat, messin' with my breathing. She's so fuckin' delicate. Sassy and mouthy and clever.

She's a survivor, no doubt. But she's a hundred pounds and change, not legal to drink, and she's got no money, no ride.

I got to find her.

If she gets away, she's not comin' back. She ain't stupid. Even if she had no idea what Chaos was doing, she knows Steel Bones wants her. She's gonna run as far and as fast as she can. And she ain't likely to luck out again with a washed-up dude like Chaos who was more interested in a payday than pussy. Oh, fuck.

"Baby! Come on. Where are you?"

We're further apart now, but I can hear Heavy call the club on his phone, asking for backup.

"No one touches her! Make it known!" I shout at him. I should have never left her. There's no sign. No broken branches or trampled leaves. She didn't come this way.

This is a fuckin' mess. The woods go on for miles. All the way to the river. I don't let the kids ride dirt bikes out here. Too many hunters out of season.

My chest tightens. What do I do?

I can't lose her.

She's—

She's perfect. I feel awake for the first time in years. She woke me up.

I backtrack, scan for signs. I see where big men tore through, but if she came this way, they've destroyed the evidence. Jesus. What am I gonna tell the boys?

Parker's still lukewarm on her, but Carter gets the same dumb look I do when she comes in the room.

My shoulders are heaving. I lean over to catch my breath, brace my hands on my knees. We gotta form a search party. She can't be stuck out here at night. It's freezing.

"Yup. Let me talk to him. I'll call you back." Heavy's hanging up his phone as he approaches through some trees.

He claps a massive hand on my back.

"Brother."

His grumbly voice echoes. The woods become still. Nickel and Jed have approached behind him.

"That was Grinder. He was coming to join us. He just passed Fay-Lee on the main road."

My heart leaps.

"She was ridin' bitch behind Brick Daugherty."

Rab's brother. VP of the Rebel Raiders.

"Grinder turned to pursue, but he got stuck behind a cop at a red light."

"I'm sorry, man." We all stare at our boots.

Everything crashes. Everything breaks.

Everything's fucking shit.

11

FAY-LEE

The old dude was right. When we pull up in front of Petty's Mill Pawn, it's closed. My luck keeps on goin'. They open at ten in the morning.

My rescuer, Brick by the name on his cut, hoists himself off his bike and lights a cigarette.

"Closed," he says, nodding to the metal grate pulled down over windows displaying a trumpet, a stack of DVD players, and a collection of those gas trucks you can buy at Christmas.

Brick is a keen observer of the obvious.

I survey the street. I haven't seen the whole town, but this is definitely the seedy section. Vacant store fronts. A package goods. A vape shop. A discount cell phone carrier.

I touch the lump in my pocket. I do have one thing going for me. A fully charged phone.

God, I didn't want to call one of my sisters to bail me out, but it'll be dark in a few hours, and already the wind's whipping up into something nasty.

"So what's the plan?" Brick asks. "This ain't a great neighborhood to be hanging out on the street."

I don't know. I can't sit on a bench and wait for the store to open. Steel Bones will be looking for me. It'd be a toss-up whether I'd freeze to death, or they'd find me first.

And oh, shit. I can't call home. Dizzy knows I'm from Dalton. I can't go back there. Steel Bones would find me in no time.

Dalton ain't like the small towns where people are tight-mouthed and suspicious of strangers. It's the kind of place where people will draw you a map to help you find what you're lookin' for and then give you a sob story about baby formula until you fork over a fiver. And they won't have any kids.

Carol or Dee might help me get home. None of my sisters would front me cash to go to New York City.

All I've got is the gold ring.

I'm so screwed, but I can't stay here, dithering. If Heavy finds me, the game's over.

"Let's go to my place," Brick says, flicking his ash. "My woman will make dinner. You can take a minute to breathe."

This guy really wants me to go home with him. Not good. But what are my other choices? Steel Bones is the rock. This guy is the hard place. He's pushin' sixty, though, and I'm fairly sure I could fight him off, if it's just him. But will it be just him where he's planning to take me?

Let me try something else.

"Actually, I need a ride."

"Yeah? Where you headed?"

"New York."

"New York?" Brick screws up his jowly face like I said outer space. "That's a ways away."

"Yeah."

"I was just headed home. Down on the flats. About five miles that way." He jerks his thumb over his shoulder.

I scrub a hand over my face. "Is there a bus stop?"

"For school buses. The closest bus line is—shit—Shady Gap? Maybe Pyle."

"I don't suppose you're goin' to Shady Gap?"

He shakes his head. "Can't say that I am." His face brightens as if he just got an idea. It's the fakest look. "Here's an idea. I'm headed out tomorrow for Stonecut County. Spank the Devil." A genuine grin splits his face. "The old lady's gonna visit her sister. I'm flyin' solo this year."

I've been hearing about Spank the Devil since I came to town. It's a biker rally in the mountains north of here. A huge deal. Not Sturgis big, but respectable. They've even got a band headlining that I've heard on the radio.

People will be there from all over. I could hitch a ride basically anywhere.

"Why don't I give you a ride there? We could hang. You could, uh, figure out your next move."

"Okay. Yeah. That would be great." I scan the empty street. "I could meet you here. Once this place opens, I'll have gas money."

Is this guy gonna go for that? I don't really wanna go to his house. But I'll need to find a place out of the weather to hunker down for the night. It's gonna be a cold one.

Fuck Steel Bones.

I didn't have shit to do with their drama.

And fuck Dizzy. I don't know exactly why I'm pissed at him, but I am. It's preferable to the horrible feeling bubbling deep in my belly, black and sour and reeking of grief and hopelessness.

So, yeah. Fuck Dizzy. I don't need him. I don't need anyone.

I do need a fucking jacket, though.

Brick shakes his head. "No can do. You ain't met my old

lady. She'd put me out if I left a kid our Becca's age alone in front of a pawnshop. Hop on. You can crash at our place tonight. We'll move out at dawn."

He offers me a reassuring smile that doesn't quite meet his eyes, and then he swings a beefy leg, remounting his bike.

"Hop on, sweetheart. Dawn ain't left for her sister's yet. She'll have dinner on by now, and she's gonna be pissed if it gets cold."

There's no way this isn't a setup.

Jed called this guy, and he was close enough to pick me up a half mile from Dizzy's. He's a Rebel Raider. I don't know much, but obviously, they're enemies of Steel Bones.

And clearly, Jed's playin' both sides. Seems like the type. He has the face of that weasel from the children's book where a mouse tries to avoid being made into soup.

But if what Jed said was true, the Rebel Raiders at least want me alive.

I could call Brick out. Ask him what the Raiders plan to do with me.

Or I could play along. Maybe get dinner and a warm place to sleep. Maybe get some cash. And what is it they say? The enemy of my enemy is my friend?

"Make up your mind, girl. I hate reheated lasagna." He revs his engine.

Shit. I've never had lasagna except for school lunch.

I wish I had a higher price, but lasagna does it. It's not like I have choices.

I get on the back of his bike, put my feet on the pegs. He cackles with glee. "Dawn's gonna shit when I pull up with you. I told her I was goin' for a six-pack."

And then we're off again, and in minutes we're navigating a winding country road through fields and half-barren trees, houses further and further apart.

A pit grows in my stomach.

I'm on my own again. Anxiety surges through my body. I hadn't noticed, but at some point, I'd let my guard down. Relaxed. And now, the fear and worry weigh down on me twice as hard. Like how you feel heavier when you get out of a pool.

When I was in the shed, I kept tellin' myself, over and over, it's only a matter of time. They're looking for me. They're gonna find me. All I have to do is hold on. Any minute now, the door will open. Any minute.

No one was coming.

Wishin' I were back at Dizzy's, tucked under the covers by his side, listening to him laugh at that stupid British car show—the sooner I forget about that, the better.

There is no safe.

Wishin' does not make it so.

I can't be stupid again. I've got to keep running 'til I get so far, I'm not even a memory.

Maybe I'll be able to forget him then.

Dawn is the bomb.

I don't know what I expected. Maybe a big-haired biker bitch. Or a nagging fishwife in curlers.

But Dawn is four and a half feet of pure fluff. Short, puffy gray-blonde hair. Apple shape, huge boobs, and a sweatshirt with a white kitten wearing a Pilgrim hat sitting next to a pumpkin. And Brick is freakin' *terrified* of her.

We pull up, and she comes out to the porch, wiping her hands on a towel. Her hands go to her hips, and he scrambles off the bike so quick, he has to do a hop-step to get his balance.

"This is, uh, Fay-Lee. Jed called while I was on my way to the liquor store, asked me to pick her up."

Dawn's eyes narrow. "What does Jed want with a girl her age?"

"Ain't like that, Dawn. Jed's tryin' to be decent. She was in some trouble. He wanted to help her out."

Dawn eyes me from head to foot. "What kind of trouble?"

Brick shrugs his shoulders, flustered. Eventually, he says, "Man trouble?"

Dawn looks at me, raises an eyebrow. What do I say?

"Yeah. Man trouble." It's not a lie.

"And Jed's helping?" She raises her eyebrows even higher.

Brick shuffles his feet.

She closes her eyes and shakes her head. After a moment, she seems to make peace with the obvious fact her husband is feeding her a line of bullshit.

She brightens and clicks her tongue. "And where is her jacket?"

I guess that means we're good. I get off the bike as she huffs and puffs down the steps—she's carrying a lot of extra weight, and her knees don't seem too good.

She grabs my hand and starts chatting a mile a minute. "And no helmet? I swear, that man. And not even a call to hold dinner. I'm not to blame if it's dry. Do you like lasagna?"

She hustles me up the stairs. Brick's still sputtering, trying to spin something approximating a story, but she's not paying him any attention. Me neither. Dawn is like a radio station. I'm tuned in, so I have no choice but to follow along.

"I hope you like tea. *Someone* said he'd bring home milk two days ago, and *someone* still hasn't bothered."

Brick hangs his head and fully gives up on explaining himself.

Dawn urges me into a half-bath. "Wash up, now. I'll cut off the edges, and it'll still be salvageable. Fewer leftovers for *him*, but if he's worried about it, he could come home on time, right?"

And she laughs, bustling off down a hall. The food smells amazing. Garlicky.

The house is small. The carpet's worn, there's a lot of wood paneling, but it's clean. The toilet lid and tank have matching pink shag covers.

I take a breath, splash some water on my face. I check the medicine cabinet, easing it open slowly so it doesn't creak, but there's nothing but an extra hand soap.

I check my phone. Eighty percent. No new calls or messages. Not for a day or so. Rab was blowin' up my phone, and then he stopped. What does that mean?

It means that I am stuck in the middle of some deep, deep shit.

Panic rises in my chest. I need to run. Wait for Brick and Dawn to fall asleep and then steal his bike and go.

Rab knows his people have me, and they must want me alive for now, but what happens when they move to use me against Steel Bones? I'm no snitch. But I also don't wanna die for folks who haven't decided yet whether they're gonna kill me or not. And what do the Raiders do to me if I refuse to go along with this little charade?

I should take the bike. But how far will I get with no cash and two MCs after me? I am *fucked.*

"Coming?" Dawn hollers.

I close my eyes and force the panic back. I will figure it out. I'm not locked in a box. I'm comin' out of this, too.

"Dinner's gettin' cold!" Brick bellows.

I go to join them. Brick's already bellied up to the table, halfway through his slice. Dawn's fussing at the counter.

There's a plate for me, a steaming slice of lasagna, broccoli, bread in a basket, and a huge glass of tea. I slide into a chair.

Cheese drips from the sides. I swirl my fork in it, blow to cool it off. The world might be shit, but this is gonna be amazing.

"Sit, will you, woman?" Brick barks at Dawn. She swats him with her dish towel.

"If I don't soak it now, are you gonna scrub it later?"

Brick ignores her, points his fork at me. "Good, ain't it?" He grins.

I mumble agreement. I can't reply 'cause my mouth is filled with pure heaven.

"I think she likes it." Brick chuckles. Dawn steps over, cups his chin, and smacks a kiss on his lips as he chews.

"We'll put her in Becca's room," Dawn decrees as she dries a casserole dish.

Brick grunts, an uneasy look, like guilt, crossing his face. "Don't get attached. I'm givin' her a ride to Spank the Devil tomorrow."

"Young hearts, run free." Dawn smiles at me and finally sits down at the table with her plate. Brick is sopping up the last of the tomato sauce with a slice of white bread.

After dinner, Brick disappears into the living room with a beer, and Dawn pours us both a tumbler of Irish Cream. She regales me with stories and opinions, and at one point, recipes.

She gives herself the time it takes to nurse two fingers of Bailey's, and then she says, "Well, it's been a long day. Come on."

She leads me to a small room at the end of the hall. There's more wood paneling, a twin bed, and a matching white desk and dresser. Except for a framed cross-stitch of a cat with a ball of yarn and a dozen marching band trophies, the room is empty.

Dawn smooths the quilt, plumps the pillows, and then plops down on the bed.

"Becca's in Spain now with her partner Leah. They're traveling the world." Dawn's chipper smile fades. "She says she might make it back for Christmas this year. Or New Year's maybe."

She pats my knee. "She couldn't wait to get out of this town."

"Is she your only?"

Dawn nods. "I only ever wanted one, and the Lord blessed me with the best, sweetest, smartest girl."

She stands and shuffles to the door, stopping to blow imaginary dust off the trophies. "She's happy now." She sighs. "Maybe I'll buy a ticket and fly over there myself. Brick says I'm nuts. I don't even speak Spanish. I tell him I got the internet. You type a word in, and it tells you what it means. Easy-peasy." She rolls her eyes. "That man. *He's* nuts."

She rearranges a trophy, moves it to the front. "I'd offer you a shower, but I started the dishwasher without thinking. I'm sure you've had a long day. You can get one in the morning."

She lingers at the door, uncertain. I draw a breath to thank her, but she speaks in a rush, cutting me off, fingers worrying the hem of her sweatshirt. "My Brick's a good man.

But that man Jed. His brothers. The other Raiders." She narrows her eyes. "They're no good. Once you get where Brick is takin' you, *keep going.*"

She exhales in a rush and hustles off toward the kitchen, shutting the door behind her.

I bolt over, ease it open. Then I breathe again. There's no lock on the outside of the door, only a push button inside.

I go back and perch on the edge of the bed, toeing off my sneakers. The house is an old rancher with paper-thin walls. I can hear Brick flipping the channels and Dawn rattling around in the kitchen.

The sun's gone down, and the overhead light's missing a bulb. I quietly pad to the dresser and ease open the drawers. They're empty. So is the desk. Becca didn't leave anything. Girlfriend got the hell out of Dodge. Except for those trophies.

There's a beige phone from the 90s on the nightstand, the kind with a curly cord. I pull up my hood and lie on my side.

What is Brick's plan? Is he really gonna take me to Spank the Devil? Or are the Raiders gonna come and grab me in the night?

And then what? They make me talk to the cops? They stash me away somewhere?

On TV, the witnesses always get taken to safe houses, and then the bad guys inevitably find them, and there's a whole shoot-out. The hero rushes in at the last minute to save the day.

Waitin' for a hero is a sucker move.

The emptiness in my chest yawns, aching.

I don't have any moves. No money, no ride, no friends. There's no sense in trying to figure it all out.

I'm logy from the Irish Cream and lasagna and bone weary. I have a bed tonight. I can escape tomorrow.

I hear Dawn finish in the kitchen, and Brick settles on hockey in the living room. The wind howls outside. The smell of woodstove seeps through the window and the heavy brown curtains.

Can I afford to close my eyes and fall asleep? This sounds and smells so much like our house used to when Gram was alive, but I'm not safe.

I should put my shoes back on.

If something happens and I need to run, I need them on.

But I don't want to put my dirty shoes in Dawn's clean sheets, though. I compromise and untie the laces, setting them well within reach. Then I lie back down and stare at the phone.

It's a landline.

If I called Dizzy's home phone, he wouldn't know it was me. I don't know the number, but he's got a landline, too. I can dial 4–1–1. I think that still works.

I could hear his voice one last time.

Cold seeps into my limbs. I burrow under the blankets, but they're too thin to keep the chill away.

I want Dizzy. I'm not angry anymore. I'm scared, and I'm lonely, and I want him. Everything feels better when he's there. Even when he's working in that garage, I feel safe. As if life is okay, and everything is going to be fine because he exists in the world.

A thought slams into me from nowhere, so ugly, so fucked up, it has to be true.

Was he holding me for them?

Was it all about keepin' tabs on me while Steel Bones decided exactly how they were gonna dispose of me?

Of course, I'd let my guard down with the guy who's got

two kids. I'd let him do whatever he wanted to me. I'd be so grateful for food in my belly and a roof over my head.

I'm sick to my stomach. This is such crap. That was the best damn lasagna I ever had, and now it's churning in my belly.

I tuck my knees to my chest, suck down calming breaths. My face burns.

I did nasty things with him. I begged him for it.

Did he tell them? Was he laughing at me behind my back? Telling them what a freak I am? What I let him do?

The phone is sitting there.

In the other room, Brick has a coughing fit. "Gimme me a beer!" he finally wheezes, and Dawn shuffles down the hall.

Tears dribble down my cheeks.

I pick up the phone. It has square, yellowed plastic buttons. I call 4–1–1. My heart thuds in my chest. I ask for Dwayne Jones in Petty's Mill.

Then, I dial *67. Dee taught me how to do that when she used to blow up her ex's phone in middle school.

It rings. Blood pounds in my ears.

And rings.

I roll over so my back is to the door. The cord digs into my shoulder.

It rings again.

My belly clenches, and my palms sweat.

It rings.

A tear tickles my nose, and I let a deep sigh escape.

Then there's a click.

"Hello."

It's him. He's pissed. Worried.

"Who is this?" he demands.

I'm gripping the phone so tight, my knuckles ache.

"Fay-Lee?" His voice gentles. "Is that you?"

I can't answer. There's a huge lump in my throat, and tears are streaming down my cheeks.

"Where are you, baby? I'll come get you. It's okay."

I sniffle. His words dissolve the knot in my chest. All of a sudden, I can draw in a full breath.

"I ain't gonna let anyone hurt you. Tell me where you are." His rumbly voice washes over me. My brain doesn't believe him—not one little bit—but my body does. Every inch.

"You gotta trust me, baby. Are you safe?" His voice rises, turns urgent. Menacing. "Is someone else there? Put 'em on the phone. *Put 'em on the phone, Fay-Lee.*"

"I'm alone." It comes out hardly a whisper.

He exhales in relief. "Baby. Where are you?"

"Is Steel Bones gonna kill me? Because of what they think I know?"

"No, baby. No. Who are with? You got to tell me. It don't matter what you did. No one's holdin' you accountable. But the Rebel Raiders are dangerous, baby. I don't know what they offered you, but you got to get out of there."

"I didn't do anything. I don't *know* anything." My voice rises and shakes.

"Okay, okay. Tell me where you are. I'll come get you. We'll sort it out."

My tears still flow. I didn't know I could make so many. I blink, but everything's blurry. He's saying all the words I long to hear, but he doesn't believe me when I say I didn't have anything to do with any of this. He never believed me.

I would be a damned fool if I trusted him.

"Was it real?" My voice cracks. "It wasn't real, was it?"

There's silence on the other end. He's searching for what to say. 'Cause he doesn't want to say the truth.

"Fay-Lee—"

"Goodbye, Dizzy."

"Fay-Lee!" he shouts as I place the phone back on the base with a click.

I cry myself to sleep, and I dream I'm in a beach-themed bedroom, tangled in smooth sheets, a man at my back giving off heat like a furnace. The colors are all bright and crisp like in an old animated fairy tale, the kind where birds sit on your hand and when you dance, your skirts ripple as smooth as cake batter.

I wake up with numb toes and blue lips, wind whistling through cracks around the window.

12

DIZZY

I love you.

That's all I had to say.

Of course, it's real. I ain't never felt this way before in my life. You're it for me.

How hard is that to say? Instead my brain whirred around like a slot machine. She's too young. You can't put that on her. She's gonna find herself and leave your ass. You don't have the right to take what you want.

I stand in the middle of this stupid fuckin' living room, fists clenched, lookin' for something to punch. And it's all goddamn pillows.

She don't know I feel this way. She's somewhere with the Rebel Fuckin' Raiders, thinkin' I'd let her be killed, and the one time I really have to find the right words, I come up with nothin'.

Fuck.

I hate this goddamn room. I hate this house.

I should have told her I'm buying her a new one. I been lookin' at the listings. There's a lot for sale on Harper and

Charge's street. It's scheduled for new construction. She can do it up however she likes.

God. She's eighteen. She don't want a house. But what does she want? What would make her stay?

She was thinkin' about it. In the woods, by the stream. She was letting down her walls.

I should have never left her alone with Jed. That fucker. He did something. I saw Heavy's eyes. He thinks so, too.

I need to get out of here. Do something. Get on my bike and go find her. But what if she calls again?

Heavy says he called out every able-bodied brother to look for her—and he's beatin' the bushes himself—but most of the club has left for Spank the Devil. He says he'll reach out when they find her. I should stay here. If she has second thoughts—or if she figures out the Raiders are dangerous—she's most likely to come back here.

He sounds one hundred percent confident that it's only a matter of time. I wish I felt the same.

Her stuff is here. The sad fuckin' backpack filled with tuna and canned soup that she thinks I don't know about. The knife's gone. Smart girl. She must have grabbed it. She didn't see the roll of twenties I stuck in the bottom of the sack, though. That's still there.

She's with the Raiders, and she's got no cash.

If she realizes who she's dealing with and she runs, she's got nothing.

My stomach sours, and I swallow down the urge to puke.

I'm gonna kill them. I'm gonna start with the dirtbag who picked her up, and if anyone else touched her, I'm gonna keep goin' until the whole club is bones and gristle under my boots.

I stalk to the window.

I can't just stay here.

I glare at the phone and will it to ring. I tried *69. She blocked me. And the phone doesn't have caller ID.

If anyone is touching her, they'll die. It's as simple as that.

I could have told her that. Would that have scared her? Or would she have told me where she was?

My body's thrumming with adrenaline. I ain't never felt like this. Not even under fire, back in the sandbox. She's got me charged up. Totally changed. And it ain't been hardly no time at all.

I don't understand this thing we got. It's nothin' like anything I've had with any other woman. She lets me do things—she *wants* me to do things that ain't right. But when it's her and me—it ain't wrong, either.

It's like I shed loose the part of my brain that's always workin' through shit. How do I set the suspension up on the new mod the way the client wants and still work within the laws of physics? What shit is Sharon gonna pull next? Do I need to set Carson up with an exercise plan, or is he gonna grow into his weight like I did mine?

With Fay-Lee, all the background noise is gone.

All the shit I gotta negotiate is gone.

I can do what I want, and Fay-Lee *loves* it. She gives me everything, takes whatever I dish out, and then she yawns like a kitten, and curls into my side. A hundred percent trust.

Like she's got no doubt I'm gonna give her what she needs.

I'm a big man, but her trust makes me feel twenty feet tall. But that trust only goes so far, don't it?

And my brothers gotta roll up like the police. Test this thing we've got that's too new to hold under strain.

Rage seethes in my veins. I love my club. Heavy is my

president. Even though he's younger, I've backed him since jump street. But he's gotta fuckin' learn. Expanding the garage, Steel Bones Construction, renovating the clubhouse. Business, money, power. *None of it* is worth a dime without the reason we do it.

When my dad was bustin' kneecaps for the Renellis with Heavy's dad, they weren't doin' it for the future glory of the SBMC. They were doin' it for us. So we wouldn't have to struggle for scraps.

We do it for family. For the women and the kids. He's gotta figure it out one day and soon. Or he's gonna die old and bitter, the king of an empire, alone in a cold bed.

I ain't goin' down like that. I go grab my keys. She ain't callin' back. And I can't stand here and wait another second.

I bound down the stairs, and as I open the front door, Sharon pulls into the drive, her high beams on, blinding me until I screen my eyes. She slams on the breaks, skittering gravel, and yanks up the emergency brake. The boys spill from the car, faces crestfallen.

Parker's been cryin'. Parker don't cry.

I hook him around the neck and tug him into my side.

"What's goin' on Sharon? It's ten at night."

Carson goes to walk in the house, but Sharon grabs him by the back of his shirt. "You don't move. We're not staying. We're gonna clear this up right now."

Sharon's cheeks are flushed like when she's had a few glasses of wine. Is she drunk? Is she drivin' my kids around drunk?

"What is this?" I pat Parker's back and let him go to step closer, try to catch a whiff. All I smell is coffee and perfume.

Parker's staring at the ground. Carson's bottom lip is quivering. He's gonna start wailing any minute. What the hell is goin' on?

"I got a call from Jess Baker," she starts.

Who the fuck is that? The kids ain't hurt.

I do not have time for this drama. That's why she didn't call. She tries this shit occasionally, and if it's by phone, I shut it down after I know the boys are okay. Click. Done.

I understand we got business together 'cause of the boys, but this here ain't business. Not past bedtime on a school night.

Sharon huffs. "Carl Baker's mother?"

"The kid who had the party?"

"The party Parker *knew* he wasn't allowed to go to. That *you* should have asked me about before making a unilateral decision. I knew something like this would happen."

"Something like what?"

Kids gettin' into it? That's normal. I knocked out one of Bullet Nowicki's teeth over a game of horse. Tooth's still gone, but we're cool.

"Jess Baker says he's not welcome over there anymore." She glares at Parker with a look of pure hate. "And a dozen people—some of them *clients*—have already sent me screenshots of the post she put on social media about the whole debacle. You don't come out looking too good, Dwayne, I'll tell you that. You should see it. A hundred reactions. Eight shares."

I give zero shits. "I don't got social media."

"Yeah, well, every single one of Parker and Carson's teachers do. And my clients. And the parents of their friends."

"I don't see the problem. There was an issue. We handled it."

"You didn't handle it, Dwayne. Not if Jess Baker put us on blast."

"She call out Parker by name?" If she did, that dad and I are gonna have words.

"She didn't have to. Everyone in this town knows who's Steel Bones. She says a biker with a barely legal girl in his truck. Everyone knows who she's talkin' about."

"Is that what you're worried about? Gossip on the internet? Jesus, Sharon. The boys should be in bed."

"It's not 'gossip on the internet,' Dwayne. It's lost business. Lost leads. If I don't have a flawless reputation, they could take the Hazleton development. Give it to someone else. Do you want me to lose that opportunity? In real estate, reputation is *everything*."

"He called the kid a pussy," I say. Parker sucks in a quick breath, and I correct myself. "He called *the player the kid picked* a pussy. And we settled it. He apologized. He shook hands with the kid. I shook hands with the dad."

"Well, you didn't bother to 'shake hands' with Jess Baker, did you? The way she tells it, you intimidated Don. Carl was terrified."

I rub my temples. This is such bullshit. "You're overreacting. You both are. The dad was fine. His cousin's got a Ducati. We talked about it. He's thinkin' about getting one, too."

She bugs her eyes and blinks. "I can't believe you're not taking this seriously."

"It ain't a big deal."

"Not to *you*. And if it isn't a big deal to you, it doesn't matter at all, does it?"

I do not have time for this. Fay-Lee's in danger, the kids are upset, they got school, and she wants to rehash the past. Again. Now.

I'm done.

The kids don't need to hear this. And they need to be in bed.

Parker's scowling, mouth tight, eyes shiny. Carson's blinkin' up at me, waitin' for me to fix it. Sharon's face has gone red. She's gonna lose it.

"Boys. Go in the house."

"Stay right where you are," she snaps. "You're gonna hear this. I will not keep standing by silently as these boys turn into trash like their father."

Oh, hell no.

And I look at my boys. "Inside. Now. Brush your teeth. Get in bed. You're sleepin' here tonight."

They bolt for the house.

Sharon opens her mouth.

I step to her. She stumbles back a step.

"Not a word."

Her eyes go wide.

I ain't never hit her. Or any other woman. But I'm a large man, and she's got to be realizing that she don't really know me. She asks for money, and I cut her a check. She asks me to watch the boys or pick 'em up or take 'em somewhere, and I say yes.

I don't think we've had an actual conversation since Carson was in diapers.

She snaps her jaw shut.

"You're gonna listen. You're gonna get back in that car, drive home, and *think*. Think about who the fuck I am. Think about what I'd do for my boys. Then think if I give a shit about Jess Baker or your leads or the Hazleton development."

For a second, she gets it. Then her chin goes up, and her eyes get that mulish cast. She ain't gonna listen.

It's my fault. I been letting her waltz around, thinkin' she gets what she gets by right, not by my choice.

"You have no right to keep the boys," she sputters. "We have a custody agreement. If you refuse to abide by it, I will take you to court. I don't have to give you all this extra time. It's a *favor*."

I shake my head. She really don't know me.

Maybe until recently, I didn't quite know me either.

"Nah. You ain't gonna do that. You like your big house. You like Steve. You like drivin' around this town in your big car actin' like you're big shit. Who owns this town, Sharon?"

I wait, but she don't answer.

"Steel Bones owns this town. Who owns this county, Sharon? Who built that development you're so worried about? Whose check pays for the car and the clothes and the lunches? Cleats don't cost three hundred dollars."

"You *owe* me," she spits from clenched teeth.

"For what?"

"For that." She points at the house, arm so rigid it could break. "For those boys. 'Cause they're the only things you cared about, weren't they? You never cared about me. *My* dreams. *My* goals."

Fuck. It always comes down to this. I didn't support her. I didn't encourage her.

"Bullshit. I paid for everything. The classes. The license fees. Business cards. Swag. *I* watched the kids. I put dinner on the table when you were showing houses. I had prospects hang your flyers up all over the county."

"Money wasn't enough, Dwayne."

Shit. She's right.

Nothing was gonna be enough.

'Cause I wasn't what was holding her back.

Whatever was stoppin' her, whatever she had to fight through to be happy, it wasn't me. It was in her own head.

There's nothin' I could have done. No magic words. Not then. Not now.

And I am done with playing along with this game where she acts however she wants, and I deal with it, 'cause it's easier to leave things the way they are. That's not gonna work anymore.

I'm gonna find Fay-Lee, and bring her home, and we're gonna be a happy family, damn it.

"I'll take the boys to school in the morning. You want to pick them up, or should I?"

"Typical. Avoiding the subject."

"You're not getting it. We're done. It's not my job to make you happy. Not my job to give a shit about your life, your beefs, whatever. You ain't my problem."

"I'm the mother of your children," she hisses.

"You want to talk about Parker? You want to talk about how that boy don't even smile no more—we can talk about that. How he don't see the point in bein' at your house anymore. Or we can talk about your husband calling Carson chunky. I got thoughts on that matter, and I will be sharing them with Steve."

"Husky," she mutters.

"What?"

She's smart enough not to repeat it.

"But we are done rehashing the past. And you ain't stirring up no more drama. Times have changed. You ain't the only one with lawyer money anymore. Matter of fact, you want to go back to court, I got my legal representation on speed dial."

She gets an uneasy look. It's a small town. She knows Harper Ruth.

I nod, but I ain't done. "From here on out, you're gonna make this as easy as can be on everyone involved. You ain't gonna speak to Fay-Lee unless it's about the kids. And you ain't gonna shame that boy for a mistake that he already made right 'cause you're mad about what some bitch says on the internet."

I take a breath. Force my voice back down. "If you can't care about these kids more than what people think, let 'em stay with me."

Her face is frozen in a sneer, her eyes cold and filled with rage. Whatever she just heard, I guarantee, it ain't what I said.

"You pick them up from school tomorrow, then." She turns, flounces to the truck.

"You know what," she spits as she climbs into the driver's seat. "Keep them all week. I have showings."

She slams the door, peels out, sending gravel flying.

I'm already on my way back in the house, phone in my hand, texting Wall to send Jo-Beth or another sweetbutt over here to watch the kids. I'm goin' to find Fay-Lee, and I'm gonna throw her over my shoulder and bring her home.

Enough of the shit I should do.

I'm gonna do what I wanna.

I trip up the stairs, fully expecting to find the boys in the bed, Carson conked out and Parker playin' games on his phone. Instead, I face the inquisition. Parker and Carson are standing in the middle of the living room, hands fisted on their hips, feet hip-width apart, like two pissed-off, miniature Supermen.

"Where's Fay-Lee?" Carson asks.

"You can't get rid of her 'cause Mom's pissed." Parker glares, tears gone.

"I didn't get rid of her."

"Then where is she?" Parker demands.

"She don't got no money, and she don't got no phone." Accusation shines in Carson's eyes. "And she don't have a jacket."

Both boys give me the stare of death, waiting. I didn't think I could feel lower. I run a hand through my hair.

"We had a—misunderstanding. She got upset and left. It wasn't her fault."

"It was your fault." Parker says it like there's no doubt in his mind.

"In a way. I didn't handle it right."

"You got to fix it. We like Fay-Lee," Parker says.

"Yeah?" I honestly didn't know they felt so strongly about her. Vonna was around for six months, and they didn't bat an eyelash when we split.

"You're happy when she's around," Carson says. "You're never happy." He frowns, and his eyes darken. "You got to get her back. She's real skinny, and it's cold out."

"She's got her phone." I don't have anything else to comfort him. He's scared for her, and so am I.

"Oh. Cool." Carson takes his phone out of his pocket, and before I can register what he's doing, he's got it up to his ear.

"Fay-Lee?" he says.

There's a distant murmuring. Shit. He's got her number.

I reach for the phone, but he ducks. Maybe I should ease off. She didn't like what I had to say earlier, and my brain's buzzing so fast, I haven't thought of anything else besides "Come home."

"Yeah. Parker's here, too. Where are you?"

More murmuring.

"You got to come back. Dad's sorry. He won't do it again."

Murmuring.

"Fay-Lee, you got to give him a chance—" Parker swipes the phone from his brother's hand.

"Listen. I'm sorry I was a jerk to you. If you want my room again, you can have it. Whatever Dad did, he's not gonna do it again. We promise."

I can't take it. I grab the phone. "Fay-Lee."

Dial tone.

I go to recent calls, try again. It goes straight to voice-mail. *This is Fay-Lee. You know what to do.*

I do. I gotta tell her, make her *believe*, that she's the most important thing in the goddamn world to me, and I would never let anything or anyone hurt her. I know *what* to do, but I don't know how.

I sink to the sofa. The boys collapse on either side of me.

"She's really pissed," Carson says.

"You probably need to buy her something." Parker leans his head back. "A purse or something."

"Did she say where she was?"

"Nah." Carson rests his head on my upper arm. He smells like wet dog again. How the hell does he always smell like wet dog when he has no pets? He's gonna need a shower before school. "She said she was gonna miss us and sorry she left without saying goodbye."

My chest tightens.

"Just track her down," Parker says.

"Yeah, get a bloodhound," Carson suggests.

"No, dumbass. Track her using her phone. That's what they do on TV. They put a chip or something on the phone, and then they get in a van, and they track 'em down."

Shit.

There's a tracker on her phone.

That's why Heavy's so sure he'll find her.

That's why he left her alone with Jed. And her phone.

He knew something's up with Jed. He knew she'd run. And she'd lead us straight to the Rebel Raiders who put Chaos up to stealing the blueprints.

That lying, Machiavellian *fuck*.

When Fay-Lee is safe at home, I'm gonna beat his ass with a baseball bat. Or a stop sign pole. I'll probably need a fuckin' fence post.

Parker sees my wheels turning. "You can go get her, Dad. I'll watch Carson."

I check my phone. "Jo-Beth's coming over to watch you. She'll take you to school tomorrow if I don't get back in time. That okay?"

"Last time Jo-Beth watched us, she made us dust all the crap hanging on the walls," Parker complains. "And I think she stole the yellow pillow that said *Live Your Dreams*."

"Yeah, but we didn't have to clean nothin' for a week after she left. Besides, I think she's pretty. I like her purple hair." Carson's easier to please than his brother. He's gonna have a smoother time of it with the ladies.

"When I bring Fay-Lee back, she's stayin'. You two okay with that?"

"Of course. We weren't the ones that ran her off." Parker stands up and stretches. "I'm going to bed before Jo-Beth gets here and makes us clean."

Carson bounces up to follow him. "Be nice to her when you find her. And bring her food. She left her snack pack here."

"Her snack pack?"

"Yeah. She took one of Parker's backpacks, and she keeps her snacks in there. It's in your closet." Carson shrugs, and then he heads off for his bedroom.

"Brush your teeth!" I call after him. "And if I'm not back, shower before you go to school!"

I'm already dialing Heavy and walking out to the deck. I'm gonna be raising my voice.

"Speak." He picks up on the first ring.

"You ain't got guys out looking for her. You're tracking her phone."

There's a pause. There's a growl of engines and shouts in the background. He's outdoors. He's probably got her in his sights. My shoulders tense and the cords in my neck rise.

"Do you want to know where she is?" he asks.

"I'm gonna kill you."

"We had to find the person who sent her."

"We knew it was the Raiders."

"We didn't know who specifically. Or where they were. Or who they were working for."

"The Raiders don't need a reason to fuck with us."

"But they needed intel to go after the blueprints."

"You think my girl was gonna lead you to the mastermind? If anything, she was a pawn."

"You have to trust me."

"I don't. Not anymore."

We fall silent. A bullfrog honks near the creek that runs behind our property. The night is clear, and the moon is almost full. The temperature's droppin' fast.

Then there's a long, weary sigh from the other end. "'First be reconciled to your brother' the good book says."

I grunt. Heavy has the habit of quoting Scripture. He picked it up from his mama who was forever hasslin' us boys with the word of the Lord. It generally means his big brain has hit a wall.

"Where is she?"

"Brick Daugherty's. Idle chatter says he's heading up to Spank the Devil in the morning."

"Brick? Is he the meth dealer?"

"That's Book Daugherty. Book moved to Delaware. Brick's the younger brother. The one that looks like a fat Willie Nelson."

"I'm goin' to get her."

"There're gonna be thousands of people there. She'll be safe. We wait. Watch. We can figure out who's behind all this. What their endgame is. Protect the club."

"Would you let Harper be bait?"

God help him, for Steel Bones, I think he would. But he's smart enough to understand that another man would not.

There's another long pause. He must be on the side of the road. I hear vehicles zip by, shouts fading in the low roar of traffic. He must already be downtown in Anvil. It's a sleepy mountain town fifty-one weeks a year. During Spank the Devil, it becomes the largest city within two hundred miles.

I'll never find her there without his help.

My fists ache to cross the distance and beat her location out of him.

"We have eyes on her. She's safe."

"She's mine."

He either gets it, or we're done.

"Head on up. I'll take you to her. You have my word, she's safe until then."

"Once I've got her, we're havin' it out."

"No doubt, my brother." He exhales. In the background, tires screech. "Everything I do, it's for this club."

"I know. That's why I ain't gonna kill you all the way."

"There's no way I convince you to hold off? Just 'til we see where they go after the rally?"

"Fuck you."

"Fair enough. Call when you're fifteen minutes out. I'll

meet you at the town sign. We'll get her. I don't suppose you'd agree to go in subtle, would you?"

"Not a chance."

"I'll call Harper then. Tell her to dress up in her lawyer clothes and bring her briefcase."

"Good idea. Oh, and Heavy?"

"Yeah."

"Make sure Jed's somewhere else."

There's a moment, a silence where the truth we've both come to separately sits between us, thick and rank.

"Ayup."

We hang up, and I pad down to the gun safe and strap up. Fay-Lee's coming with me if I have to fight my way through a mob of Raiders. Honestly?

I welcome it.

13

FAY-LEE

I'm sitting in a lawn chair on Rab's gross bony-old-man lap. His leathery arm is a steel band around my waist, and his hard dick is poking the small of my back. He smells like cheap beer and mothballs. I want to puke.

He stirs the campfire with a long stick and embers go flying. A few greasy, younger guys are squatting nearby, eyeing me like dogs under the dinner table.

I'm in deep trouble.

Everything was fine on the ride up to Anvil. I've heard of Spank the Devil. Everyone has. The biggest biker rally on the East Coast. Four days of motorcycles, music, and mayhem. A hundred opportunities to lose Brick, five-finger some cash, and make a friend who'll give me a ride when the thing's over.

And the morning was fine, a two-hour road trip on a mild fall day. Brick is a cautious driver, and his touring bike has big, comfy seats. Before we left first thing in the morning, Dawn gave me an old quilted jacket of her daughter's. She'd hidden ten bucks in the pocket.

As soon as we hit the Anvil town limits, bikers swarmed

us, a dozen men in cuts with the Rebel Raider's red-and-white patches. The man from the bar—Rab—pulled into the lead. When I first met him, he'd struck me as a grizzly old head. Weathered and harmless. The kind of guy you find sitting for hours at a lunch diner counter.

I was wrong. He's sharp. Nasty. And these men follow him without question.

All chance of bailing disappeared in an instant.

When we got to this campsite, situated among dozens of others demarked by lines of bikes, tents, and trucks with the tailgates down for kegs and coolers, Brick gave me a weak smile.

He said, "It'll be fine, girly." Then he hustled off toward the stage and vendors, and I haven't seen him since.

My hand reaches for my phone on instinct, but I don't have it anymore. Dober, a bald guy with a thick neck and a VP patch, took it. He took my knife, too. A dude with a prospect rocker pinned my arms behind my back, and Dober searched me, mauled my tits and grabbed my pussy, took my shit, and laughed. The prospect pocketed my ten bucks.

I'm so screwed.

"What are you going to do with me?" I ask.

Rab jiggles his knee, jostling me against his hard-on, and slides his arm up so he's holding me right under the boobs. He gives my left tit a rough squeeze. "Be patient."

He laughs and stirs the fire. He's close-mouthed. The others aren't.

Nearby, Dober is running his mouth to a guy named Scratch.

"I still don't get it." Scratch digs his nails into his crusty neck. Dude comes by his name honestly.

"It's fuckin' simple," Dober explains. "Dizzy gets the

blueprints Chaos was goin' after. We trade the blueprints for the girl."

"Why the fuck couldn't Jed just get the blueprints, like, months ago?"

"'Cause if Jed gets busted like Chaos did, we don't have an inside guy, no more."

"And Dizzy's gonna do his club dirty for this skinny bitch?"

"That's what Jed says. He swears the guy's fuckin' stupid over her. Gone."

He did? I can't help but lean forward, and Rab's arm digs into my ribs.

"So we're just waitin' for Dizzy now?"

"He ain't answered the texts yet."

"You sure you got the right number?"

Dober slaps the back of Scratch's dirty neck. "We got the right number. Dumbass."

"You called that gash for weeks about Chaos. She never answered." Scratch jerks his chin towards me. I'm the gash. Fuck him. And fuck any man who sees women that way.

I stiffen without thinking, and Rab cackles. "Don't make me jizz my pants, now, girlie."

I want to unzip my skin and run like hell. But even if I manage to get free of Rab—bite him, maybe, although yuck, gross, ugh—I'd have to get past all the others. Some are drunk or high, but it's early in the day. Most aren't too impaired yet. I wouldn't get five feet.

"Why do we want blueprints?" Scratch asks. "I seen Dizzy's ride. Sweet mod. He's got cash. If he's gone for her like Jed says, he'd pay for her."

"Knocker wants blueprints."

"Fuck Knocker. He's in Supermax. He ain't gettin' out anytime soon." Scratch talks big, but he lowers his voice when he says Knocker's name. Rab's gaze flicks to him, and his eyes narrow.

Dober casts a nervous glance this way. Underneath me, Rab shifts. I think Scratch might be talkin' himself into a hole.

Dober spits. "Fuck you. You wanna give up your cut? Feel free to black out your ink anytime."

"Cut of what? Knocker's insane, man. Fuckin' conspiracy theories. 'Destroy Steel Bones. Revenge our fathers. Split the spoils.' Dude sounds like the bad guy in a comic book." Scratch is muttering under his breath, but he seriously misgauges his volume.

"You got a better plan?" Rab asks. Scratch's face pales, but he screws up his courage and pulls back his shoulders.

"What I always say. Move more weight. It's bullshit that we don't deal in Petty's Mill. Those country tweakers drive all the way to Shady Gap for our shit. If we weren't so fuckin' afraid of Heavy Ruth, we'd be making bank."

Rab raises his eyebrows. "You got a big mouth for a man smokin' his own profits."

Scratch dials it down, shoving his shaky hands in his pockets. "All I'm sayin' is we could be knee deep in pussy and hard rock right now—and rakin' in cash—but we're over here grillin' hot dogs with the weekend warriors, our dicks in our hands, babysitting that skinny bitch."

When I get out of this, I'm knockin' that guy's last three teeth out.

My heart sinks.

Am I gonna get out of this?

What do they do to me if Dizzy doesn't come through with the blueprints? And he won't. Of course, he won't. He's not going to betray his club. Especially not when he thinks I'm involved with the enemy.

I need to focus. Look for a window to escape, a weakness. Dizzy's not riding to my rescue. You can't rely on anyone but yourself.

In that shed, I wasted hours, thinkin' someone was coming for me. It was only a matter of time, right? I sat in the corner. Picked off my nail polish.

By the time I realized I was on my own, I was weak. Hungry. Thirsty. But I didn't give up. I dug at the seams of the metal walls. I pried at the bottom. I banged with my fists, lay on my back and kicked at the door, and screamed.

I didn't give up until my body did.

Goddamn, how did I not learn my lesson?

Dizzy is *not* comin'. I need to come up with a plan.

My brain won't cooperate. I try to catch the eyes of the people milling in the distance, drinking from red plastic cups, chatting around their own fires. To a man, they avoid my gaze. Everyone's hangin' out, but they steer clear of this campsite like there's a fence around it. No one's gonna challenge these guys. Eventually, I quit trying, and my eyes are drawn to the fire.

There's so much noise. Competing radios blasting, and a few acres away, the dull roar of the metal band on the main stage.

People shout. Laugh. Engines rev and roar. Panic rises, flailing in my chest.

No one's coming.

I'm on my own, and I'm as trapped as I was in that shed.

I drop my head and close my eyes.

And then the roar of an engine splits the air.

It's a Raider, barreling into camp, tearing up the frozen ground. His beady eyes are shining.

"They're here. He didn't come alone."

What? Dizzy?

The men come alive, rising to their feet, patting the obvious gun bulges under their shirts. Guys who'd wandered off to talk to neighboring groups trot back. There are more than a dozen men surrounding me now.

Rab is still sitting. His dick is still hard. "Chill out. We're in the middle of a thousand people. They ain't comin' in guns blazing."

"Dizzy is a dumb fuck." Dober spits. "He could have made himself a cool three thou."

"Three Gs ain't nothin' to the patched-in brothers of the Steel Bones MC anymore." Rab chuckles, bitter. "They're big time, now. Billionaire developers and big-time politicians. Drug lords and mafia kingpins. Greed ain't gonna turn 'em. Except our friend Jed. He was lookin' for a reason, though. He's got the heart of a rat." Rab spits.

A few of the other men follow suit.

"Why'd you offer Dizzy the cash, then?" Scratch asks. He's fixated. The other guys are shuffling closer. Cracking their necks.

Somethin's about to go down.

Butterflies go wild in my stomach.

Is Dizzy here for me?

"Common negotiation tactic. Open with a low-ball bid. When they don't bite, lower it. This gash's life is our low-ball bid. Now he knows it's worth less to us than a used beater. I figured it would've put some fire under his ass. Jed fails again, though. He said Dizzy would do anything for this bitch. Apparently not."

Rab finally stands, setting me at his side.

"We gonna kill her here?" Scratch asks. My heart slams against my ribs.

"You really are a dumb fuck, ain't you?" Rab sneers.

"Nobody's killin' anyone in this crowd of witnesses. You got her?"

Dober's hand clamps around my wrist. He nods.

"I suppose we're movin' to a new phase of negotiations," Rab sighs. "Guess we ain't gettin' those blueprints."

The sound of engines grows louder, echoing. A dust cloud blooms behind us where a line of port-a-pots form a boundary of the festival.

The beady-eyed guy is on the phone. "They're headed this way."

He's gesturing away from the port-a-pots, down an incline, toward the main gathering area. You can see it now. People parting like the red sea, crowding under the vendor's tents. Another cloud of dust rises in the air.

The death metal band is still raging, but the radios have been shut off. Everyone's craning to see what's going on.

"There's ten of 'em. No eleven."

"Relax. We outnumber them. This is just gonna be a conversation."

"Heavy Ruth and Dizzy Jones are riding lead."

He's coming.

My body sags. Dober jerks my arm. "Try anything, bitch, I'll shank you in the back." He takes my knife from his pocket, flicks it open, and presses it flat between my shoulder blades so my hair hides his hand.

Oh, fuck.

Dizzy's coming, and I'm gonna die in front of him. My eyes burn.

I can see them now. Oh, my gosh. It's like a movie.

The terrain's too uneven for full speed—and there are too many people—but they're coming steady. Dizzy's hair and beard are wild in the wind, and his face is terrifying. My belly clenches and my heartbeat breaks into a gallop.

Heavy rides beside him, glowering and fierce, and seeing them side-by-side like this, there can be no doubt. They share blood. And they are intent on the same purpose.

Dizzy's dark eyes meet mine. A shiver courses down my spine.

He's coming for me.

He is righteous fury personified, and he is comin' for what's his. He thinks I'm working for the enemy, and he doesn't care.

He loves me. Holy shit. He loves me.

All of a sudden, voices rise, and there's a charge in the atmosphere.

"Fuck. Is that a pump-action shotgun?"

"They ain't gonna open fire in the middle of Spank the Devil," Dober says, but he doesn't seem so sure.

The Raiders firm their stance and free their pieces. A few of the less sober guys look wildly for an exit, but the camps are pitched too close. We're hemmed in by a line of bikes, a city of tents, and a bonfire.

Rab grabs my arm and drags me in front of him. There's no knife at my back anymore, but I'm staring down a mob of armed bikers. Shotguns. Pistols.

I hope they know what they're doing.

Or what if they don't care if I'm collateral damage? Wouldn't that be just what Heavy wants? If I get caught in the crossfire, I can't tell anyone about Chaos.

My gaze darts back to Dizzy. His mouth is cast in a grim line, but his eyes speak. My panic ebbs. He's not gonna let anything happen to me. I *know* it.

"They ain't stoppin'," a prospect squeaks. "Fuck this." He vaults over a bike and races off.

"Stand your ground, men," Rab urges. "They ain't gonna shoot in front of all these people."

Dizzy's focus has turned to Rab. He's still yards away, but I can read his face like a book. He's gonna destroy this man who dares to touch me.

He's come for me. My heart soars.

Everything slides into place as he skids to a stop about an acre away, resting his shotgun on his forearm, aiming it straight at my head.

"Trust me," he shouts.

"I do." It's a whisper. He can't possibly hear me over the roar of men and engines, but he smiles, keeping his eyes glued on mine.

It's so clear. What he said that day at the stream, he meant. I belong to him. He'll always come for me.

And he'll take these motherfuckers out, one way or another.

"He's gonna shoot!" Dober shouts.

"Run!" Rab bellows. Someone digs his hands into my shoulders. "Leave her, you dumbass! They're behind us! Scatter!"

"Drop!" Dizzy roars.

I fall to the ground. Before I hit the dirt, I catch a glimpse as he raises the shotgun, pumps it, and fires a shot into the air with a firm and steady hand, his leather jacket flapping open in the wind, every inch a cowboy on a steel horse.

I curl up and cover my head, squeezing my eyes closed, and a thunderous crack echoes in the mountains.

"He's crazy! He's racking another round! He's aiming. Go! Go!" a man shouts, and there's pandemonium as everyone left in the vicinity scatters.

Feet pound by my head, and I huddle as small as I can. There's scuffling, grunts, but no other gunshots. I peek up.

Shouts and screams ring out in the crisp air. The wail of

sirens swells in the distance. The music plays on, and the crowd chants the lyrics, oblivious.

It's anarchy. Tents have toppled. One fell and caught fire. Flames shoot up, along with a column of pitch-black smoke. Fights have broken out. Bikes are roaring through the confusion as people flee, and others rush over to save their shit.

A few dudes, high as hell, are whooping as they pitch burning logs into the tents that are still standing.

It's mayhem.

Miraculously, no one seems to have been hurt.

I find my feet. There's so much shit going on, my brain can't sort through it all.

Where is Dizzy?

There.

Still forty yards away. The anarchy has spawned a chain of brawls, and another club is riding through off to the side —slow as shit and very careful—trying to escape the chaos.

Dizzy sprints for me, bulldozing men out of his way. Heavy, Charge, and Wall are behind him.

"Wait there. I'm comin'!" he shouts, pointing at me, and by some miracle, I hear.

A drug-addled dude stumbles into his path. Dizzy picks him up with his one free hand, pitching him out of the way like a ragdoll. Right into one of the bikers trying to ride out.

The man's bike wobbles. Topples. The druggie scampers off.

The rider roars, untangling himself from the machine and bolting for Dizzy. The guy is not that tall, but he's wide, solid, and really fuckin' pissed. His rocker reads *Los Insurrectos*.

All his brothers lower their kickstands, and now it's a melee.

Wall plows through dudes like a mad bull. Heavy's

knocking men over with single blows. And Dizzy's a rabid dog, ripping and tearing through anyone in his path, heading straight toward me, eyes burning, his gaze never wavering, not for a second.

I'm so struck that I don't notice Dober.

Not until his fingers dig into my upper arm and the cold tip of my knife dents the tender skin under my chin.

"Don't move." His breath is hot on my ear.

It's like someone hit pause.

Everyone around the campfire freezes mid-motion. Around us, it's pandemonium, but within this circle, time has stopped. From the corner of my eye, I see Nickel and Bullet creeping closer.

Steel Bones are behind us. Dizzy and the others are facing us, guns raised.

All the other Raiders are gone. Dober's alone.

Fear grips my chest and squeezes. He's trapped. Desperate. I'm fucked.

"Back up!" He raises his elbow until the knife is perpendicular to my jugular. I shallow my breaths, stay as still as I possibly can, but I'm shaking.

Heavy is the first to drop his weapon. He takes a small step forward and lays it carefully on the ground. The knife pricks my skin.

Heavy freezes, squatting, holding up his palms. "I see we're at an impasse."

"What the fuck is that?" Dober spits.

"A stalemate."

"Speak English, motherfucker."

"Let her go," Dizzy orders. I've never heard him sound like this. His voice is a rumble, as deep and resonant as Heavy's. Everyone's gaze flies to him. Among all these armed outlaws, it's crystal clear. In this moment, he's the most dangerous. "Let her go now, and you live."

"You ain't gonna let me walk out of here." Dober's losing it. The knife is nicking me, and I don't think he means it to, but a trickle of warm blood drips down my neck. Dizzy sees. His jaw tics every time the knife touches me, and he readjusts his grip on the shotgun.

"You can ride out of here. You have my word," Heavy says. "But if you don't lower that knife, my brother here is going to blow your brains out. You have my word on that, too."

"As soon as I let her go, you're gonna shoot me."

"In front of all these witnesses?" Heavy scoffs. "That would be crazy."

Dober snorts.

Dizzy clears his throat, and when he has Dober's attention, he slowly squats next to Heavy, lowering his shotgun to the ground.

"See? Everything's cool. It's gonna be fine." He smiles gently. It's meant for me. "Don't move," he says, low and calm. "I love you. I've never felt this way before in my life. You're it for me."

A strangled sob escapes my lips. "Now?"

"Now," he says, but his gaze darts over my shoulder.

And then there's a grunt, the knife falls from my throat, and there's a weird gurgle. Dober staggers backwards, and Nickel's there, catching him, slamming a hand over his mouth. They stand together for a long moment, Dober swaying, and then he crumples.

Nickel takes his full weight, and with Wall's help, they drag him to the lawn chair Rab was sitting in, and set him carefully in it.

Dober's eyes are open, unblinking. Unseeing.

My stomach heaves.

There's a quiet snick, a flash of red and metal, and Nickel stalks off, wiping his hands on his black jeans. Wall looms in front of Dober's body, obscuring it from view.

Oh, shit. He's dead.

I shove my fist in my mouth to muffle a scream.

It was so quick. So quiet.

I gaze wildly around at the camps, the fires, the fights breaking out and petering off. No one noticed. How is that possible?

"Baby." Dizzy's in front of me, filling my field of vision. My teeth are chattering. I'm freezing cold. "Baby, breathe."

I can't.

In the background, Heavy's barking orders. "Cuts off now. Hand 'em to the prospect. Charge, go borrow someone's truck. Everyone, empty your pockets. Hand Charge all your cash now. Bullet, go find a tent we can use as a tarp."

The men burst into action, soldiers under orders.

Dizzy grabs my hand and leads me to his bike. "Can you hold on to my waist, baby?"

A hysterical sob slips from my lips.

"Baby." He grabs my chin, tilting my head until I meet his eyes. "You need to keep it together for a little while longer. You were so brave. You did a great job. You didn't do nothin' wrong. You're safe now. I only need you to hold it together a few more minutes so I can get us out of here. Okay?"

He brushes a soft kiss across my trembling lips.

"He—he—" I can't spit it out. All the terror bowls into me at once. I sag. Dizzy gathers me close, wraps me in his big, strong arms. "He almost killed me," I mumble into his chest.

"You're okay. Be brave for me a little longer. You ain't

never gonna be afraid like that again, okay?" There's a tremor in his voice.

He was scared, too.

For me.

I could have died.

I blink, and his face becomes clear. The creases in the corners of his darkened eyes. The snarled wildness of his hair.

"You were afraid." My fingers reach out to touch his bearded cheek.

"Of course, I fuckin' was."

"You came for me."

"I always will. I told you I would, woman. Don't know why you won't listen."

"I want to go home." It's too much. There's blood dried on my neck, and I saw a man's throat slit, and I almost died, and I am so tired. Tears well in my eyes.

"Okay. I got you." He helps me onto his ride, guiding my feet to the pegs. "You sure you can hold on?"

He mounts, drawing my arms around him.

I rest my cheek against his back and inhale the leather. "For a little longer," I whisper and wind my arms around his waist. "I got you, too."

WE DON'T GET AS FAR as Petty's Mill. After about an hour, Dizzy pulls off at a motel near the Stonecut County line and gets us a room.

It's a dump. It reeks of air conditioner and stale cigarettes.

Dizzy flips the dead bolt behind us.

I'm so numb, the surge of panic almost doesn't register.

"Please unlock it."

"Shit. I forgot." He slides it open. "Okay?"

"Okay."

And then we stand there, staring at each other.

Dizzy's stance is wide, his chest rising and falling as if he's run a marathon, his eyes burning.

I hug myself.

The heating unit sputters a few times and the fan cycles off.

It's dead silent.

He explodes.

"What the fuck were you thinking, Fay-Lee?" he shouts, starting for me. I jerk away, and he growls, balling his fists and pacing the room. "You could've been killed! These guys aren't jokes. They deal meth. Pills. Fuckin' fentanyl. Women are dogs to them. Less than dogs. Jesus Christ! Did they touch you?"

My nose burns.

"Did they touch you?" His voice raises. "Did they make you do anything?"

"No!"

My answer doesn't calm him at all. "Why did you run? I told you. I wasn't gonna let anything happen to you. Why didn't you believe me?"

Hot tears dribble down my frozen cheeks.

I hate this. "Stop yelling at me," I sob.

"Fuck." He stops, his back to me, and tries to run his hands through his hair. It's all knotted from the ride, though, so he gives up and stares at the water-stained ceiling.

I cry harder.

Now I wish he would start hollerin' again. The silence is worse. My stomach aches.

"You wanna spank me?" I ask. "Would that make you less mad?"

"That's not—" He exhales, but he turns back around. "We ain't gonna do that now. That's for play. Not for when we got to figure shit out."

His face is bleak. What do we need to figure out? He came for me. He said he loves me. That means we're together, right?

"What do you mean?" There's a lump in my throat.

"I mean if you don't trust me or believe me or whatever, what's the fuckin' point?"

"You don't believe *me*! I didn't know about Chaos. I swear. I didn't know that guy was callin' me. I met him one time. At a bar. Jed was there. That was before I even came to the clubhouse or met any of you guys."

"Jed was there?" He doesn't seem that surprised.

"Yeah. They talked. I thought you knew. He's in your club." A chasm opens in my chest. If he's gonna dump me, send me on my way, I wish he would. I'm tired. I can't stop the tears, and my nose is stuffing up.

"Baby, stop crying."

"If you don't like it, you can fuck off."

"Don't use that tone of voice with me."

"Don't talk to me like you own me." Now we're both shouting, and I start pacing. "Don't act like I'm the one to blame. I had nothing to do with any of this. You all made this my business."

"I do own you." He crosses the room. I lunge for the bathroom, but I don't have a chance. He throws me on the bed, face down, and pins me.

I buck and flail, but I've got so little energy left. And I don't want to fight with him.

He easily pins my arms with one hand above my head.

My jacket bunches up, exposing my bare sides to the air. His weight presses me into the mattress, his leg between my thighs.

We're both panting.

His hair brushes my cheeks. He smells like woodsmoke and leather. I stop struggling and relax.

"That's right, baby. Calm down." His voice is a rumble in my ear.

I can feel his hard cock nestled against my ass. I work my hips, my pussy growing slick with cream. I love this. He's covering me completely. Except grindin' against him, I can't move.

I'm helpless. He can do whatever he wants. I moan.

"Not yet," he pants. He rises on his knees, flips me onto my back, but he keeps my wrists pinned to the mattress. "We're gonna sort this out."

He's not mad anymore. And that bleak, disappointed look is gone, too. I wriggle, but I can't get any contact. I whimper.

"I'll give you what you want, baby. But first you're gonna give me what I want."

"What's that?"

"If you're gonna be my old lady, you gotta trust me. It don't work otherwise. You got to know I love you. I'll fuckin' die for you, woman. Kill for you. But if you ain't in this—" His hands tighten on my wrists and his lips turn down. "If you don't want this, I understand. I'll take you wherever you want to go. Set you up. I'll—Why you cryin' now?"

He lets go of my wrists to run his hands down my arms, as if he's checking to see if I'm hurt.

"You love me?"

"Yeah." His forehead's creased in confusion. He has no idea why I'm sobbing.

"You want me to be your old lady?"

"I been sayin' that."

"You said I was your woman."

"You are. Woman. Old lady. Wife. Same difference."

"There's a difference."

"Why are you crying?" He smooths my hair back.

"I'm happy."

The corner of his lip turns up, but his brow is still furrowed. "Strange way to show it."

"Okay." I smile back. "I guess I'll trust you then. In the future. I'll be sure not to run for my life when your club comes accusin' me of being a rat."

"I was handling it."

"I'm not a rat. I only met Rab that once, and I had no idea what Chaos was doin'. I would have split if I'd known. That's the truth."

He smooths my hair. "I know."

"I was only with that Raider 'cause I needed a ride. I wasn't workin' with them."

"I know," he says again.

"How?" I wipe my eyes. "I mean, *I* know I'm telling the truth. How do you?"

"'Cause I know you. You're honest as shit."

That kind of stops me in my tracks, but the tears still flow. The hurt's still there.

"In the driveway, Jed said the club was gonna convince you to kill me."

"Never would have happened. Babe, you're the best thing that ever happened to me. You, Carson, and Parker. You guys are my reason. For everything."

"You mean that?"

He nips at my neck, and my pussy clenches. "You got to believe me when I speak."

"Okay. I believe you."

"You just tellin' me what I want to hear?" he asks. I feel his lips curve into a smile against the crook of my shoulder.

"If you're gonna be my old man, you gotta believe what I say," I imitate his gruff voice. "It don't work otherwise."

"I guess it don't." He pushes up and takes my lips, kissing me so thoroughly my toes point. "Push your pants down, baby. I can't wait no longer."

I do as he says while we kiss each other desperately, hair catching in each other's mouths, fumbling with buttons. I use my feet to shove down his jeans and tug my bra to my neck. He suckles my tit, drawing the nipple in his mouth, lapping with his raspy tongue as I guide his cock between my legs.

"You ready enough, baby?"

"Yeah. Do it now." I lift my hips, and he slides home. My eyes roll back in my head. It feels so good to be filled by him, surrounded by him, caught in his arms.

"Don't think you ain't gettin' paddled for this shit when we get home," he grunts in my ear as he strokes into me harder, working my clit with a calloused thumb. My orgasm's coiling, making my mind mush.

"You gonna punish me?" I bite my bottom lip and let my knees fall open. He bucks more vigorously, nailing a spot that has me clawing his shoulders. "I'll never do it again. I'll be good," I gasp. "I promise."

It's a bold-faced lie.

He knows it, too.

He grabs my hips, thrusts hard and fast. "Cum for me, naughty girl. Do it now."

I explode, my ears ringing, and then his hot seed splatters my bare belly, and he shouts his release.

Next door, a pissed off guest bangs on the wall.

"Get a room!" he shouts. The walls are seriously paper-thin.

We both dissolve in sticky laughter, tangled together. He's still wearing his white socks. He looks ridiculous and hot and all mine.

He tucks me under his chin and kisses my forehead. "Sleep now. I'll get food when you wake up."

"Dizzy?" I yawn and scrub my eyes.

"Yeah?"

"I love you."

He holds me tight and throws a leg over my hip. "You ain't never gonna have cause to regret it."

"I ran," I mumble, drifting off to the buzz of the overhead light.

"I caught you."

I fall asleep with a smile on my face, in Dizzy's arms, a whole new world waiting for me when I wake up.

"Those brats?" Charge asks.

"Yup. Brats. Keilbasa." I adjust the meat with my tongs. You don't want to overcook sausage. "This here is some Cajun shit. It's spicy."

Charge pops a squat on the cooler next to the grill. He has the weary look of a hunted man. Or a dude who's got some explainin' to do to a woman.

A few minutes ago, Fay-Lee pecked me on the cheek and went to rescue his new girl Kayla from an onslaught of sweetbutts lookin' to lay prior claim on their favorite pretty boy. Kayla's got a six-year-old, but she's sheltered. Naïve almost. She don't know what to do when a bitch steps to her. Fay-Lee will fix her up.

When we got together, Fay-Lee had the females in line tout suite. Someone—Danielle, I think it was—sat on my lap one night when Fay-Lee was in the bathroom. Fay-Lee dragged her off me by the hair.

She would've lost the ensuing fight, and I'd have had to step in—no matter how much I feed the girl, she still don't have much weight to her, except that ass—but Story Jenkins leapt in to back her up. Ended up with Bullet takin' bets. My girl won.

Story and Fay-Lee have been thick as thieves ever since. I bet they're in the clubhouse now, recruiting Kayla into their shenanigans. Story strips at The White Van, but my woman's the bad influence. It's commonly known.

I grin. Can't help it. She's somethin' else. Never a dull moment.

"What you smilin' about?" Charge grumps, cracking a beer.

"A juicy brat's a beautiful thing." It's the truth. Nothin' like a spring day, grilling out, kids runnin' and hollering. Parker and Carson have taken Kayla's little one under their wings, showin' him all the trouble he can get into around the clubhouse. Life is good. "What crawled up your ass?"

"Every fuckin' sweetbutt in this place."

"Must be hard. You need a stick to beat 'em off with?" I'm raggin' on him, but I sympathize. He's a goner for his woman. She's gonna tear him up when they get home.

"She's got to get used to it." Charge glares at the back door the women disappeared through. "If they see they can rattle her, they'll keep doin' it. And if I handle it for her, she'll lose respect."

"Ah." I nod my head. "You're letting other pussy crawl all over you so your woman can earn her own respect. Solid plan, my man."

Charge flips me the bird. "You got better advice?"

"Every man must chart his own course in life." I turn the sausages. Perfect char. I'm the master.

Carson and Kayla's boy, Jimmy, comes flying over, careening to a halt a foot from the grill. They make quite a pair.

Jimmy's got a mean mug, and Carson's twice his size and

all smiles. Since Carson's growth spurts, he's almost got a grown man's size, but he's still got a little kid's heart. Steve don't say shit to Carson about his weight anymore. Not since Carson got big enough to bench press him if he wanted.

"Dad," Carson pants. "Can we take Jimmy ridin' out in the woods? He ain't never been on a dirt bike before."

"No!" Charge and I answer at the same time.

"Can we get a brat then?"

"Ain't done yet. Go get a hot dog from Ernestine."

"Okay." They tear off for the picnic table buffet the old ladies have laid out, but they get distracted mid-way and head off toward Parker who's sittin' under Shirlene and Twitch's tree, playing games on his phone.

That boy's face is stuck to a screen way too much. Maybe dirt bikes ain't enough of a challenge anymore. Maybe he's ready to restore his first motorcycle. Big George has a basket case he took off a divorced lady cleaning out her garage. I'll ask Fay-Lee to look into it.

She likes to act as if she don't care—and she hates it if anyone calls her a stepmom—but she loves doin' things for the kids. She's always goin' on about how she ain't old enough to be their mother, so they best pick their own shit up and close the damn door—we ain't air conditionin' the neighborhood.

Gets real pissed when I point out she sounds just like my mother.

We been gettin' into it ourselves a bit—Fay-Lee and I. I'd like another kid. I want her waddling around the house, front heavy and about to tip. She's an amazing mom already. In her folding chair, cheerin' for Parker and Carson at every game. Sneakin' them cash whenever they ask. Pickin' them back up when life throws 'em disappointments.

When Sharon's "opportunity" out of town turned into a

fulltime job in Pyle, she suggested the boys stay with us most of the time—to keep their schooling consistent, she said. Fay-Lee didn't bat an eye. She was up at the next PTA meeting. Got disinvited, too, 'cause she motherfucked a mom who made a remark about her age.

Anyway, I know she'd love havin' a baby of her own, but she don't wanna lose her freedom. She don't want to be a drudge, doin' for other people all day. Unappreciated.

What with managing the office at Big George's, fixin' up the new house I bought her last year, and fussin' over the boys, she does do for other people all day. I don't think she'd be happy to hear it, though, so I keep it to myself.

I brought up havin' a kid one time, a few months back. She said no. I dropped it. She brings it up at least once a week. Almost daily now. Tells me all the reasons she don't want to be a mom.

She don't like coffee dates with other women and book clubs and paint nights. She thinks organic food is a scam. She likes cussin' too much.

I don't see what that's got to do with havin' a baby, but I'm a man. I'm sure she's got her logic.

While Charge and I been grillin' and commiserating in silence, Nickel has ventured over. His eyes are flickin' all over the yard. He's lookin' for Story.

"She's inside," I say.

He grunts. Doesn't respond. But his eyes narrow on the back door.

"Beer?" Charge asks, half-rising and grabbing three cold ones from the cooler.

Nickel and I hold out our hands. Charge slaps icy, wet bottles into our palms. I sip as I take off the sausages and lay them on a plate lined with a paper towel. Perfect.

I beckon the ladies, and Deb sends Angel over to grab

them. I put a few more on the grill. Don't want anyone to go hungry.

"Why don't you go in there, Dizzy? See what's goin' on?" Charge nods toward the clubhouse.

"I'm cookin', man. And *my* woman's fine."

"What's goin' on?" Nickel tenses and swells, pumped with adrenaline. Instantly, he's ready to kill. Jesus Christ. It's a handy thing—one I'll always be grateful for—when a man has a knife at your woman's throat. Or when a former brother turns on his club for mere money and needs to be put down.

On a random Sunday afternoon at a family picnic? It's unsettling.

I clap a hand on his back. "Relax. It's nothin'. Charge has got woman trouble."

Nickel sniffs and cracks his neck. You can see it. He's got this dark energy now, and he don't know what to do with it.

"Looks like Bullet's tryin' to get something going over by the fire pit," I point out. It's early for the sparring to start, but Wall and the prospect Roosevelt are gathered there, messin' around.

Nickel nods. "Peace," he says as he stalks away.

Charge shakes his head. "I don't get why he don't claim her. Story's been after him forever. She ain't gonna turn him down."

"I'm sure the man has his reasons."

We're quiet a while, soakin' in the sunshine. It's the kind of early May day that's bright but cool. Everything's chatterin'. The birds. The crickets. The women and the old dudes at the horseshoe pits.

A glorious day. I'm a blessed man.

And then a whistle rings out in the yard, and the chattering turns to hoots and hollers.

"It's Fay-Lee, ain't it?" I try hard to fight the grin. I've been grillin' a while now. I figured she'd be demandin' my attention sooner or later.

"Ayup."

I look where folks are pointing. She hanging out an upstairs window, unbuttoning her shirt.

"Who wants to see my tits?" she shouts. Thank goodness Ernestine herded all the kids inside a few minutes ago to wash their hands and get sundaes.

There's a hue and cry. I slap the tongs in Charge's hands. "Give 'em a minute or two then turn 'em."

She takes off her shirt, swings it in the air, and lets it fly. She's wearin' her white lace bra with the little pink rosebud.

"Hurry up, sugar!" Grinder shouts. "Dizzy's headin' up!"

I'll beat his ass once I'm done with Fay-Lee's.

She smiles at me, easing her hands behind her back, widening her eyes each time she pops a clasp.

"Get outta that window, baby!"

"Make me!" She holds the bra to her chest and lets the straps fall down. "Oops."

"Heads down, motherfuckers, or I'm collectin' eyeballs when I get back out here!" There's a chorus of tough talk and laughter, but I make note of who listens and who don't.

I bust through the door and pound up the stairs, grinnin' from ear-to-ear. By the time I reach the room—the same one I found her in that first day we met, although it's been redone since then—she's naked and bent over the bed, ass high in the air, gigglin'.

I crack her ass cheek with one hand while I unzip my pants with the other. She shrieks, tilting her hips for more.

She loves it. She loves me. It's a miracle. *She's* a miracle.

Thwack. Thwack. I make that ass wobble, leave a handprint I'll admire later. Maybe make her show everyone. Remind them so there is no doubt she belongs to me.

She's panting, her hand shoved between her legs. I let the next one catch wind, and she shrieks as my palm makes contact. Then she kind of shakes her head and scrambles forward on the bed. I drag her back.

"Uh, uh, baby. You're gonna take what you asked for."

"Leave off, Dizzy. I got to—ouch!" She swats at my hand and flips to her back. "Hold up. *Broccoli! Orange Crush!* Fuck!"

I squeeze in one last slap, and I quit. The current safe word's *parmesan*, but she's always forgettin' it and changing it. She knows *hold on* or *stop* works just fine.

"I wanted to tell you something."

"That why you decide to hang out the window and strip for the whole damn club?"

"I needed your undivided attention."

"My ears work fine."

She pouts, scooting up to the head of the bed. I sit at the foot. She's adorable. I love the scar at the corner of her mouth. I love her big brown eyes and her long black hair and her stubborn chin. I love her pointy elbows and her long legs.

"Well? You gonna tell me what's so important that I had to leave Charge Denney with the brats and come up here?"

She chews her bottom lip, glancing up at me from under thick lashes. "I changed my mind."

"Okay."

"That's all you can say?" she huffs.

"It's a woman's prerogative?"

She tucks her knees to her chin, and rubs the tattooed stars on her wrist. She had Creech add three. One each for me, Parker, and Carson. Then she had Creech turn Sharon's name on my back into barbed wire.

She's nervous about somethin'. I want to go to her, drag her into my lap, kiss her 'til she remembers there's nothin' she can't tell me. She ain't alone in life anymore. I got her back. In everything.

But I wait. I think I know where she's goin', but I remain calm. She has surprised me before. Often.

Finally, she sighs. "I want to have a baby. Your baby. Dumbass."

My heart leaps in my chest.

"But not right this minute. I got to get used to the idea. I'm gonna stay on the pill until at least this prescription runs out."

"Okay." A grin splits my face.

"And there's things I want to do first."

"All right."

"And we got to make sure Parker and Carson are okay with it."

"They will be." Both boys have asked me when we're gonna have a baby. They're outgrowing their stuff, but they're attached to it, so instead of donating it to the Goodwill, they want to pack it away "for when you and Fay-Lee have a kid."

"I don't want stretch marks."

"I'll love your stretch marks."

"We should probably get married first."

"I've asked you a dozen times," I point out. "Bought you that ring."

"Rings don't mean anything. And it's just a piece of paper."

"We can go to the courthouse. Don't need to be a big

deal. If you're worried about family bein' there, you know Steel Bones are your people now."

She gets maudlin every once in a while after she's had a glass of wine. She'll call one of her sisters, and they'll go on about themselves, won't let Fay-Lee get a word in edgewise, and then they ask for money. She ends up cryin' in the bathroom with the door shut.

"I'll think about it," she concedes. "I don't want to be a boring married mom. I still want to do kinky stuff. In bed."

She crawls over to where I'm sitting and tucks herself under my arm.

"I'll fuck you however you want."

"You're an infuriatingly simple and easy-to-please man." She's smiling now, too. I push down my pants to past my knees and scoop her up into my lap. She squirms until she's straddling me, arms wrapped around my neck. Her pussy's hot and wet against my belly. My cock is nestled in her ass crack.

I kiss her. She tastes like ginger ale. "Want me to show you how I'm gonna put a baby in your belly? When you're ready?"

"Yeah," she pants, guiding my cock through her legs so she can rock her wet slit up and down the shaft. I take her mouth, twine my tongue with hers, breathe in all her smells and sounds.

Before this woman, I was gettin' by. Making do.

Now, I'm livin'. She's given me everything. And as I slide home, burying myself to the hilt in her heat, I swear in my heart, as I have every day I wake up beside her—I will give this woman the world.

My woman. I caught her. She's mine.

∾

THE STEEL BONES Motorcycle Club saga begins with Charge.

A NOTE FROM THE AUTHOR

Will Ernestine ever take Grinder back?

Will Creech ever find someone who can love him?

Who was Boots' "California Girl" and why did she leave?

I have no idea! But you will be the first to know if you sign up for my newsletter at www.catecwells.com.

You'll get a FREE novella, too!

ABOUT THE AUTHOR

Cate C. Wells indulges herself in everything from motorcycle club to small town to mafia to paranormal romance. Whatever the subgenre, readers can expect character-driven stories that are raw, real, and emotionally satisfying. She's into messy love, flaws, long roads to redemption, grace, and happily ever after, in books and in life.

Along with stories, she's collected a husband and three children along the way. She lives in Baltimore when she's not exploring the world with the family.

I love to connect with readers! Meet me in The Cate C. Wells Reader Group on Facebook.

Facebook: @catecwells
Twitter: @CateCWells1
Bookbub: @catecwells

Printed in Dunstable, United Kingdom

71437880R00161